A fan...

As his assailant came at him, Bishop glimpsed his face. It wasn't a *he* at all, but rather a *she*. He caught her around the waist and held her so that they were eye to eye.

Her strong legs wrapped around him. Wisps of black hair brushed his cheek as her arms went around his neck.

Snarling, he grabbed her wrists and yanked. She was strong, but he was stronger.

She scuffled backward as he stepped toward her.

Bishop looked at the woman on the ground. She stared at him with a mixture of fear, awe, and triumph.

"What . . . ?"

He hit the ground with bone-jarring force.

Then there was nothing but the darkness of the night and the smell of his attacker. When he heard the soft victory of her laughter, he kr

Other AVON ROMANCES

Kathryn Smith

NIGHT OF THE HUNTRESS

AVON BOOKS
An Imprint of HarperCollinsPublishers

AVON BOOKS
An Imprint of HarperCollins*Publishers*
10 East 53rd Street
New York, New York 10022–5299

Copyright © 2007 by Kathryn Smith
ISBN: 978–0–06–084991–7
ISBN-10: 0–06–084991–6
www.avonromance.com

First Avon Books paperback printing: February 2007

Avon Trademark Reg. U.S. Pat. Off. and in Other Countries, Marca Registrada, Hecho en U.S.A.
HarperCollins® is a registered trademark of HarperCollins Publishers.

Printed in the U.S.A.

10 9 8 7 6 5 4 3 2 1

This book is dedicated to Kim Lewis.
Thank you for constantly pleading, "Kathy, tell me a story." You can stop now, though.
Thank you for always believing in me—and for believing that I'm a goddess even when I feel like dirt.
But most of all, thank you for liking Nick and not John because you know I don't share well with others.
Love you.

And of course I have to mention my husband, Steve, because seeing his name in print makes him happy and he makes every day a gift.
Thanks, Babe.

Acknowledgments

I need to thank the fabulouos Roxi "Roxstar" Fleschin for helping me with all things Romanian, including some swearwords that didn't make it into this book. Also, thanks to Roxi for all the decadent and terribly delicious food she used to bring me in Toronto. I miss it! And I miss her.

Any errors are my own, either by mistake or by bending details to suit my story.

NIGHT
OF THE
HUNTRESS

Chapter 1

Fagaras mountain region, 1899

The spinning gold coin fell at Marika Korzha's feet. Rather than reach for it, her hand instead went to the knife strapped to the outside of her thigh.

"You . . ." She thought for the right word in English, "*insult* me."

The man smiled smugly, narrowing his pale eyes. His confidence told her that he thought himself safe with his men flanking him, backing him. He thought because she was a woman in a tavern filled with men, he was in control.

He was wrong.

She was not alone; her own men sat at a table waiting. All she had to do was give the signal and they would come to her side.

1

She would have three of these men dead by the time her own arrived.

"You are insulted by gold?" The man's voice was smooth, mocking.

She didn't reply. She merely watched him. He knew full well what the insult was.

He flashed his arrogant grin at his companions before turning it back to her. "Aren't you going to pick it up?"

The English came easier this time now that she remembered the language. "Pick up what?"

"The gold at your feet."

Marika's gaze remained fixed on him, but she shifted her right foot so that the toe of her boot caught the coin. It sailed across the uneven floor to bounce off the man's leather-covered shin. His eyes widened at the force of impact. "Perhaps you should pick it up."

Some of the smugness left his narrow features. "I shall take it out of your payment then."

"Payment?" She lifted her shoulders in a casual shrug, the light wool of her collar brushing her cheek. "How can I be paid for something I have not yet said I will do?"

The man approached her—only one step. Some of the patrons of the little tavern watched the encounter with interest. Others wisely kept their attention on their own affairs. "We had an agreement."

Her shoulders drew back, straightening her spine. She wasn't as tall as he was, but that didn't mean she would be cowed by him. She wasn't afraid of him, or his money or his men. "I agreed to meet you. I agreed to listen to you. I may agree to work for you. So far you have done nothing to convince me to accept."

Indistinct eyes narrowed. "Pretty cheeky for a woman, aren't you?"

Marika wasn't quite certain what "cheeky" meant, but she could tell from the man's expression that it wasn't a compliment.

Her head tilted as she regarded him, her face carefully blank. "If I were a man you would not talk to me as if I were an idiot."

Had he no other expression but that irritating smirk? "But you're not a man."

No, she wasn't. It would take more than trousers and boots to conceal her sex. Her hair was too long, too thick, held in a braid that fell far down her back. Her skin was too pale and unshadowed, her features too delicate and fine. She didn't want to be a man. It was far more advantageous to be what she was.

It made it all the more satisfying to see the expression the moment her opponents realized they had underestimated her.

"Neither am I an idiot. You try my patience. This meeting is over." She turned purposefully, presenting him her back. Would he shoot it? Bury a blade in it? Would it kill her, or would her men wonder yet again at how quickly she healed from injuries that might have been fatal to lesser mortals?

Over the voices and raucous laughter in the tavern, she heard the step, the scuff of a boot on the floor. She felt the air announce a coming danger with a subtle shift, raising the hair on the back of her neck.

The man wasn't the first to attack her when her back was turned. Men always waited. They wanted to prove themselves her superior, but they always waited until she couldn't see them coming to do it. She knew without looking that the Englishman had sent one of his minions after her rather than make the attempt himself.

She whirled, seizing the man's arm as he reached for her. Had she not been expecting this tactic she might have broken his wrist, but she held back, bringing him to his knees with the force of her grip.

Her own brethren rose, coming to stand beside her in case the situation intensified.

Her gaze met that of the narrow-faced man. He stood with the remainder of his men, watching her with barely concealed wonder.

"The stories about you are true." He spoke as though suddenly realizing she was more than just a woman—more than human.

Marika didn't like it. The patrons of the tavern were watching as well. Whispers started. Whispers about her—a woman who dressed like a man and fought like a soldier. Was it *her*? Was she hunting? Were they in danger? Fear raised their voices, heightened the smell of their sweat.

It was time to leave.

"You are a man who always sends others to do what he is afraid to do himself." She released her captive's wrist, flinging him away from her. "I do not trust that."

"I am not asking for your trust," he replied.

Marika snorted. This man had no honor, and she would not lessen her own by associating with him. "We are done."

Her men followed as she turned to leave, clustering around her as though she needed their protection. They knew better, but they were simple men and their habits were ingrained to the bone.

"Does the name Saint mean anything to you?"

It was a desperate demand, but it had the desired effect. Marika froze. Her lungs, as still as death, refused to work. She couldn't blink, couldn't think. But her heart thrashed in her chest, like a bird flailing against its cage.

Slowly, she faced him once more. Anxiety colored his features, but that familiar arrogance was slowly coming back. "I see that it does."

Fingers clenched into fists. "Tell me what you know."

He missed the dead calm of her tone, ignored the flatness of her gaze. He was far too confident—or stupid.

"I think not. I think you will sit—"

He couldn't finish, not with her hand wrapped around his throat. She had started moving as soon as he opened his mouth, crossing the space between them like a pouncing cat. She had him bent backward over the table, gasping for air as his fingers clawed at hers. A tankard had spilled, its fragrant contents soaking into the aged wood near the man's head. Pistols pointed at her—one pressed against her temple.

"Kill me and you may be certain that I will take your master with me." She looked into the Englishman's eyes as she spoke to his men.

Pale eyes stared at a point over her shoulder. She saw the command given in those gray depths. She saw fear also, but then he would have to be an idiot not to fear her. The pistol at her temple lowered, as did the others.

Marika loosened her grip, allowing him to draw breath. She took one . . . two steps backward, aware that the men around her moved as well. No one wanted to be too close now that she had shown the more feral side of her nature.

It had been foolish of her to reveal so much of herself, but at least this Englishman would think twice before underestimating her again.

Now that it was obvious there wasn't going to be any bloodshed, the patrons of the tavern went back to their business—or gave the appearance of doing just that. Most of these people were peasants and they stayed out of that which did not concern them, but they kept watch just in case.

Marika gestured to the empty table and the chairs around it. "Sit. Please."

Rubbing his throat, the pale-eyed man gave her a wary glance before doing as she bid. Marika took the chair across from him and called for drinks and *placintele prajite*—little meat pies—for her companion and his men, as well as her own.

Once they were all seated, the mood among the English eased. This was good. She wanted this man to fear her enough to speak truthfully, but not so much that he was afraid to speak at all.

She could smile, could make herself seem more feminine and approachable, but that was stupid and would undermine her very nature. Instead she settled for a more direct—but relaxed tack. She wrapped her hand around the cool mug and took a deep swallow of the beer. They would drink for a bit before she pressed for information, even though she wanted to beat it from him. Spirits didn't affect her the same as it did regular humans, but this man didn't know that. He would think alcohol made her slower, weaker. He would relax, maybe become a little arrogant again.

Stupid man.

She picked up a small package of fried meat-filled dough and bit into it. The savory flavor filled her mouth, rich and hot. She chewed and swallowed. "Please, tell me what you know of the creature called Saint."

He helped himself to the plate as well. "I know you would very much like to find him."

Marika's gaze narrowed. "I hope you know more than that." He would pay for wasting her time if he did not.

He must have heard the warning in her voice

because he paled. "Not much, but I believe the creature I want you to capture for me does."

Could it be so? Was she finally getting close, or
would this too prove to be a fruitless endeavor?

"It is not my way to hunt for payment." She was
many things, but someone's servant she was not.

The man took a small bite of pastry and nodded.
"I understand that, but I have not the . . . resources
nor the skill to track and capture him myself."

"And I do?"

"You are familiar with the habits of vampires, no?"

Marika glanced around to make certain no one
had heard him. Superstition was still very strong in
her country, and people tended to take talk of monsters very seriously.

"I might be." She wasn't yet prepared to fully admit her identity, not until she knew for certain what
he expected from her.

He seemed to take that as an affirmative answer.
"You are also from this area. Bishop has a history
with this country. He could go to ground where I
would never find him. Your *talents* make you more
difficult to hide from, I think."

Talents. She had never thought of it quite like
that before. "Bishop?"

"That is his name."

Saint and Bishop. How dare these abominations
take such holy titles as their own? Had they no
shame? She could rage against it for a long time, but
she had other concerns to deal with at the moment.
"He is here? In Romania?"

The man nodded, his cheek bulging with pie. "He arrived last night. We expect him to enter this area tomorrow evening."

Marika's heart flipped. Tomorrow. "We?"

"My associates and myself."

Associates? What kind of word was that? Friends. Companions. Family. Those were words that bespoke connection and loyalty. Associates meant nothing except a common interest. There was no bond there.

Sometimes she wished her father had never sent her away to be educated in the ways of England and the rest of the world. Ignorance would make her mind so much more peaceful.

If she were ignorant, she would not think to ask her next question. "What do you want with this Bishop?"

He wiped his fingers on a handkerchief. "He has something I want."

Simple enough. She was right not to trust this man, but the information he gave her was invaluable. If she left now she could hunt this Bishop on her own, find out the whereabouts of Saint, and then rid the world of not one but two vampires.

The man obviously thought of that as well. "I need him alive, madam. Torture him if you must to get the information you need, but I *must* have him alive. I guarantee you that I will not permit him to live when he has served his purpose."

For the first time since he had walked through the door, Marika sensed complete truth in his voice and manner.

Her jaw tightened. "You have payment?"

Her companion smiled and withdrew a small pouch from inside his coat. It landed on the table before her with a heavy clunk. A look inside verified that it was filled with gold coins.

"Half now, half when you bring him to me."

Half? This was only half of what he intended to pay her? Good Lord, she and her men could live like kings on one quarter of this! She schooled her features to keep her shock from showing.

"I do not usually capture vampires." Usually she simply killed them. "I have no way to subdue him."

His thin lips curved. He still looked extremely pleased with himself, but Marika didn't find it half so annoying anymore. "I believe I can help with that. I have restraints as well."

He seemed to have thought of everything. "And I may keep him as long as I need?"   .

"Within reason."

It shouldn't take more than a few days for her to break the vampire, if that. The creatures were notoriously disloyal to their kind, turning on each other like rats to save their own hides.

A long, clean hand reached across the table, offering itself. "Do we have an agreement then?"

He'd never once asked for her to prove she was who he thought. If she put her hand in his, he would know that she was exactly the person he had come looking for. He would have something to hold over her. He could just as easily send a hunter after her someday. There were plenty of monsters who would leap at the chance to spill her blood.

But he had given her the chance to find Saint, the very creature she had been hunting since she was old enough to kill.

Marika placed her own hand in his grip, applying enough pressure that he would remember which of them was the stronger.

"We do," she replied in a low voice. "I will give you this Bishop."

And Bishop would give her Saint—the vampire who had killed her mother.

Three centuries had passed since Bishop last saw the Fagaras mountains. He hadn't ever planned to return, but those plans went the same way so many others had over the vast span of his life. Plans changed. Countries changed. Even he, immortal as he was, changed.

Regret, however, did not.

He had arrived last evening but it had taken a day's rest and a great deal of courage gathering before he had been able to leave town and make this particular journey. He would not be able to concentrate on what he came here to do with the ghost of this place hanging over him.

Night hung like a sooty veil over the countryside. The bold peaks of the mountains were black silhouettes against the sky as they reached for silvered clouds. A pale moon brushed fingers of light over the grass, over the discarded mortar and stone.

He walked in the darkness, amid the wreckage of what had once been a fine country house. All that remained was the battered outer structure, the inside having been gutted by fire hundreds of years earlier. Birds nested in the higher, more sheltered areas, while nocturnal animals made their homes in the lower. The remnants of a campfire bespoke Gypsies, long since moved on.

His former home was a ruin—an ancient one at that—something travelers remarked on and locals used as fodder for tales. He remembered when this house had been alive with music and laughter and love. There had been a large hall where he now stood. An iron crucifix had hung above the door, hung there by his own hand. Elisabetta had selected the window hangings herself; rich, bold colors and fabrics. The house would have been old-fashioned by today's standards, but back then it had been the epitome of style and elegance.

It had been a home.

How many nights had he stood on the balcony—on the very roof—and watched the clouds swim by with the woman he loved by his side? Her skin had been like the palest ivory in the moonlight, so fragile and warm.

There was nothing left here for him but memories. Nothing left here that belonged to him but the pain and regret of a night long ago when fire had destroyed this house and a group of ignorant and frightened men had destroyed his life.

This shell meant nothing to him, and yet, as he

stood among the dirt and rubble, he could almost hear Elisabetta's voice on the breeze. Cursed with an excellent memory, he could call up the delicate sweetness of her features without effort. He remembered loving her and being loved in return.

Loved so much that she put his safety above her own, the little fool. But not loved so much that she would give him her soul, no matter how badly he had wanted it.

She had given her life for his. Centuries later he still had trouble forgiving her sacrifice.

Tentacles of gloomy light made this place ethereal and maudlin—as beautiful as it was decrepit. He saw it all clearly—even those things the shadows sought to conceal. This was no longer his home. There was no life here—none that touched his own.

He left the ruins. The farther away he was from them now, the better he would feel. The bits of wood and stone that crunched beneath his boots gave way to the soft swish of grass against worn leather. Wildflowers bloomed around the house's foundation, pretty dots of pastel color in the rich, black-green grass.

In spots the grass brushed his thighs, but he eased through it as a warm knife cuts fresh butter. Each step was easy and unhurried as he walked toward the forest at the back of the property. It was thicker than he remembered, the trees of course larger and farther reaching than they had been when he lived here.

He had missed the smells of this place. Spruce. Beech. Rich, damp soil and fragrant grass, heavy with dampness. The wild sweetness filled him, easing his regret, reminding him of how he had always loved it here.

Reminding him of all he had before the men came and took it away.

The grave wasn't far from the forest's edge—a lopsided stone, etched with painstakingly carved letters that were now dull and littered with moss, was the only marker. He had wanted to give her an angel, but he hadn't the talent to chisel anything beyond her name and the date. He had destroyed three slabs of stone—taken from the ruins of their home—and two chisels, and had almost lost his mind making this monument, and it was far from perfect.

Although on reflection, he rather thought Betta would have liked this rough stone. She always preferred simplicity to his tendency for the dramatic. She would have liked how the forest had grown up around her resting spot as well. She liked the country and the quiet, had loved these wild, uncompromising mountains. Loved them so much that she refused to leave them, so he stayed there with her. After all, there was only so much of the world he could see before it became repetitive.

Her love was contagious. They had been settled for years before he started talking about travel, about wanting to show her the wonders of the world. He had seen so much, and he wanted to share it with her before the end of her frighteningly mortal life.

Things might have turned out differently if she had left when he wanted, or if she had allowed him to make her like him.

But she hadn't. And the pain of that was much like the grave he stood on—a pale reflection of what it once had been. Time really was a great healer, it seemed.

Damn it.

He cleared debris and weeds away from the stone, picked the moss from its weathered surface. He left the wildflowers with their purple and blue petals.

"I know you are not here," he murmured, brushing dirt from inside the curve of an S. "But I want those who pass by here to know that you are remembered." Such attention was sure to spook the locals, if any saw the grave, but he was past caring.

He worked for an hour, until the little grave was as tidy as it could be without landscaping and fashioning a new stone. He could have straightened the marker, but thought better of it. Then he bade Elisabetta good-bye—just in case he was wrong about her not being there anymore—and rose to his feet.

It would be dawn soon, and he needed to return to his lodgings before the sun rose. Anara, the friend for whom he had made this journey, had given to him, for the duration of his stay, a house in a village near Fagaras with a small staff who knew what he was. He could trust them to attend to his needs and maintain an illusion of normalcy.

He might not care if people saw Elisabetta's tended grave, but he wasn't so haughty that he wanted to flaunt himself in front of them. He wasn't afraid of the people there, but the place itself and the memories it held made him uneasy. He would make his time in Romania as brief as possible and be on his way.

Anara's brother was missing. These things sometimes happened, but more frequently this past year. Anara was worried that her brother had fallen victim to some hunter called the Huntress. Apparently this Huntress had taken it upon herself to rid the world of all shadow world creatures, particularly vampires. She took the task very seriously, it seemed, and without mercy. It didn't matter if the killing was deserved or not; if it wasn't human it was evil, and therefore had to be destroyed.

Bishop knew the kind all too well.

Most vampires—himself included—killed by accident because they were too hungry, not because of some twisted sense of righteous morality. That wasn't to say there weren't vampires who were cruel or vicious, but they weren't often the ones trying to live a quiet life.

This Huntress killed without provocation, and was credited with more than one hundred killings and disappearances spanning south into Bulgaria and east to Moldova. Vampires and others were becoming increasingly frightened. They had made this woman into some kind of mythical monster, something lurking in the shadows waiting for the right moment to strike.

Bishop had taken it upon himself to solve the mystery of the Huntress and put an end to the creature's reign of terror. He was against senseless killing regardless of the victims or culprit. Long ago he had made a promise to stand against such crimes, and he intended to go on keeping it.

When he and the Huntress finally crossed paths, one of them was going to die.

It would not be Bishop.

He hadn't gone any farther than the road—a rutted wagon path that cut through the hillside—when he heard the clomp of hooves and the rumble of a cart some distance away.

His first instinct was to take to the sky, fly away before he was found and dragged off to be staked in the middle of the town to await the dawn, but he shook off the irrational fear. With the moon this full and the night this clear, there was too much of a chance that the occupants of the cart—or anyone else in the vicinity—would see him. A flying man was bound to cause a sensation, and he did not want any hint of his presence getting out. He was better off hiding, or pretending there was some reason for him to be on foot so far from town.

A familiar scent reached his nostrils. Not human. Vampire. Another vampire? No, the scent wasn't right. He didn't have time to process it before something shifted in the corner of his vision—a swift shadow pouncing from the darkness.

He whirled, plucking his attacker from the air and tossing him to the ground.

The man hit the dirt with a grunt, but he rolled to his feet with unnatural grace and speed. This was the creature he had caught wind of just moments before.

As his assailant came at him, Bishop glimpsed his face. It wasn't a *he* at all, but rather a *she*—a curvaceous, strong, rather pretty *she* who seemed intent on fighting him.

Their gazes locked. Her dark eyes widened, and for a second she faltered. Had he not been so shocked, he would have used that second to his advantage, but she had the upper hand. She struck swiftly, coming at him with a fist that glinted in the moonlight.

Silver. She had a silver chain wrapped around her hand.

Bishop dodged. She tried to follow with a kick to his ribs, which he deflected with a swipe of his arm. She spun but didn't fall.

Her next punch landed, sent a jolt of pain through his jaw as the silver burned his flesh. Instinct kicked in as the beast inside him roared to life. Fangs ripped from his gums. His vision sharpened. When she came at him again, he was ready.

Her head snapped back when he landed a blow of his own. Blood trickled from her mouth as she faced him. She smelled of earth and strength and something familiar that called to him even as she kicked him in the side of the head. His fangs scraped the inside of his mouth, and he tasted his own blood. Hunger blossomed within. He wanted to sink his teeth into this woman. He wanted to glut himself on her, wanted her whimpering in his arms.

Pain lanced his arm. One of her companions had cut him with a silver blade. Bishop didn't stop to think, he simply reacted. The man sailed through the air and landed on the ground with a cry and a loud snap.

He faced the woman once more. "Do you suppose I broke him?" He didn't know why she attacked him and he didn't care. He had done nothing wrong, had done nothing to provoke this violence, but he had run from humans once. He would not do it again. If it meant his own preservation, he'd kill every last one of this gang.

The sound that came from her throat sounded very much like a battle cry. She launched herself at him. Bishop caught her around the waist and held her so that they were eye to eye.

Fear tainted the otherwise sultry scent of her. Underneath that there was a taste of desire. She was ruled by instinct as well, so it seemed her beast was every bit as enthralled by him as his was by her.

Her strong legs wrapped around him. He held his ground. Too late he realized that she wasn't trying to topple him, but ensuring that he didn't toss her as easily as he had her man.

Breasts pressed against his chest as her thighs held him. Wisps of black hair brushed his cheek as her arms went around his neck. Releasing his hold on her waist, he reached up to seize her hands, but he was too slow. Just as his fingers touched hers, a sharp stab punctured the side of his neck.

Snarling, he grabbed her wrists and yanked. She was strong, but he was stronger. He slammed her back against the wagon, once, twice. Her grip on his waist loosened, and he shoved hard enough to knock her to the ground.

She scuffled backward on her hands and heels as he stepped toward her. His fangs were fully extended. His heart clamored wildly as the last vestiges of control slipped from him. He was going to kill her. He was going to kill them all.

God, forgive me.

His knees buckled as he took another step. The moonlight dimmed as fog rolled in. The fog didn't belong to the night—it was in his head.

He looked at the woman on the ground. She stared at him with a mixture of fear, awe, and triumph. She swam and blurred before his eyes.

"What . . . ?" That was all he managed to ask before his tongue stopped working.

He hit the ground with bone-jarring force. All he could hear was the sound of his own raspy breathing, the roar of his own heart pounding in his ears.

Then there was nothing but the darkness of the night and the smell of his attacker. When he heard the soft victory of her laughter, he knew the awful truth.

The Huntress had found him.

Chapter 2

He had the sign of the cross branded on his back. The sight of the pale scar burned into his golden skin made Marika's heart quicken with anticipation. The Englishman had been right. This Bishop bore the same mark as Saint and the rest of his vile brethren. They had been marked by the church with heated silver—a sign of their supposed penance.

There was nothing penitent about this . . . thing, no matter how angelic he might look while asleep.

She was sore and bruised from their battle, but Dimitru had suffered the most. He had managed to wound Bishop with his blade, but he had paid for his bravery with a broken arm. It would be a long time before he was able to fight again.

"Is that him?"

Marika took her attention from the vampire long enough to glance at the girl in the doorway. "Hello,

Roxana," she replied in Romanian. "Yes, it is him."

The girl came forward, stepping into the torchlit cellar that served as a hideout, storeroom and cell. At sixteen she was tall, willowy and beautiful. Dimitru had high hopes for his oldest daughter's marriage, but Roxana wanted to be a vampire hunter like Marika.

Marika sincerely hoped the girl chose marriage instead.

Roxana's dark eyes narrowed as she stared at the prisoner. "I thought he would be ugly."

They had taken his shirt and his shoes in case he had weapons concealed within. The clothing wouldn't fit over the manacles they had clapped on him, so it had been left off. Now Marika wished they had at least put a blanket over him. Roxana shouldn't be looking at a half-naked man, even if he was a vampire.

Especially not a vampire like Bishop, who was no doubt very skilled at seducing his prey into his dark embrace.

"He is ugly," Marika informed her coolly. "On the inside."

But his outside was beautiful—something she would never, ever admit. He was tall and muscular, tanned and graceful. His hair was tousled brown silk with a touch of auburn. His mouth was as sensual as it was cruel, and his eyes were like a hawk's—wide spaced and greenish-gold. When he had looked at her earlier he had taken her breath away. The only imperfection had been the dirt underneath his fingernails and ground into the calluses on his hands.

Her reaction to him was disgusting. She should not find him the least bit appealing, but she did. When they were fighting she even felt heat stirring low within her abdomen. She had never reacted to a vampire that way before. Never that way to anyone—human or non.

Were it not for her agreement with the Englishman—Armitage was his name—she would kill Bishop right now. Were it not that he might give her the location of Saint, she'd take him outside to greet the coming dawn, and then there would be nothing left of him for her to find pretty or sensual.

Roxana peered over Marika's shoulder at the vampire, but maintained a safe distance. "What are you going to do with him?"

Marika placed an arm about the girl. Roxana was almost as tall as she was now. "He will tell us where others like him are hiding. Then we will give him to an Englishman in exchange for gold."

"An Englishman? Gold?"

Chuckling, Marika gave the girl's slender shoulders a squeeze. "Yes." Then an idea occurred to her. "Later we will go to town and buy you a new dress with the Englishman's payment. Would you like that?"

"Oh, yes!" Roxana hugged Marika fiercely—it was like being embraced by a kitten. "Thank you!"

Yes, a dress. Get the girl out of the trousers she favored because she emulated Marika in every way she could. Put her in a dress, make her as pretty as she could be and hope that some kind farmer with a comfortable income would take a liking to her, marry her and give her fat babies. That was what Marika wanted for her. Better that—better anything—than seeing her killed by a vampire or something equally evil.

"Go get some sleep then. It will be dawn soon. We will go after breakfast." The daylight would be difficult to face on so little rest, but before noon there was less risk of getting a headache. She was unnaturally sensitive to the sun, though she could bear it if she took the necessary precautions. Generally it wasn't much of a bother, as her "occupation" called for her to be at her most alert at night.

Roxana went without argument, a little skip to her step. Ten years separated them in age, and yet it might as well be fifty. Marika had never been that young, that innocent. Life had made all her choices for her.

"May I have a new dress too?"

She jumped at the sound of his voice—flawless Romanian with just a hint of a foreign accent. It wasn't a surprise that he knew her language given his history with this country, but the sound of it on his tongue angered her all the same.

He shouldn't be awake this soon—it wasn't even dawn yet. Armitage told her the injection would make him sleep until well into the day—when the sun was too high in the sky for him to consider attempting escape.

She faced him with her chin high. She would not show fear. She would not show anything.

He sat on the narrow cot—the chains hadn't even rattled when he moved—his back to the stone wall, one knee bent, his heel braced on the edge. The other knee listed to one side, giving her an ample view of his muscled chest. The thinly padded silver around his ankles was tarnished but it would hold him, as would the matching cuffs around his wrists. The chain holding both sets to the wall and floor was stronger, with thick links. It should be too strong for him to break, but just to be safe, a thinner silver chain was wound around it.

Why silver was so effective, she didn't know. All she knew was that vampires didn't like it.

Neither did she.

His head was tilted to one side as he watched her. His face was completely expressionless, yet she could feel his anger, his hatred. She stood her ground—well out of his reach.

"What happens now?" he demanded. "Am I to be tortured? Maimed? Perhaps you and the other women plan to ravage me?"

She didn't ask how he knew there were other women about. He could no doubt hear them—she could, although not well. She hadn't wanted to bring him back to the village, but it was the only place where they had the means to hold him. And the people there believed that she could actually protect them from this monster.

She sneered at him. "None of the women here would have a creature like you."

He smiled—something that made him look uncomfortably human. And altogether too attractive. "But you're not a woman, are you? Not completely."

She didn't answer. She couldn't. She should have anticipated this.

His smile never wavered, but his eyes seemed to glow in the torchlight. "Do your people know you're half vampire, Huntress?"

"A halfling." His tone was vaguely mocking. "I've never met a dhampyr before."

Marika flinched at the word. Instinctively she checked the doorway, where the graying approach of dawn eased into the cellar. No one was there to hear his damning appraisal.

Chains clinked as he straightened, his narrow feet touching the rough floor. "They don't know. Isn't that interesting."

The look she gave him was one of pure malice. "If you think this gives you power, think again. They will never listen to you." God, she hoped they wouldn't.

He was still smiling, a fact that brought a chill to the base of her spine. "Of course they wouldn't. But you are wrong, little halfling, I do have power. I know your secret."

He did. She had never kept a creature alive long enough for him to know what she was. No one but her father ever knew, and even he didn't know the full extent of what the vampire attack on her pregnant mother had wrought.

"I wonder why you keep it from them."

His expression told her he knew exactly why. How could she tell her men that half of her was the very monster they sought to destroy? They wouldn't understand. Many of these people's lives had been touched by the *vampir* either literally or by stories. Marika never asked for this curse. It had been forced upon her by the one who killed her mother.

Saint.

"Your time might be better spent, *vampir*, by telling me what I want to know."

He cocked a brow, mocking her with his humor. He was the one in chains and yet he made her feel as though he were in charge of this exchange. "Which is?"

She could strike him, wrap silver around her hand and suffer the discomfort just to see him bleed. Take her power back. "Where is Saint?"

He frowned. "Saint? Never heard of him." His tone was hardly convincing.

Fingers fisted at her sides. "You bear the same scar on your back."

His upper body slowly reclined to rest his head against the wall; his dimpled chin lifted defiantly. "Isn't that a coincidence."

If she didn't know better she would be tempted to believe him; he sounded so sincere, even as he silently laughed at her. "You will tell me where he is."

"Why don't I fuck you instead?"

She didn't think, she simply reacted, launching herself across the floor to aim a fierce kick at his head. He took it as if it were nothing more than a slap. She realized her error a second too late as he grabbed her boot in his hand and flipped her.

Marika hit the dirt on her front, the air rushing from her lungs with a force that left her dazed. She had done exactly what he hoped and now he was going to kill her.

Dirt gathered under her nails as he pulled her to him. His fingers bit into her calf. If he wanted to he could snap her leg like a twig, but he didn't. A part of her knew that he wanted her sharp and aware for whatever he did to her—not numbed by shock or pain.

She tried to turn over onto her back, but he was stronger than she was. The bolts in the wall groaned as he strained against them. Good God, he wasn't strong enough to break them, was he?

That scared her.

There was a wooden crate near the cot for just such an emergency. Her hand fumbled inside as she slid by, grabbing what she sought. When he stopped pulling and seized her by the back of the trousers, she arched upward, twisting in his grasp to smash the holy water against his shoulder and upper chest.

He threw her like a hot poker. She heard him grunt as the smell of burning flesh met her nostrils. She hit the dirt floor hard, but self-preservation had her rolling to her feet despite the throbbing in her limbs. She ran to the door. Only once she stood in that patch of watery dawn did she turn to look.

He was slumped on the cot, his flesh smoldering and blistering where the blessed water had hit it. There was blood as well—the bottle had cut him when it broke. The smell of him called to her, awaking a hunger she refused to feed.

There was such pain in his features as he met her gaze, but his eyes were as cold as ice. She would not feel bad for hurting him. She was not the monster. She was not an abomination. She was half human. She did not drink blood. She did not kill without reason.

"You will tell me where Saint is," she told him. "Do not make me hurt you further."

"One of us is going to die," he told her, his jaw clenched. "You know that."

She nodded. "I also know that it will not be me."

Then she closed the heavy door, bolted it and walked up the steps to meet the dawn.

"Did you find the dhampyr?"

Victor Armitage looked up from the rare roast of beef on his plate. His employer—a gray-haired man with eyes like slate—stared at him expectantly. "Yes, my lord. She came to the tavern just as you said she would."

"And she was agreeable to our offer?" The older man refilled Victor's glass as he asked.

Victor chewed the tender, succulent beef and

swallowed it with a sip of wine. Cecil Maxwell always employed the best chefs no matter where he resided, and this backward country was no different. "Indeed. Very predictable, that one." He pressed a napkin to his lips. "She behaved just as we anticipated."

Lazily swirling his own glass, Maxwell watched his wine, but Armitage knew where his attention truly was—on him. "Did you anticipate that bruise on your throat?"

Instinctively Victor's hand went to his neck. His collar and cravat covered where Marika Korzha's hand had choked him. How did Maxwell know? He always knew.

The older man was smiling—a self-satisfied smile rather than one of genuine pleasure. "You give yourself away, Victor. The proper response would have been, 'What bruise?'"

Victor managed a strained smile of his own. "Indeed, my lord. I see there is much I have yet to learn from you."

Maxwell's smile faded. "There always will be, Victor."

His appetite faded under the weight of that meaningful stare. For years Victor had followed this man—and others like him—hoping to raise himself into the upper ranks of the order. It never happened. Maxwell had just as much as told him it never would. Lesser men would quit, but there was no leaving the Order of the Silver Palm. The only way out was death, by causes natural or otherwise.

Victor didn't want out. He wanted to prove himself. If all went as planned with the dhampyr, the elders would have to take notice of his work. Maxwell himself would be forced to admit that he had done well. The promise of that alone was worth the struggle.

"When will you contact the dhampyr again?"

"In one week's time," Victor replied, cutting into his beef once more. His appetite was returning. "By then she should have the whereabouts of Saint."

Maxwell smiled at his wine, pleased now. Better the wine felt the weight of those cold eyes than Victor himself. "And we will know them as well."

Victor nodded. "I have men monitoring her movements. If she discovers anything or goes anywhere, they will follow and report back to me. If she goes after Saint, we will know."

"If Bishop gives him up, she will go." Maxwell sounded certain. "She will not be able to help herself. Her curiosity and need for revenge is too great. We will have to watch her closely. If she gets to Saint before we do she may very well kill him."

Roast seemed to stick in Victor's throat. That would not go well for him. He swallowed hard. "I will not allow that to happen."

For the first time Maxwell looked at him with something other than distaste. "That is what I like to hear."

It was time to take attention off himself. "How can we be certain Bishop will betray his friend?"

"Betray?" Maxwell chuckled. "Oh, our friend

Bishop has far too much honor to *betray* his friend, Victor."

Wasn't that very betrayal the hinge upon which this whole operation hung? "But I thought . . . that is, I was under the impression—"

"Try not to think, Victor. You need only do what I tell you. It will make both of our jobs less complicated that way."

The younger man flushed. "Apologies, my lord."

Maxwell topped up Victor's glass again, even though he'd barely touched the wine already in it. "Once Bishop realizes the truth about the dhampyr's identity, he will give her the location of his friend without hesitation."

"He will?" Silently he cursed himself for asking what his employer would no doubt deem a foolish question.

But Maxwell showed no derision. In fact, he seemed pleased to have the opportunity to elaborate. "He knows that Saint will want to see her, and he will believe that his fellow vampire is strong enough to withstand any attack the dhampyr commits, and he is correct in his assumption. But Saint will not be able to resist both the dhampyr and our agents. By then it will be too late."

Victor smiled. "And the Silver Palm will have both Bishop and Saint."

Maxwell smiled also, and lifted his glass once more. "And the dhampyr, Victor. Do not forget that we will have the dhampyr as well."

* * *

While out with Roxana, Marika realized the gold cross that had belonged to her mother was missing. She never took it off so the only thing she could think of to explain its disappearance was that it must have come off during last night's capture of the vampire.

It was a short distance out of their way and the cross meant a great deal to her, so after buying Roxana's dress—a pretty rose frock that complemented her dark coloring—Marika drove the buggy up the rutted hillside. Midday was still two hours away and the sun, while annoying, was not too bright or hot for her to stand. One of the more negative aspects of her "condition" was this accursed sensitivity to daylight.

Of course, everything about being a dhampyr was negative. She'd trade all her strength and abilities in a second to be a normal, human woman.

Or at least that's what she believed when she didn't give more thought to the consequences of such a trade.

The spot was easy to find. The grass was trampled from their fight and the boots of the men as they had collected the wounded Dimitru.

Roxana didn't even seem upset that her father had been hurt. Perhaps there was some hardness in her yet. Or perhaps she—like all young girls—simply didn't believe her father would ever die. Strangely, neither thought offered the comfort it should have.

"You search that side of the road," Marika directed as she climbed down. "I will search the other."

Wordless, Roxana jumped to her bidding. Sometimes Marika thought she could tell the girl to jump off a ledge and she would do it.

Would Roxana be so keen to mimic her, to idolize her, if she knew what Marika truly was? Bishop's remarks about her secret had made her paranoid. She had given him power over her, and that had been foolish.

The events of the previous night came back to her as Marika searched the grass where she had fought with Bishop. The look on his face when he saw her had been one of surprise with a little bit of appreciation. He had found her attractive until she attacked him.

She'd bet all the Englishman's gold that he had changed his mind on that account rather quickly. Too bad she couldn't say she now found him ugly as well. He should be ugly—twisted and gaunt like the evil he was. At the very least she should be immune to his charms, being what she was and knowing what she did.

He would have killed her this morning and instead of being terrified, or even angry, she'd thrilled at his strength. It had been too long since she'd encountered an adversary with the skill to better her. Usually the fact that she was a woman caught them off-guard, made them lazy. Bishop didn't let the fact that she was female stop him. He treated her like a true threat.

As odd as it was, she appreciated that he didn't underestimate her.

"I found it!"

Grinning proudly, Roxana bounded through the grass and across the road. The sunlight glinted off the gold chain dangling from her hand.

Marika took it from her with a hug. "Thank you. I was beginning to think it lost forever."

Roxana pointed to a spot over Marika's shoulder. "What is that over there?"

Glancing over her shoulder, Marika saw the remains of two stone chimneys and what appeared to be the walls of an old house. Surely it couldn't be a coincidence that this place stood in the exact spot where they had found Bishop? This might be his daytime resting place. There might be something here she could use against him—something that would help her in her quest to find Saint.

She glanced at the girl with a grin. "Want to go exploring?" She shouldn't. The sun was only going to get more and more difficult to bear, but she could not pass up the opportunity to investigate, especially if snooping yielded information about her mother's murderer.

Roxana didn't even reply, she simply started running for the ruins.

Laughing, Marika followed. God grant her half the enthusiasm of youth.

If she suspected there might be any danger to the girl, she wouldn't let her run in like that, but since vampires rarely shared a hiding spot, there was very little chance of their stumbling upon anything that might injure either of them. Even if they did, daylight would soon make an end of it.

There were footprints in the ash of an old campfire, but other than that there was nothing fresh at the ruins. Nothing was disturbed. There was the entrance to an old cellar, but it had caved in years ago. If anyone or anything had burrowed through it, they had managed to conceal it perfectly.

Marika placed her own boots in the ashen indentations. Her feet were small by comparison. The person who made these was a man with large feet and a wide stance. A man secure in his own strength and arrogance.

The prints didn't belong to a man at all. They belonged to Bishop. She knew it to be as true as the air she breathed.

If this wasn't Bishop's hideout then why had he been here? He hadn't been out for a leisurely stroll, and he couldn't have been hunting prey, not in such an isolated spot. Had he met someone there? Another vampire? Saint?

No, there was no trace of anyone else. If Saint had been here, she would have known it—of that she was certain. His presence would have been a slither at the base of her spine.

She looked around, eyes narrowed against the bright sunlight as a slight throbbing began in her skull. There had to be something. . .

There. In the woods.

Roxana was quick on her heels as Marika waded through the deep grass. The sea of green was disturbed in places, as though someone had walked through it recently. Her heart sped up. This was where she would find whatever it was that had brought Bishop there.

Her hopes were dashed when she saw the grave. Vampires Bishop's age didn't rest in graves—unless it was his own crypt. Only the vilest of creatures would desecrate a grave. She herself had done it only once and only because the person buried there—the person who was supposed to be dead and at rest—was about to rise a vampire.

This wasn't Bishop's grave. The ground here hadn't been displaced—unless she counted the weeds tossed to one side and the little mound of moss beside them. This grave had been recently tended, not disturbed.

"Elisabetta Radacanu," she read aloud. "Born 1583, died 1624."

Roxana's hand flew to her mouth. "It is her!"

Marika frowned at the girl's reaction. "You know who this woman is, Roxana?"

A quick nod was her answer. "She was *his* lover."

"Bishop's?" She shook her head. Calling him by name detracted from what he truly was—made him more human. "The vampire's?"

Another nod—accompanied by a glance back the way they had come. "This must have been their house."

Turning her attention behind them as well, Marika studied the ruins. It could have been a fine house at one time but now it was nothing more than pitiful shelter for traveling Gypsies and animals.

The vampire in her cellar had lived here? It was impossible to imagine him in a domestic situation. No doubt he had meant to mock the nearby village with his very presence, pretending to be human when in fact he preyed upon them.

"Some stories say she died as he tried to save her." Roxana's eyes were wide as she spoke. No doubt she saw this as a ghost story come true. "Others say he sacrificed her to save himself."

Marika snorted. "I know which version I believe." No vampire would ever put a human's life above its own.

Roxana stared at the ancient grave. "I wonder who buried her."

"Her family, I suppose. Whoever made the stone." It had happened hundreds of years ago, it shouldn't matter.

"But it says 'Beloved.'"

"You think the vampire buried her?" She spoke sharply—but she didn't like the assumptions her mind was making. "You won't make much of a hunter if you think they have feelings, Roxana. If you do not want to end up dead, or worse, a vampire yourself, you have to remember that they're not human."

The girl looked as though Marika had slapped

her. "They were once. You said yourself that under-standing your enemy makes you a better hunter."

She stomped off, leaving Marika watching af-ter her. Beautiful, she had hurt the girl's feelings. Marika spoke the truth, though. Roxana might have been right in that sometimes it was good to remem-ber one's own humanity, but the girl's naive and romantic nature would get her killed. She wouldn't last two minutes against a true monster.

Elisabetta Radacanu had died because she'd aligned herself with a vampire. She couldn't have been an innocent. No matter how she had died, she had brought it about by her own actions.

Marika would have a talk with Dimitru when she returned to the settlement. Roxana needed to meet young men from the nearby villages. The sooner she was married and living under her hus-band's roof, the sooner Marika could breathe a sigh of ease.

And judging from the pressure in her head, and the warmth spreading across her cheeks and nose, she would do well to get out of the sun. The last thing she wanted was to burn—it would make go-ing out again anytime soon painful.

Fastening her cross around her neck once more, Marika cast one last glance at the grave. Some-one had been here recently and tidied the site. It looked too well kept for a grave so old. Who would take such care of a woman centuries dead and forgotten?

There was only one person—*creature*—and she didn't want to believe him capable of such sentiment. She wouldn't believe it.

Although, she thought as she walked away, he *had* been there the night before.

And it would explain the dirt underneath his fingernails.

Chapter 3

Adhampyr who hunted vampires. Jesus Christ, what had he gotten himself into?

Lying on his back on the cot, Bishop listened for voices above him—anything that might give him some clue as to what they had planned for him. There was nothing. Earlier he had caught a bit of conversation, but nothing of any import.

Perhaps the dhampyr knew enough to talk about him elsewhere, so he couldn't hear. He'd like to think he might cut the tongue right out of her pretty head, but that would be a waste when there were so many other uses for it.

Asking her to fuck had been a ploy, but he wouldn't have said no if she'd taken him up on it. That said a lot about him—none of it flattering.

He hadn't planned to sleep when the sun rose, but pain from the holy water and anger eventually bowed to fatigue and his body's need to heal itself.

Sometime during his rest someone—and he had a good idea just who might be stealthy enough—had come in and suspended a large silver cross just inches above his chest. He had room to breathe, but just barely. Any other movement would burn him. His hostess was quite determined to keep him there.

Why was he there? More importantly, why had she kept him alive? And what in the name of all that was holy did that half-breed witch want with Saint? Even though he knew where the son of a bitch was, he wasn't about to just hand him over to the Huntress.

He was in her camp. Was this the only dungeon or had she others? Were there other prisoners here—Anara's brother, perhaps? He hadn't heard anything to indicate that he wasn't alone, but that didn't mean much. Other prisoners might be housed somewhere else. Or maybe he was the only one she had yet to kill. He served a purpose.

He only had to figure out what that purpose was to gain the upper hand. He knew her secret, but that did him little good unless he could force her to reveal herself in front of her men. Even then, such a revelation might only serve to get them both killed.

What had Saint done to earn this woman's wrath? Why did she target shadow creatures when she was half of that world herself? He could understand if she hunted evil as he did, but there seemed to be no pattern. She hunted without provocation.

She hunted those who should be her allies, not her enemies.

She was dangerous to his kind and others like him. With her dhampyric abilities she could track them, fight them. Her followers helped her with silver weapons and traps. She could not be allowed to continue this reign of blood or the shadow creatures of Eastern Europe would be culled severely.

Footsteps sounded on the ground outside, approaching a spot just above his head. Someone was coming. Were they coming to kill him? Feed him? He needed blood soon. Maybe it was his hostess. He'd very much like the chance to repay her for the baptism she bestowed upon him earlier.

The above-ground door to the cellar opened with a low groan. Sunlight flooded down the steps to pool on the floor, a man's shape silhouetted in the center.

Boots scuffed on the stone steps. Bishop watched as the lone man entered his prison. Perhaps he should have been more on guard, less sanguine, but having lived six hundred years he was more or less relaxed about whether he lived or died. That didn't mean he'd go easily, but he wasn't afraid of it either.

The man was tall and fair-haired. He had the thick build of a laborer or warrior—something Bishop could respect. He stood at the bottom of the steps—in the safety of the sun—and stared at Bishop.

Bishop stared back. When minutes had passed and the man hadn't spoken, hadn't moved—had done nothing but breathe and blink, Bishop spoke, "*Ce este?*"

The man shrugged. "I came here to look." His Romanian was rural, but not peasantish. Like his mistress, this man had something of an education. From the way the Huntress spoke English he would wager she had been born into a wealthy family.

Why would a lady dress herself up in trousers and hunt vampires?

"You have looked." Bishop arched a brow. "Finished?"

"All my life I have heard the story of how you were chased from this country."

Bishop's jaw tightened. "What of my wife? Did you hear what happened to her as well?"

"You sacrificed her to save yourself." The man spoke with such conviction that Bishop almost believed the lie himself.

"Do you truly believe I need to hide behind a woman?"

The man just stared. Did he believe that Bishop could have him for lunch and not feel an ounce of remorse? Because right now he could.

"No," the man said finally. "But it does not matter now, does it?"

"No." A faint stab of pain pierced Bishop's heart. Poor Elisabetta. It didn't matter for her, not now.

"You are a legend," the man went on. Did he ever plan to leave? "I thought you would be more frightening."

Grinning, Bishop held out one manacled arm. "Free me and see how frightening I can be."

The man actually paled at that suggestion.

"You people need to feed me, you know."

A frown puckered the man's brow. "I do not—"

"I'm no use to your mistress if I'm starved."

That seemed to make sense to the man. "I will tell someone to bring you food."

Good. Then he didn't have to worry about killing anyone. "Thank you. Now get out."

He expected the man to leave, but he didn't. Educated he might be, but he was dumb as a coffin nail. Bishop jerked at his chains, as though he was going to leap off the cot. The cross above him swayed but didn't touch him.

His visitor jumped, turned on his heel and ran up the steps. Darkness closed in once more as the doors fell shut with a loud bang.

Alone once more, Bishop lay back on his narrow bed and smiled. He didn't have much to be amused at, but sometimes it was convenient to be scary.

"Most dhampyrs die shortly after birth, did you know that?"

The woman—he didn't even know her name—didn't look at him as she entered his cell with a plate of food and a jug of ale that evening. His statement, however, had her gaze shooting to his before she could think.

He lay on the cot, his hands folded demurely over his stomach. "Your mother must have taken every precaution with you."

She set the plate and tankard on the floor just out of his reach and then used her toe to nudge them closer.

"I was raised by my grandmother."

Interesting. Had the mother died? Not wanted her half-vampire baby? "Then she obviously took very good care of you."

"She did."

He watched her for a moment, studying the slight tilt of her fine nose, the curve of her full pink lips. Under different circumstances he would have found her attractive, perhaps even intriguing. Wanting to screw her didn't count. As it was he simply wanted to learn as much as he could about her in order to find her weakness.

"What is your name?"

She didn't look at him. "You already know what they call me."

"Your real name."

Her chin lifted. She looked at him now—direct and right in the eye. "Why?"

"Because I want to know what to call you." Christ, he wished he could sit up. "You know my name."

"I know what they call you." She said it as if it made a difference. "That makes us even."

"It is my name. It has been my name longer than the original."

She looked away. "There is no need for you to know my name, nor do I need to know yours."

"Makes it easier, doesn't it?" Christ, it would be so much easier to be intimidating if only he could move. "Then you do not have to think of me as a person."

Her jaw tightened. He had struck a nerve. "Like your name, you have been a monster far longer than you were ever a person."

"And you have been both and neither since the day you were born."

She reacted as though he had slapped her. "Marika," she whispered. "My name is Marika."

It was a pretty name—and surprisingly it suited her. She was far too pretty to be the killer she was. For some reason, her confiding this to him warmed him a little. He didn't want to warm toward her because he knew she'd kill him in a blink.

"My name was Blaise." That was all the apology she would get for his earlier remark. She didn't deserve his guilt or sympathy. He didn't care if she had never belonged, if she straddled two worlds. That was no excuse for murder.

She nodded, her dark braid falling over her shoulder as she composed herself once more. This tougher side of her was much easier to deal with. "Tell me where Saint is."

Was Saint truly the reason for this abduction? And how had she known he would be in Romania? Who had told her and why? "Why do you want him so badly?"

"He killed my mother."

Shit and damn. Never mind warming toward her; that was almost reason to feel sorry for her. "I am sorry."

"So am I." She hesitated one second as her black gaze bored into his. "Tell me where he is."

"Even if I wanted to tell you I couldn't. I don't know where he is."

"You lie."

"I haven't spoken to him for almost twenty-six years." He and Saint had met shortly after the woman Saint loved had died. Saint had been inconsolable. Not only had the woman died, but the child she had been carrying as well. Saint had tried to change her to save her, but it hadn't worked. He had given the woman his blood, but she was too weak to survive the process. Even though Saint hadn't been the child's father, he had grieved as if he were.

That had been in Brasov, not far from here. The child would have been a dhampyr had it survived, as Saint's blood would have run in its veins. Bishop stared at Marika. Surely not. . .

But there was something familiar about those dark eyes of hers. Dhampyrs often took on traits of their vampire sire, though no one knew why. The truth was, dhampyrs were simply too rare to know much about them.

It wasn't impossible that Marika was Saint's get. What were the odds of Saint being involved with two pregnant women? But Saint was so sure the child was dead, and he had seen his lover die. If Marika was the child, wouldn't she know that Saint hadn't killed her mother, he had been trying to save her?

Unless, of course, she had been told a different story.

"You know for a fact that Saint killed your mother?"

"Yes." Determination lit her eyes. "Tell me where he is."

"I told you I do not know."

"And I call you a liar." Her face was flushed in the torchlight, her eyes bright with anger. "You want to protect your friend."

Friend? Had Saint ever borne or aspired to such a title? They had been more brothers than friends—loyal to the death if not particularly close. It was that loyalty that protected Saint even now. "I wouldn't be much of a friend if I didn't, would I?"

"He killed my mother."

"And killing him won't bring her back." Six hundred years made it easy to be sage. But he spoke from experience on that count.

"It will give me great satisfaction."

"No it won't." Six hundred years had driven that point home as well.

"You mean to say that if you were given the chance to avenge your wife's death that you would not?"

Bishop's blood ran cold. How dare this woman talk about his wife. "She was killed by people much like yourself and your men, and I do not need the chance to take revenge. I killed them all almost three hundred years ago."

Her face turned even tighter. "So you say. There are those who would believe you killed her yourself."

It was a cheap shot, spoken to rile him. It didn't. There were so many other ways she could bait him, but she was too angry to see them. "I do not deny it. Her relationship with me was what got her killed. I offered her immortality but she would not take it. She was Catholic." Why was he telling her all this?

"She knew she would be damned."

"You believe I'm damned?" It wasn't a surprise really. Everyone thought that—even the church he and the others had turned themselves over to. Bishop didn't believe it, not for a second.

"I know it."

"And what of you, little half-breed?" He made it sound as distasteful as he could. "There is no claiming both worlds when we die. Will you go to Hell or Heaven?"

"I hope to go to Heaven."

"By slaughtering innocent people? I think not."

"There is nothing innocent about anyone I have killed—nor were they human."

"You're not human, and by that same rationale, you deserve to die as well."

She didn't say anything, but he could feel her animosity—and her confusion. It couldn't be easy being two-natured. He wasn't about to pity her—after all, she had wrapped him in silver and dumped holy water on him—but she would never truly belong with humans and she had made herself an outcast with the shadow world.

She nudged the plate again. "Ivan said you wanted food."

Bishop stared at the plate. It had stew on it. "That's not the kind of food I meant. Not that it doesn't look and smell delicious, but it won't quiet the hunger I feel."

She looked horrified. "I will not bring you blood."

He almost chuckled at her expression. "Then we're going to have a problem."

"Are you threatening me?"

He searched her face; there was no guile in it, no feigned innocence. "You really don't know, do you?"

"Know what?"

"My God, how many vampires have you killed?" What else didn't she know, and how could he use her ignorance to his advantage?

She shrugged. "One hundred perhaps."

Good Lord. "And you never once kept one like you are keeping me?"

Hesitation. Then, "No."

"Do you never crave blood?"

Her hands clenched. "Of course not!"

She was lying, he could see it in her eyes, but that didn't matter right now. "So you have no idea what happens to a starved vampire?"

"I assume they grow weaker."

That cockiness would get her killed someday. "Some young ones are like that, yes. But I am not young, little halfling, nor am I like vampires born from a bite."

"How?"

"Starvation doesn't weaken me, it makes me more like an animal. In a few days I will be stronger than normal. I will also have less control. I will be ruled by my hunger, driven to feed. Your chains and crosses won't be able to stop me when that happens."

She was frowning at him. "You lie. You want to frighten me into letting you go."

"Don't be stupid!" He struggled upright, and the cross burned his chest. He fell back on the cot with a snarl, singed but not scarred. He would kill her if he had to, but he didn't want to take innocent people along with her.

"I do not scare that easily, nor am I so foolish as to believe you would tell me the truth about such matters." She nodded at the stew. "That is all the food you will get from me, *monstru*."

She had no idea just how much of a monster he could become. She would starve him for the sake of her pride, think he would become more malleable to her demands. Oh, yes, she was going to get herself killed one of these days.

She left him there, a niggling hunger deep within him and irritation smoldering there as well.

Eventually he reached for the stew and ale. He

even managed to work himself into a semisitting position to eat. Then he lay back down and started thinking about escape.

And he hoped that if he lost control before he could escape, the village was away for the night—even though he knew that was unlikely.

Sometimes, it *wasn't* so convenient to be scary.

Irina Comenescu lived in the nearby town of Fagaras, for which the mountains that Marika called home were named. She used to live in the village with Marika and the others, but Marika hadn't liked having her grandmother so close. Her enemies could use her *bunica* against her, and Marika would rather spend eternity in Hell than put the woman who had raised her in danger.

Irina bore the harshness of her life on her heavily lined face. The past twenty years had seen stability and progress blossom across the country where before there had been unrest and a desire for reform. Marika knew little of that struggle. Her grandmother had lived through it. The old woman lost a son who went off to fight on the side of the Russians against the Ottoman Empire in '77, a mere three years after her only daughter died in childbirth and one year before she lost her husband to a wasting illness.

Whenever Marika wanted to see true strength, she went to her grandmother, who had also been both mother and father to her.

The house was a little, tidy pink dwelling in one

of the better neighborhoods in the city. Marika's father hadn't wanted anything to do with his daughter, but he wanted her brought up in a manner befitting her birth—when she wasn't at one of the schools he sent her to. She and her *bunica* had lived in comfort, with a housekeeper and houseman, but poverty was everywhere, and since Marika had never been told to think of herself as someone's better, she had friends who didn't enjoy the same life she did.

This little pink house was where she ran whenever she needed guidance. And she needed guidance now.

Bishop had said she was half monster, that her own code marked her as one of those who deserved to die. She could deny it all she wanted to, but when he said it, he had made her realize that if she ever met another like herself and if that other was not a hunter as she was, then she would kill it. She would kill it even though it was half human.

Of course she would kill it. No one should have to live like this. That didn't make her a monster; it made her . . . merciful.

She tethered her horse to the fence where it could graze on the lawn and knocked on the door. This was not her house anymore, and no matter what her grandmother said, she would nòt enter without invitation. And even if she were to try, the door should be bolted from the inside as she instructed her grandmother to do always.

From the other side of the door Marika's sensitive

ears heard the approach of shuffling footsteps. Her grandmother was by no means young, but a hard life had aged her more than her years. "Who is it?" asked a clear, strong voice in lyrical Romanian.

Marika smiled, as she did every time she heard that voice—and pleased that the old woman took the precautions she had asked of her. "Marika, *Bunica*."

There was the sound of a bolt sliding and then the door opened. Before she could speak, Marika was enveloped in strong arms, her cheek pressed against gray hair that smelled of sweets and baking.

"Papanasi prajiti," Marika almost sighed the words. The little balls of raisin-filled batter fried and sprinkled with sugar were her favorite treat.

"Da," her grandmother replied, releasing her. "I had a feeling you would come today."

They sat in the front room, which looked much the same as it had when Marika was a child, with its sturdy furniture and blue drapes. They drank thick, strong coffee with their sweets and talked of the comings and goings of the neighborhood. Half an hour or more had passed when her grandmother finally said, "So tell me, child. Why have you come?"

Marika swallowed the last of her pastry. "I captured a vampire the other night."

Her grandmother shook her head and muttered something under her breath. Marika didn't want to know what she said. Her grandmother had never approved of what she did. She had wanted her to marry years ago—even had the groom picked out. It might have happened if the groom's father hadn't risen from his grave a vampire. Perhaps "risen" wasn't quite the right word. He had clawed and dug his way out, rising to the surface a dirty, snarling creature half mad with bloodlust.

Seeing your fiancée drive a stake through your father's chest was more than most men could stomach. Grigore called the wedding off, despite the fact that she had prevented his father from making a meal of him.

"He is a friend of the one who killed Mama."

The old woman froze. The hand that rose to her mouth had a slight tremor to it. Her shock was almost palpable; Marika felt it slip over her like powder.

"Marika, why do you chase these ghosts?"

"Because the creature that killed my mother must pay for what it did to her—what it did to me!"

Her grandmother shook her head again. Her lined face was pale and sorrowful. "Your mother would not want this."

"You do not believe she would want her killer brought to justice?" The very idea angered her.

"No, especially not by you."

That was an odd way to phrase it. "What do you mean?"

Her grandmother thought for a moment, collecting herself and her thoughts. "I do not like this violent life for you. I do not wish to lose you as I lost your mother."

Guilt pierced Marika's heart. Undoubtedly that had been her grandmother's intention. They never talked about the death of Marika's mother. Her grandmother avoided the subject whenever it came up. Why? Was it simply that painful? Or were there things her *bunica* knew that she wouldn't—or couldn't—share with Marika?

"You will not lose me." Even as she spoke she thought of how close to death she had come the other night when Bishop had tried to escape. How fair of her was it to risk her life when her grandmother had already lost so many loved ones?

"Your father came to visit a few days ago. He asked about you."

This was her grandmother's way—moving from an unfavorable subject to something diverting. She knew how Marika felt about her father, and she knew that anger would overpower curiosity about her mother. It always did.

"Did he?" More likely *Bunica* had offered information to him. Her father didn't care where she was or what happened to her. He never had. He saw her as a reminder of the monster that had killed his beloved wife. As a child Marika had prayed for him to love her. Now she thought of him as a little more than a man she barely knew.

"His wife was delivered of a new baby just last month."

Marika's jaw tightened. "Was it a son?"

Her grandmother nodded, her expression uncertain.

"Finally, an heir. One that is fully human and the right sex."

"Marika." It wasn't reproach, but sympathy.

"I am fine." It was an old wound, one that should no longer sting, but it did. "I hope he will be happy now."

Perhaps now that the old man has his precious son he'd finally die—that was what she truly wished. Die so she wouldn't have to think about the fact that she was such a disappointment and shame that he didn't want to see her.

Now if he could just be killed—and turned—by a vampire, she would have an excuse to shove a stake through his unfeeling black heart. He had cast her aside like rubbish, and every time she killed a vampire she thought of him and how he would have to approve of her now.

The bastard. He was such a large part of her life for someone who was never in it.

Some of her thoughts must have shown on her face because her grandmother looked almost afraid.

"Your face frightens me when it does that."

That was a subtle shift of her features, a brightening of her eyes. It was how the vampire side of her reacted in times of high emotion.

Marika stared at her feet, willing herself back into a state of calm. "I am sorry."

"Do not apologize for what you feel, my child. You mustn't think of him, he does not matter."

I would if you would stop talking about him. She kept

that thought to herself, of course. Her grandmother seemed to think she deserved to know about her father's life, but she hated to see Marika upset by it.

"Bunica," she asked, lifting her head, "am I a monster?" It had been her father who first called her such. Bishop was the only other person to do so to her face. No one else knew what she was, no one but her grandmother.

That wrinkled face fell in sorrow. "Oh, my dear child, no." She held out her arms, and Marika went to them. On her knees in front of the old woman's chair, she pressed her face against her grandmother's shoulder, felt the comfort there and wept.

Chapter 4

The only thing Marika despised more than vampires was being wrong.

As she sat on the foot of her bed in front of the fireplace, the flames drying her hair, she very much feared she was wrong to not give Bishop blood.

She was alone in her little cottage, fresh from a lukewarm bath, and it was late. She was dressed in a nightgown her grandmother had given her. It was soft and demure, and Marika had ripped almost a foot off the bottom of it so that she would be able to fight in it if her little village was ever attacked.

Her little village. Her home and pride. It was just a few houses along a lane, really, and for now it was silent. Everyone was safe and in bed where they belonged. There were the usual sounds of night, the fire crackling in the hearth, nocturnal animals on the prowl and horses snorting softly in the barn, but there weren't any voices—and absolutely no sound from beneath her.

If Bishop knew it was her cellar he was prisoner in, no doubt he'd try to keep her awake as much as he could. Either he hadn't bothered trying to sort the sound of her footsteps, or she had done a better job at insulating the cottage against noise than she thought. Thick rugs covered the floor. Heavy drapes covered the windows, and she had learned to move as lightly as a cat—it had kept her alive on more than one occasion.

She didn't even talk or sing inside the cottage. In fact, the only things she did there were sleep and bathe. She ate with Dimitru and his family and occasionally with her grandmother. She despised cooking, and cooking for one was even more despicable. Sometimes she would lie in bed and read a bit, but even then she worried about making some sort of sound that would identify her.

But she was growing weary of being so cautious, and the vampire in the cellar did nothing to ease the feeling.

Days had passed since he'd first made the request for blood. He had been in her possession for almost one full week, and he had changed radically since his capture. He had become more agitated, more venomous.

More like an animal than a man.

Never had she seen such a change in a vampire. By now he should be lethargic, weakened from fasting. Blood was what sustained a vampire, and lack of it should drain the strength from him. That was what she had learned in her research, what all the books and stories said. Not so with Bishop. If anything, he seemed stronger, more powerful. Her fear now was that he would break his restraints.

If that happened, she and her people were dead. She didn't fool herself that she could defeat him—not alone. It had taken her and her men and Armitage's poison to capture him under normal circumstances. They might be able to destroy him were he to escape, but he would take as many of them with him as he could.

There was something in his eyes that pulled at her heart in a most guilty fashion. She couldn't bear to look at him, because it was always there looking back at her. It was as though he knew all was lost—like a tiger in a cage that a child was about to fall into. Bishop might not want to kill them, but he would.

She didn't want to feel for him, but a small part of her had to admit that she might have been wrong to assume he was the same black-hearted killer as Saint. That didn't mean Bishop was innocent—for a vampire that was impossible.

Lately she had come to think about how he looked the night she had first met him—when they had fought and she knew the thrill of a true adversary—that brief flicker of doubt. For a second she had wondered if she would win. She rarely thought that—but she would think it from now on. She wouldn't be so arrogant about her own abilities.

If she had faced Bishop alone he would have bested her, and not just because he was a full-blood, but because he was simply stronger and faster than any other vampire she had ever encountered.

It wasn't that she was impressed, she told herself, because she wasn't. She was simply acknowledging a formidable opponent. His power was what she needed to think about, his skills and abilities. Those were what she needed to be familiar with so she would know how to retaliate against them.

She wouldn't think about the lines of his mouth, the wide set of his eyes, the texture of his hair. She was looking at him as a man, and that was more dangerous than letting him free of his shackles.

Tomorrow she was to meet the Englishman—Armitage—again. She was supposed to have Saint's location by now. Instead, she had nothing but Bishop's growing animosity and his repeated insistence that she knew something about the disappearance of someone named Nycen. Apparently there were others he thought she should know about as well, creatures she had never known existed, let alone encountered.

There was no hint of a lie in his tone or gaze, nothing that made her suspect he was trying to distract her with this information. Someone was giving her credit—or blame—for the disappearances of these creatures.

The shadow world—that was his term, not hers—now considered her enough of a threat that they had sent Bishop after her. His mission could not have been to kill her, else she would have been dead that first night. He would have snapped her like a twig before she managed to inject the poison into him.

He was not a normal vampire, that she had established. He was like nothing she had ever seen. Was Saint the same? More importantly, was that the kind of blood that had poisoned her own?

God, what did that make her?

Bunica said her mother would not want this for her. What would her mother think of what she had become? Would she be proud that she had died bringing such a child into the world, or would she turn her back on the *monstru* as her father had?

She could forgive her father for thinking her a monster. As much as she despised him for it, as much as his abandonment hurt her, she understood the fear and hatred behind it. But Bishop had insinuated as much himself; a vampire thought she was a monster. What kind of person did one have to be to be termed a monster by those who were soulless?

The kind of a person who starved someone who had never done anything against her in order to get information.

Ridiculous. She must stop thinking of these things as human, as innocent people. They weren't. *He* wasn't. She might not be guilty of the crimes Bishop accused her of, but that didn't mean she disagreed with whoever *was* responsible.

All she needed to remember was that *she* was the kind of person the monsters feared. She was strong and determined and she was not afraid. She was the kind of person who would not rest until she had killed every vampire and monster she could.

The kind of person she was certain her mother never dreamed she'd ever become.

.

She was starving him to prove a point she might not live to enjoy.

"Our Father, who art in Heaven . . ." he mumbled the prayer under his breath to take his mind off the gnawing in his gut. In all his years he had never been given any evidence that God hated or loved his kind. As far as he could tell, he hadn't suffered more or less than other creatures, human or otherwise. He'd just had more time to spend suffering.

And more time to ponder it.

There had been an equal amount of joy in his life as well, so he couldn't be that despised by the Almighty.

And when he died, Bishop suspected that his soul would be weighed the same as everyone else's. He had a fairly good idea where he would end up. What would his little halfling Marika think of that if she knew where? Would she worry that she might end up some place decidedly warmer, or would she send him to his Maker right then and there to test his theory?

The thought would have made him smile at any

other time, but fear kept his humor at bay. He was very much afraid—and didn't mind admitting it—that he was going to lose control soon.

Days had passed since he told her what would happen if she did not feed him, and on each of those days she had come to him and asked him where Saint was, promising him blood as a reward if he told.

Had he been stupid enough to believe she'd keep her word, he might have lied and made up a location for Saint, just so she'd give him what he needed to regain his equilibrium.

But every day she came, looking more and more appealing in her worn trousers and man's shirt. The clothes were shapeless, but sometimes when she moved, the fabric would mold itself against the curve of a hip, a breast. She was undeniably woman.

". . . and forgive us our trespasses as we forgive those who trespass against us . . ."

Perhaps it was the hunger that made him find her so arousing. Maybe he was losing his mind, because he ought to be thinking of ways to kill her, not imagining the weight of her breasts in his hands.

The idea of killing her was not so appealing as it had once been. Now he didn't want her blood for any sense of revenge or justice, but for the simple taste of it on his tongue.

Perhaps it was because they were of a similar nature, or perhaps it was because she had become increasingly desperate to discover Saint's location—so much so that he felt sorry for her. Sympathy made her methods easier to understand.

But it wasn't sympathy that made him wonder what all that black hair would look like loose and tumbling down around him as she rode him. Sometimes—and he knew this from experience—dislike made for fabulous sex.

He ignored these desires as best he could. The only thing she seemed to feel for him was disgust, and he used that to center himself.

"For thine is the kingdom . . ."

Every day that she asked about Saint, he looked her in the eye and demanded to know the location of Anara's brother, Nycen. Either she didn't know what he was talking about or she was a better liar than he was willing to give her the credit for being.

He wasn't prepared to find her innocent just yet, not when there was so much blood on her hands already. But denial seemed strange behavior for someone so seemingly proud of her kills. If she had taken and killed Nycen, why not crow about it? Why not rub his face in it? That seemed more her style, since she was so damn righteous.

And she had the nerve to call him a monster. *She* was the monster, and if she didn't feed him soon, she was going to find out just what kind of monster he could be. The blood he spilled would be on her hands—not that he would leave much to spill.

"*Amen.*"

He heard the hatches of the cellar open and familiar footsteps—almost inaudible—click on the steps.

"Please," Bishop's voice was hoarse, desperate as she came into the cellar. He was done with pride. He'd crawl if she wanted him to. "Give me blood."

His control was slipping. Hunger threatened to consume what humanity was left in him. Something that had been buried deep within him was writhing to the surface. Whether it was self-preservation or self-destruction that drove it, he didn't know, but it was becoming nigh on impossible to fight it.

He didn't want to let it loose.

Marika didn't look at him—she rarely did—as she set the plate of food on the floor as was her habit.

"Where is he?"

This was their usual game—one Bishop was tired of playing. Tired and angry. He bolted upright on the cot, the cross suspended above him hitting him square in the chest. Smoke rose.

Snarling, he seized the silver as it seared his flesh and yanked it free of its chains. He threw it hard enough that it embedded itself in the wall on the opposite side of the cellar.

"I told you I do not know where he is."

Staring at Marika and her wide, dark eyes, Bishop strained against the metal that bound him. The little idiot didn't even have the sense to move.

For days he'd let her needle him, endured her questions and accusations, all because he thought there might be something more to his abduction than a mere vendetta against Saint, but there wasn't. Whatever agenda she had, he served no other purpose to her than as a means to finding the vampire she believed killed her mother.

He was being punished for something Saint had done. Hell, Saint might not even be the one she was looking for. If he ever ran into the bastard, he'd make sure the other vampire knew what Bishop had suffered on his behalf.

Links stretched as the chains began to pull from the wall and floor. The silver cuffs around his wrists and ankles burned, but it only fed his strength. Her restraints wouldn't hold him once the beast rose.

Any second now, what little control he had left would disappear. He would be free. Free to do whatever he damn well pleased. Free to feed.

Marika would be the first one he killed. God, he wanted to do so much more than kill her.

He snarled at her. "Get out!"

She looked surprised that he had spoken. To be honest, he was a little shocked as well. He was more in control than he thought.

Or at least he had been.

"Now!" A low growl escaped him as the chains began to pull apart.

His vision a haze of red, Bishop watched hopelessly as Marika ran to the door, but instead of fleeing, she began calling for her men and their weapons. She told them to bring something she called "the English poison." He could only hope it was the same stuff she had taken him down with that night she captured him.

He prayed that it would be strong enough to act against him now.

And he prayed that she either killed him this night or that when he woke up he was as far away from innocent people as he could be.

The demon inside him knew it was in danger and it pushed harder. Chains popped and snapped, ripped from the walls with the sheer force of Bishop's will. They dragged on the dirt floor as he stalked toward Marika. He didn't hurry, even though he knew her men would come. She didn't move, but she was poised to fight. Reaching around her, he closed the door—either to protect her men from him, or to buy him a few more minutes before he killed her; he honestly didn't know which.

There was a very good chance that both of them might end up dead before this night was over.

"I do not want to hurt you," he rasped, "but if you do not stop me, I will kill you and anyone else who gets in my way. Do you understand?"

She nodded, her face stark white.

"Good. And you do realize now that you could have prevented this?"

Another nod.

"I wanted you to know that—just in case you happen to survive."

She swallowed, her long, elegant throat constricting beneath her ivory skin. Her pulse fluttered like sparrow wings at the base of her neck. How he wanted to place his tongue there, feel the rush of blood through her veins. Sink his fangs into her and feel her hot and slick in his mouth. Glut himself on her.

Wetness burned his eyes—either tears or blood. How long had it been since he'd lost himself to the hunger? He hadn't killed a human in centuries—not one who hadn't deserved it.

Marika was a cold killer—why feel any guilt for what he was about to do?

With that thought, the last of his control withered, overcome by the lust flooding his senses. His fangs slid from his gums with one painful push. His skin was hot and tingling, as though every nerve was alive and on fire.

He met Marika's terrified gaze. She might be afraid, but she was in a fighting stance. He had been right. One of them was not going to survive having met the other.

"Kill me." It was his final request.

And then he pounced.

She could still feel the heat of his breath on her skin, the heavy weight of him pressing her into the cellar floor. The silver manacles on his wrists had burned and bit into her arms as he held them pinned out to the side. Helpless as a kitten, her heart pounding so hard she could hear it, she had waited for the fangs scraping her neck to bite and when they had. . .

"Surely you're jesting."

Shaking her head, Marika stared stupidly at the Englishman. She was shaking, and the spot beneath the bandage on her neck throbbed in time with the pulse between her legs.

Oh. God.

Thankfully she didn't have to ask what he was talking about. He went ahead and refreshed her memory. "Whatever do you mean you need more time?"

Her fingers trembled as she placed them against the bandage hidden beneath a scarf around her neck. Pressure did nothing to ease the ache, it only made it worse. She swallowed and squeezed her thighs together beneath the table. "He hasn't told me where Saint is yet."

"That wasn't part of our agreement." Armitage looked angry, worried, and a little confused. "I say, are you quite all right?"

Did she laugh at his perception or take his eyes out just for spite? "I'm fine."

Fine so long as she didn't think about Bishop wrapping her braid around his hand, pulling her head back. . .

"You do not look fine."

"I am." Her voice was hoarse but firm.

Bishop's hips had pressed against hers, his legs between hers. The hardness that made her arch against him as his fangs pierced her throat.

Killing him had been the last thing on her mind.

It made her sick just to think about it—not that she couldn't kill him, but what she had wanted to do instead.

Wanted him inside her where she was hot and wet for him. Wanted his hardness thrusting inside her as he drank her life away. She wanted *him*.

Thank God her men had come with the poison. Thank God her blood seemed to cool Bishop's ardor.

If only there had been something to cool hers.

The Englishman gave her an odd look. "You are very flushed. Would you like some water?"

She doubted the tavern had any fresh water. "No." Then she added, "Thank you." Her grandmother had raised her to be polite.

"I do not like this." Armitage gave his head a little shake, then raised his finger. "We agreed you would have the vampire one week, no more."

His tone grated on her nerves, and that was a welcome diversion from thoughts of Bishop and the things she could have done to him. "We agreed that I could have him until he told me Saint's location."

"Which we also agreed should not take more than seven days."

She shrugged. "As you can see, however, it has."

The Englishman's mouth thinned, becoming nothing more than a slash in the lower half of his pale face. "That is no concern of mine."

"I could refuse to bring him to you." The idea of losing Bishop filled her with such anxiety and fear that her throat tightened with it. How would she find Saint without him?

How would she ever experience the promise of such ecstasy again without him?

The arrogance she was coming to associate with Armitage revealed itself full force with the curve of his smirk and the mocking glint in his gray eyes. "I could tell every shadow creature from here to England where to find the Huntress as well."

The shivering, cloying warmth of Bishop's embrace melted entirely away to cool aggression. "I do not like threats." She didn't like this little man acting as though he had power over her either. Surely he knew she could kill him and no one would ever be the wiser? She could hide him where no one would ever find him.

"Nor do I. One more day, that is all I can give you."

She would accept that for now. She would play by his rules for now. It would take Bishop almost that long to recover from the amount of poison Sergei had injected into his system. She would find a way to buy more time if she needed it later.

It had been easy for her men to sneak up on Bishop. He had been too busy suckling at her throat to worry about them. The taste of her blood had seemed to calm him somewhat, taken some of the aggression from him. After that first bite he had become almost tender with her—not at all brutal as she had expected. His mouth had been hot, his lips seductively warm. He had jerked against her when the needle pierced his flesh, sending jolts of pleasure through her groin.

She had to bite her own lip to keep her men from hearing her moan.

"One full day and the night," she countered. "It will be safer to transport him during the day."

"For you, perhaps." Pale eyes narrowed. "How do I know you will not kill him?"

She blinked. "If I wanted him dead, he would be." But inside, she asked herself the same question. What was stopping her from simply killing Bishop? Why hadn't she allowed her men to kill him last night as they had so feverishly wanted?

The money, of course. The men and villagers who supported her put their lives in danger for her cause. They had children and wives to feed.

And he was her only link to Saint, of course. That was all there was to it.

Her answer seemed to appease him. "Very well. One full day and night and you will bring him to me the following morning."

"Where?"

Armitage thought for a moment. "The site of his former dwelling. That seems fitting."

It seemed cruel to hand Bishop over to this man on the very spot where she had captured him and where he had lost so very much, but what did she care? For all she knew Bishop wouldn't even realize where he was.

She shouldn't care about his feelings. He had tried to kill her. He would have killed her had her men not come to the rescue.

Wouldn't he have?

That death, she suspected, would have been

more pleasureable than anything else she had ever experienced.

"Fine." She rose to her feet. Her legs shook a little. If she wore skirts it wouldn't have been noticeable. As it was, she thought the Englishman saw her slight sway.

"You really ought to get some rest," he told her without his usual mockery. "I think you are pushing yourself farther than your constitution can support."

Her gaze locked with his, letting him see just how close she was to shoving her boot down his throat. "Would that be my delicate, *feminine* constitution?"

Now it was he who placed his hand against his throat, no doubt remembering how she had pinned him to the table on their first meeting.

He shook his head. "I meant no disrespect."

Of course he hadn't. She almost snorted in derision.

Marika left him without a farewell. Stomping out of the tavern, she met Ivan and Sergei outside, where the sun was thankfully hidden behind thick clouds. The two had insisted on accompanying her. Did they think she was a weak woman too? They should know better. Of course, they had no idea what she truly was.

She didn't even know what she truly was. This encounter with Bishop had aroused feelings and sensations she had never experienced before.

"Everything all right?" Sergei asked, his native

Romanian more gruff than usual. Was it just her imagination, or did he look at her differently now after last night?

Marika nodded. "For now."

She swung herself into the saddle of her black mare and nudged the horse into motion with her heels. When she was enough in the lead so that the men couldn't see her face, she touched her lower lip. It was tender where she had bit it, but it was already healing. No one would notice the strange marks her teeth had made.

She had felt them behind her lips—felt them ease from her gums as Bishop's hot, wet mouth worked against her throat.

Fangs. She had started to grow fangs.

And she had wanted to sink them into the taut, golden flesh of his bare shoulder as his had into her neck. She wanted to taste him, wanted his blood in her mouth and his body inside hers.

At that moment, entwined with Bishop on the dirty cellar floor, she had wanted to know the taste of blood.

She had wanted to be a vampire.

"What are we going to do?"

Maxwell applied a match to his cigar. The pungent aroma of expensive tobacco soon wafted around him. He believed you could tell a lot about a man from the cigars that he smoked. His were expensive, exotic and smelled of power.

"Always have a contingency plan, Armitage." He shook the match to extinguish it. "It's the only way to guarantee success."

The younger man was confused, and of course he would be, having neither Maxwell's intellect nor his experience in these matters. "Sir?"

"In truth Saint is someone else's problem. Wherever he is, our brethren there will track and capture him." He drew a mouthful of smoke and slowly exhaled. "Our goal first and foremost is to bring in Bishop and the dhampyr."

Armitage seemed surprised. "So we just wait?"

"Of course not." No, the boy really had no talent for thought. Orders, Armitage could follow, but thought was a mystery to him. It was both a virtue and a flaw as far as Maxwell was concerned. "The head of our order in Italy informs me that Temple is already on his way into their custody. He wants the others as quickly as possible."

"But we haven't the number of men it will take to capture both the vampire and the dhampyr."

Maxwell smiled. As dull as Armitage's intellect could be, he enjoyed enlightening the young man. "The vampire, no. The dhampyr, however, will be easier. Bishop will be easy prey once we have her."

"I don't understand."

"Of course you don't. I will use smaller words perhaps?"

Armitage flushed, shame and indignation heating his blood. "Forgive me."

No, the boy wasn't terribly bright, but he knew

his place. That would serve him well. "We have already used the dhampyr once to entice Bishop. He believes her responsible for many of the disappearances we orchestrated in this area."

"But when she is taken he will know she wasn't responsible."

"Yes, and he will set out to find who is. We will leave enough of a trail for him to come right to us. And when he does . . ."

"We will have the means to hold him." Armitage's youthful face lit with a grin as he finally put it all together in his little, narrow mind.

Maxwell smiled. "Two birds, one stone."

"Brilliant, sir."

"Yes, I know." He pushed the cedar wood box across the desk. He felt like celebrating. "Cigar?"

Chapter 5

The first thing Bishop saw when he opened his eyes was Marika. She sat on a chair in the center of the room, one booted foot crossed over the worn thigh of her trousers. Call him old-fashioned, but he couldn't help but wonder what she would look like in a pretty dress.

That thought alone told him his demon was under control once more. And that perhaps he had been kicked in the head, because he shouldn't be thinking of this woman as attractive, especially when he had, for all intents and purposes, tried to eat her.

They were in the familiar confines of the cellar. He was on his cot, chained as usual. He might have thought the night before a dream were it not for the fact that the shackles were new—and someone had finally thought to give him a shirt.

And of course, there was the bandage on Marika's neck. Dhampyrs didn't heal as fast as vampires apparently.

"Are you all right?" he asked.

She nodded, her dark braid shining with blue highlights under the lamplight. "You seem to have recovered as well."

"Yes." He didn't have to tell her the reason for it. From the way her fingers stroked the linen on her neck, she already knew the answer. He wasn't even scarred from the silver that had burned his skin.

"I suppose I should just be thankful that you didn't kill me."

"I suppose." He could have told her he wouldn't have killed her, but he couldn't—not and have it be the truth. "I did not want to kill you. Not like that."

She nodded; whatever she took from that explanation she kept to herself.

"That little bit of blood was all you needed?"

It was odd having this conversation with her— it was too surreal, like talking about debt with a friend who had just given you a shilling.

"Because it was yours, yes." There was no point in adding that hers was the most potent blood he had ever tasted. And he would rather drive a stake through his eye than admit that he was still intoxicated from it.

She would no doubt kill him if he told her he'd sell his soul for more. That one taste of her had only made him hungry for another.

Marika seemed to understand what he meant. He watched the changes in her expression as she processed what the fact that he had tasted her and taken so much strength from it meant. "You will be leaving here tomorrow."

"I assume you do not mean that I will be free to go on my merry way?"

She actually turned pink at his sarcasm. That wasn't guilt coloring her cheeks, was it?

He tried another approach. "Are you going to kill me?" He certainly wouldn't blame her for it. That didn't mean he intended to make it easy for her either.

She seemed shocked by the suggestion, as though she hadn't killed before. "No."

"Then you either plan to hold me elsewhere or you're going to hand me over to people who will kill me."

She looked away. Fair enough. Tonight was the night then. No matter how much damage he sustained, he would have to escape before dawn. He hadn't tried before this because he wanted to discover what she wanted with him and to determine whether she was lying about not knowing Nycen. Now that he knew it really was all about Saint, and that she wasn't responsible for Nycen's disappearance, there was no more need to put himself through this hell.

"I would have thought you'd do the job yourself." He kept his tone light, but the venom was there all the same.

She surprised him by meeting his gaze. "Would you have killed me last night? If my men hadn't come?"

"Perhaps. Eventually." His jaw tightened. "I really don't know."

Her cheeks flushed even deeper. She knew what he would have done before he killed her, just as he knew she would have let him. Feeding was very sensual to his kind, an act every bit as intimate as, if not more so than, sex itself.

"It was the first time you've ever been bitten, wasn't it?"

Her face must feel as though it was on fire. She didn't even speak, just gave him a terse nod. Even if she hadn't answered, he would have known from the way she held herself and the subtle heat of arousal that teased his senses.

In a way, he had taken her virginity last night. Too bad he hadn't been of the right mind to truly appreciate it.

"No one ever told you?"

Defiantly she stared at him. "There was no one to tell me—no one around me knew anything about vampires and even if they did . . . very few knew what I was."

Poor little halfling. "No wonder you hate what you are."

"Half of what I am."

He smiled sadly at her. "There's no such thing. You cannot take half of what you are away."

"How do you know?" She sounded like a child. Compared to him she was.

"I'm six hundred years old. I've never seen it work."

Her arms folded beneath those taunting breasts of hers. "But you do not know for sure. There may be a way."

"If it makes you feel better, you believe that. You might be happier if you just accept what you are. You're going to have a very long life—unless someone kills you of course."

"You failed."

"I haven't truly tried," he replied honestly with a bit of a shrug. "The next vampire or whatever that comes along might succeed where others have failed. Maybe they'll bring friends to make sure the job is done properly."

She paled, but her posture lost none of its rigidity. "I would rather die at the hands of a monster than become one."

He smiled, partly mocking, partly in true sympathy. "I may be a monster, but sweetheart, your heart is as black as they get. Too bad you can't see it."

She recoiled from the verbal slap, flinching as his words hit home.

"I knew someone who was very much like you once."

She sneered at him. "And they did not kill you?"

"I wonder if your mouth would be so smart were I not in these chains. No, he didn't kill me. He was my friend."

She cocked a brow to tell him what she thought of that, but was otherwise silent.

"He was obsessed with the idea of becoming a monster. He feared that we were damned. Like you, he thought a cure might be possible, but in his eyes the cure was constant prayer and denial of what he called his 'demonic 'urges." While Bishop and the others tended to think of the demon inside them in more metaphorical or benevolent terms, Dreux had believed it pure evil.

He could see from the expression on Marika's face that she agreed with Dreux's thinking. It made Bishop wonder just what kind of urges his little captor denied herself. Were the situation different, he would offer to help her with that.

"My friend would go for days, weeks even without feeding. He would cloister himself in a cell with his Bible and rosary while the rest of us fed and indulged in other appetites."

"So far you have told me nothing that makes me believe being compared to this 'friend 'of yours is dishonorable."

"No, I suppose I can't expect you to make the logical assumption on your own." He almost laughed at her murderous expression, but thoughts of Dreux kept him sober. "It always ended the same way when he engaged in this self-destructive behavior."

When he didn't immediately continue, she arched both brows. "I seem to be missing this 'logical 'assumption as well."

"Indulging in our appetites allowed the rest of us—"

"You mean there's more than you and Saint?"

That's what he got for opening his big mouth. "It allowed the rest of us to feed without killing, mate without maiming." She winced but he continued, "Dreux denied himself until he couldn't stand it anymore. He would be so starved that he would kill the first human he stumbled upon. It didn't matter if it was man, woman, or child, although he usually preferred those who were sickly or weak—or those who would not be missed come morning. Are you seeing my point now, little one?"

She nodded, her expression suddenly appalled.

"By trying to deny what he was, my friend turned himself into the very thing he feared becoming most."

"That will not happen to me."

"No?" How certain she sounded, and yet how afraid. "Tell me, the last vampire you killed, what was his or her crime?"

"What do you mean?"

"Your last kill—what was the reason for it?"

"It was a vampire."

He noticed she hadn't said it was a being from the shadow world, and that only enforced his belief that she wasn't responsible for Nycen's disappearance. Nycen wasn't vampire, but of the Fae Folk. "Only that?"

"That's enough."

He held her gaze for a long time. She believed what she said. "I do not know who taught you to hate so deeply, but I'm sorry for it."

"Sorry?" She huffed. "I'm not."

"I know. That's why I'm sorry." And he was. So much that his heart was heavy with it. "Please leave me now."

She blinked. "What?"

"I cannot look at you any longer. Please go." He turned his face away from her then, and pretended not to watch as she slowly rose to her feet.

"I know what you are trying to do," she said as she walked toward the door. "You are trying to make me despise myself. It won't work."

He allowed himself to look at her one last time, and he let her see the pity in his gaze. "I know. Someone long before me already succeeded."

"Marika, I want to stay here with you!" Roxana's dark eyes, bright and pleading, damn near softened Marika's resolve.

"It is too dangerous," Marika replied, handing the girl's satchel up into the wagon. She and the rest of Dimitru's family were the last to leave the village. The others had started relocating themselves after Bishop's near escape—at Marika's request. It was a precaution they sometimes took when they feared an attack.

Only Marika and a handful of her men remained. Dimitru should have been one of them, but with his injured arm, Marika worried that he might get hurt again. His wife would never forgive her if that happened.

And if anything happened to her only daughter, Ioana would kill her.

"But I can help!"

Marika steeled herself against the girl's tears. "I am sorry, Roxana, but I would put your safety above all else and that might get me—or someone else—killed. You have to go." With that, she turned her back on the girl calling to her from the rear of the wagon and walked the short distance to her own dwelling.

The wagon rumbled away; the sound of its wheels faded along with the sound of Roxana's plaintive voice. Someday she would understand. Even if she didn't, it did not matter. She would be safe, and that was all Marika wanted.

Correction—all she wanted was Roxana safe and Bishop's words out of her head. Ever since she left the cellar, all she thought of were the things he had said, the way he had looked at her. His hatred and his anger she could handle. If he had been afraid, she could have accepted that as well, but not that pity, not his disgust. How dare he be disgusted with her! How dare he look at her as though she were some loathsome creature so far beneath him, she'd have to climb up just to touch the sole of his boot.

He was the lowlier of the two of them. He was the full-blooded vampire—a creature bred of pure evil. She was still half human. The blood on her hands could be excused. It wasn't innocent.

Except that Bishop claimed that some of it was.

The very thought turned her stomach.

She stood outside the door of her home and looked up at the sky. There wasn't a cloud to be seen, just a curve of the moon and more stars than she could ever hope to count. She stared at their twinkling light, breathing the cool night deep into her lungs, driving all the fear and doubt away.

It was late by human standards, more like midday to vampires. For her, it was simply too early to go to bed and too late to do anything else. Once again she was set apart.

Of her men that remained, only two were not asleep. They had helped Dimitru and his family with their departure, but soon they too would be in bed, knowing full well how alert they would have to be come dawn. And then Marika would be the only one left awake except for the vampire beneath her house.

She would give him no more thought. She would dwell no longer on the things he said to her. It was a trick. He wanted to make her doubt herself by having her entertain the idea that nonhuman didn't equal evil. He would have to try harder if he wanted to succeed in that.

Of course she wasn't evil. Of course all her kills were justified. She had saved lives—destroyed vampires just as they were about to rip out the throat of an innocent human.

Well, perhaps not as they were *just* about to rip out someone's throat, but it was inevitable. Vampires were killers. It was their nature. Even Bishop himself had been unable to say he wouldn't have killed her when he attacked her.

She did a good thing ridding the world of vampires. She would think about all the people she had saved—all the innocent humans. She wouldn't think about the shadow creatures who might have mourned the loss of a loved one.

There was no such thing as an innocent vampire. They did not know anything about loss or love.

It was that thought that took her inside her house to prepare for bed. She'd curl up beneath the blankets and the soft quilt her grandmother had made and read for a bit. Reading was a luxury she rarely afforded herself—not just because it was hard to get books in such a rural area, but because there always seemed to be something else that needed to be done. She would take the time to indulge herself, and she would not think about the fact that in the morning she was handing Bishop over to men who would eventually kill him.

Marika would not think of the things they might do to him before they actually got around to the killing.

He deserved to die for his crimes—for what he was. But it didn't seem fair to truss him up like an animal for it. He deserved a fair fight.

But who could possibly give him one? No human, that was for certain.

She had one foot inside the door when she heard the distant pounding of hooves. They were some distance off, but her hearing was more acute than a normal human's—not as good as a vampire's but good enough that she knew the horses were approaching her village, not leaving.

Was it Dimitru returning despite her wishes? Was it Roxana? If that girl defied her, Marika would personally tie her up and hide her in the outhouse till she returned tomorrow.

She listened carefully. It wasn't just a wagon she heard. There were more horses as well. It couldn't be Dimitru or Roxana unless they had company. The rest of her men would not defy her in this manner, unless something terrible had happened.

It wasn't her men, of that she was certain. She knew it wasn't her own people because the hairs on the back of her neck rose even though there wasn't a breeze.

If not her men, then who?

She stayed in the doorway, but reached her left hand inside to grab the rifle that stood by the entrance. It was loaded and she wasn't afraid to use it.

When the men finally rode into view—thank God for her excellent night vision—she counted easily a dozen of them. A few of them were Romanian, some looked like they were Greeks or Turks. The others were decidedly English.

Was her *friend* Armitage behind this?

"Who are you?" she demanded of the one who headed the group. She asked in English, assuming that was his language.

"I'm no one you need to know the name of," he replied. She had been right to assume he was English. His accent, while not as crisp as Armitage's, was undeniably the same.

Marika's fingers tightened around the rifle, inching it closer to her side. "What do you want?"

"What do you think?"

What was it about these men that made them play games? Why not answer the question as she wanted? Why always with more questions?

"I have no idea." If they wouldn't be honest, then she would pretend ignorance.

The man smiled—it wasn't pleasant. "Well, sweetheart, we came for you."

Her heart gave a little thump, but Marika ignored it. "Me?" Truthfully she had expected they would tell her it was Bishop they wanted, not her.

If they thought to defile her, they would be in for the fight of their lives.

The man nodded; blond hair gleamed under what little moonlight there was. "We've never bagged ourselves a dhampyr before. I look forward to discovering what you're capable of."

He knew what she was. The realization hit her at the same time that she pulled the rifle out into the open and up to her shoulder. She fired, knocking the man off his horse. Then she dove inside the house, hitting the floor hard, and yanked open the drawer of her dresser where she kept more shot.

Loud voices rose up outside. Her men would wake up soon. Would they be quick enough to arm themselves against these intruders?

On her back on the floor, she reloaded her rifle and raised it. When the door to her house opened, she took a split second to ascertain that she did not know the man and shot him in the neck. He went down with a heavy thud, his body bracing the door wide open.

Others were coming. Shots rang out, and she heard a cry. It sounded like Ivan. Was he dead? No time to think or even check. She needed to reload.

Below her she could hear thumping. Bishop. Had they gone down into the cellar? Fear—unexplained and unwelcome—filled her for but a second, only to be replaced by an almost smug certainty that it would not be Bishop who died in that cellar.

Another man appeared in her door. She raised the rifle, but a blink too late. He fired first.

Pain exploded in her left shoulder as she fired her own shot, knocking her back against the floor. Her aim went a little wide, but she still managed to graze the side of his head. It was enough to make him stagger backward and trip over the legs of the dead man behind him.

Marika's head hit the floor with a crash. Light burst behind her eyes as pain engulfed her from the shoulders up. Nausea swam in her stomach and blackness swamped her mind. She could not pass out. If she passed out they would take her.

Gritting her teeth, she groped blindly for her ammunition and reloaded the rifle. There would be more coming shortly. She had to be ready.

She would not be taken.

He was becoming accustomed to the smell of his own flesh burning.

As silently as possible, Bishop forced himself to endure the agony of breaking free of the bonds that held him. Sweat, laced with blood, beaded on his brow and back.

Were it not for Marika's blood, this would have been much easier. In a feral state he had ripped through these chains like paper. But where Marika's blood lessened that primal side of him, it strengthened him in other ways, gave him back his precious control.

Above ground he heard the sound of horses. There had been a lot of traffic in and out of the village all day. Had Marika sent people away so they wouldn't be hurt when the evil vampire was handed over to the innocent murderers in the morning?

Hypocritical little brat. She had no idea what she was doing—and was too stubborn to see that *she* was the closest thing to evil in this village.

Some of what he'd said had gotten through to her; he had to believe that. He refused to believe she was beyond hope. Why he wanted to believe she could change, he didn't bother to wonder, because he knew it had much to do with his attraction to her, and the memory of how she had felt beneath him, writhing as he drank deeply of her.

He heard her above him. Was she in the building that stood over this cellar? Was it her he heard there sometimes, walking around, sighing in her sleep?

She was talking to a man, the tone of her voice hostile. The man responded—something about being there for her. What the hell?

A shot rang out, then something hit the floor above him hard.

Marika.

Pulse roaring in his ears, Bishop strained against the chains, clenching his jaw against the urge to scream as the rending silver pressed into his flesh. He had been burned so much in the last week, he should be used to it by now, but by Christ it hurt!

The shackle on his right wrist broke first. Silver was mostly effective against his kind because of how it reacted to their skin. Marika's blood strengthened him against burns. As a metal, silver was fairly easy for him to break, though it did offer some strange resistance to his strength.

When both arms were free, he reached down and snapped the manacles on his ankles. His feet were bare and his ankles raw as he ran to the door. One kick and the heavy wood flew off its hinges. The outside hatches followed, bursting outward and scattering wood and bits of chain halfway across the village.

It was pandemonium outside. His eyes needed no time to adjust to the darkness—he could see better than a cat. One of Marika's men lay a few feet away from him, bleeding from a chest wound. He wasn't dead yet, but he soon would be.

There were other bodies—men he didn't recognize. Those that were still alive ran through the village, taking cover where they could, shooting when the opportunity arose. Two men fought beside the well—one had his hands around the other's throat.

Bishop turned as another shot echoed from inside the building behind him. A man stood in the doorway, illuminated by lamplight. The side of his head was bleeding, but that didn't stop him from going inside.

He was going after Marika.

A running leap took Bishop from the cellar entrance to the steps of the house. The man was just a few feet away from Marika, who was bleeding on the floor. The man turned, surprise turning to fear in a split second as he saw Bishop. It was the last thing he saw because Bishop grabbed him by the head and twisted. The man fell lifeless to the floor.

He went to Marika, knelt beside her. "Are you all right?"

She nodded, wincing at the movement. Her right hand came up to gingerly touch the back of her head. "Tie something around my shoulder and I'll be fine."

The only thing close by was his shirt, so Bishop yanked the linen over his head and used it to fashion a tourniquet for her arm. The shot had gone through her shoulder to lodge in the floorboards beneath her and she was bleeding profusely. The scent of it called to him, but it didn't awaken his hunger. It awakened another urge—one far more dangerous and unstable.

He wanted to kill the man responsible for this, but he was already dead. His was one of the two bodies lying on the floor just inside the house.

He would have to settle for killing the rest of them then.

"Stay here," he told her.

"And wait for one of them to come and take me? No." She struggled to her feet.

"Take you? Or kill you?"

She met his gaze. Aside from being a little pale, she didn't look seriously hurt—one of the advantages of her blood, no doubt.

"They said they had never captured a dhampyr before. They were interested to see what I am 'capable' of."

Something clicked inside Bishop's mind. A band of men roaming the countryside hunting shadow creatures. Were these the men who had captured Nycen? And what were they doing with the creatures they took?

There was only one way to find out.

He ran from the house, straight for the first man he found. He didn't have to go far, because there was one coming up the steps. He had blood on his face and in his pale hair, and one arm hung limply at his side where he had been shot.

He seemed surprised to see Bishop. "You're supposed to be locked up."

How the hell had he known that? Seizing the man by the lapels, Bishop pulled him close. "What do you want with the dhampyr? What have you done with the others? Tell me or I'll kill you."

The man stared into his eyes without fear. "Their deaths will serve a higher purpose."

So this man was among those responsible. It

hadn't been Marika at all. Bishop allowed his fangs to lengthen to full extension. "What purpose? Where are they?"

His answer was a loud bang and then a splash of warmth on his face. The man had a pistol—and rather than answer Bishop's questions or face the consequences, he had killed himself instead.

Bishop dropped the body and wiped his arm across his face. "Jesus Christ."

He looked up to find six men facing him down, rifles trained at his chest.

Bishop smiled. "You weren't a match for the dhampyr. You think you're a match for me?"

Six trigger fingers flexed. And fired.

Chapter 6

Ivan was dead. Sergei was wounded, but not fatally. That there had been only one death given the scope of the attack was a good thing, but Marika couldn't bring herself to feel any joy over it.

Those men had been after her. She'd never been hunted before, and the experience left her with a tremor in her muscles that refused to go away—a chill that settled deep in her bones. Had it not been for Bishop, those men would have taken her.

Just as she had taken Bishop. He had no reason to defend her, yet he had.

None had survived his wrath. Every man who came to the village intent on taking her had died. She had killed some herself, others had been killed by her men, but at least seven of them had been killed by Bishop alone. They shot at him and he still managed to defeat them.

Marika had never seen anything like him in all

her life. It had been both frightening and beautiful to watch him fight. He had been nothing but single-minded grace. So fast, so deadly. He had saved them all. Saved her.

And how did she repay him? By pulling bullets out of his chest with a small pair of pincers she used specifically for such tasks. Normally when she did this, her patient was unconscious—or soon fell into such a state. Bishop was wide awake and it made her anxious.

"Does it hurt?" she asked, as she rummaged in his torn flesh for the first shot. It was difficult work because his body was already trying to heal itself with unnatural speed and ease.

He was on her bed with several lamps illuminating him. Battered, bloody and beaten, he still looked better than most human men on a good day. It wasn't right.

He met her gaze. There was pain in his eyes, mixed with what she took to be mockery. "The shot they used is silver, and you are digging inside me like you're digging a shallow grave with a butter knife. What do you think?"

The silver would explain why her own wound had hurt so badly—and why it still burned, even as she felt it slowly begin to heal. Bishop healed faster than she. If she didn't act quickly, he'd heal with the silver inside him—burning him from the inside out, until it eventually killed him.

She dropped her gaze back to her task. "I have not thanked you for saving my life."

"I hadn't noticed."

He was being caustic again—she didn't have to look at him to know that.

"I suppose I deserve that." She found the jagged ball of silver inside him and gripped it firmly with the pincers. "But I want you to know I appreciate that you helped fight those men."

"You are welcome."

No mockery that time. She pulled the shot from his chest. He grunted and his body tensed, but other than that he gave no indication of how badly that must have hurt.

Blood eased from the wound, warm and rich. She watched it pool on his flesh, red and inviting. She wanted to . . . taste it.

Her gums itched, ached as though she had a tooth that needed pulling. It was her fangs, extending for the taste.

Swallowing hard, she pressed a cloth over the wound and dropped the silver ball into a small bowl on the bedside table.

"You're pale," he remarked. "Does the sight of blood bother you?"

Coming from anyone else she could answer that question as a human and pretend that she was but a weak female, but not with him. She knew exactly what he was asking.

"Yes," she admitted.

"Have you ever fed?"

The very thought made her stomach cramp. "No. And I never will."

He made no more attempts at conversation as she worked at removing the remaining silver from his body, and Marika was glad for it. She worked as quickly as she could, but still she had a difficult time with the last wound as it had already started to close up.

She wiped her hands on a towel and finally raised her gaze to his. "I've never seen a vampire heal so quickly."

He looked tired and drawn. "This is not normal, even for me."

There was something he wasn't telling her, something he expected her to realize on her own . . . Her throat tightened. "My blood."

Bishop nodded. "I believe so."

If her blood was this potent for him, what would his be for her? Would it merely heighten her vampire nature for a time, or would it turn her completely?

"If you took more of my blood, would you heal even faster?"

He frowned. "I imagine so, yes."

She could give him her blood, let him bite her again—she practically shivered in pleasure at the thought, damn her own hide. Then he would be strong enough to leave here. She could tell her men that he escaped—tell Armitage that he had gotten away during the attack.

She would never have to see him again—could forget all the things he made her wonder and feel. She could go back to the way she had been before capturing him.

Go back to hunting for the one that killed her mother and wonder if Bishop would tell him about her. Go back to thinking all vampires were soulless and evil and forget that one had actually saved her life.

"What are you thinking?" There was wariness in his tone. "I have come to hate that expression. It usually means you are going to try to kill me."

"You cannot stay here," she replied. "You have to go."

He eased himself into a sitting position. "You've changed your mind about handing me over to your friends?"

"They're not my friends, and yes."

He watched her for a moment, his eyes scrutinizing as he tucked his lips together in a strangely endearing manner. "Why the change of heart?"

"You saved my life." She splayed her hands wide as though that should say it all. "The least I can do is spare yours."

Hawkish eyes narrowed. "You'd let me go?"

"Yes, if you promise to leave the area tonight."

He shook his head—just once. "I cannot do that."

"What do you mean?" He couldn't be serious? After all she had done to him and he was refusing to leave? He had been shot at!

"I promised to find out the truth about my friend's disappearance and I mean to."

"I thought you said those men were behind it." He had told her his theory as she'd prepared to remove the bullets from his chest. She shivered, thinking once again of how she might have become part of some monstrous collection of unnatural beings.

Would anyone be so loyal to her that they would search for her as Bishop did for his friend?

"I did."

She tried to ignore how the muscles of his stomach bunched as he sat like that. Tried to ignore the smooth, golden perfection of his skin. Why wasn't he pale and sooty-looking like the undead should be? "They're all dead."

"There could be more."

More that might yet come for her. If they took her and put her in a room with the other creatures they'd taken, she'd be killed as soon as they realized who she was and how many of their kind she'd destroyed.

Odd, but she'd never cared about how hated she must be, until now. And even now she only cared because it could cost her life. No, that wasn't quite right. If she was honest with herself—and she was forced to be—she would have to admit to a certain amount of guilt for her past actions.

She didn't like feeling guilty. It made her second-guess herself, and she liked that even less.

"It is my fault Ivan is dead. My fault the men are wounded."

"They followed you willingly."

"Tell that to Ivan's widow."

"I do not have to. She knows. Your men follow

you because they want to. After all this time, each of them knows the risks involved."

She watched him, looking for some hint of mockery in his expression, but found none. "And now they know what I do—that not all vampires are evil. I wonder if they will wonder how many we wrongly killed."

He watched her as well—a little too closely. "The past is done. Better to think about what is coming."

He was right. There would be time for regret later—if she lived that long.

"You are certain there are more humans involved?" God, she wished she had a shirt to make him put on. The sight of his bare flesh distracted her. All thoughts of regret—all thoughts of *anything*—evaporated when she looked at him.

"One of them told me there was a 'higher purpose' behind these abductions." He rose to his feet a little stiffly, but with still far more grace than he deserved. "That makes me believe it is not a small concern."

God only knew how many more there could be out there. When the men who had attacked her did not return more could be sent. . .

"You cannot stay here." Even as she said the words she knew they were foolish and pointless. He already knew that it wasn't safe for him. It wasn't safe for any of them. Her men she could trust to scatter and stay away. She could look after herself—find a small place where they wouldn't be so quick to find her while she looked for them.

"I have a house," he told her. "In Fagaras."

"Go there. I will come as soon as I can."

He looked surprised. "What for?"

"You want to find your friend." She went to the closet to find fresh clothes for herself. "I want to know why these men want their actions attributed to my name. The sooner that happens, the sooner you can leave Romania."

He stared at her; she could feel the heat of his gaze burning into her back. She paused, staring deep into the dark of the clove-scented closet. "I would like to help you find your friend, and these men."

He didn't respond right away, and when he did, it wasn't how she expected. "I will be the first you've ever let get away, won't I?"

She nodded, glancing at him over her shoulder. "I do not like it, but it seems you and I have a common enemy, and I am willing to try to put my prejudice aside and trust you if you are willing to do the same."

Bishop actually smiled then, a soft curve of his lips that made Marika's heart double its pace. "That's awfully tolerant of you, little halfling."

"Tolerance has nothing to do with it." She tried to sound sharp and failed. "I owe you a debt and I do not want to live my life wondering if these men will try to take me again. I would rather die than be part of some sideshow collection."

"Is that what you think it is?"

She shrugged and grabbed a shirt from a hanger.

"Who knows? That is my fear. There could be any number of distasteful things going on. I refuse to be a part of it."

He braced his hands on the lean curve of his hips—where the waistband of his trousers seemed inclined to sit. "What about your friends? Won't they come looking for you when you don't deliver me to them?"

"They are not my friends, and what I tell them is no concern of yours." She yanked off what was left of her shirt—he had already ripped it to get to her wound. "I will think of something."

He said nothing. He was totally silent as he blatantly watched her change. It wasn't as though she was naked before him. She wore her little demi-corset that kept him from seeing too much. But it *felt* as though she was bare to his gaze, so acute was his attention. Her entire body tightened with it. She yanked the new shirt on as quickly as her stiff and throbbing shoulder would allow.

"Why?" she asked finally, after too much tense silence had passed. If one of them didn't speak, she feared something far more intimate might happen.

His gaze lifted to hers. She didn't want to know what he had been staring at. "Why what?"

"Why did you save me?" She tucked the shirt into her trousers.

"Would you rather I had let them take you?"

"I would have preferred to save myself."

"Ah." His lips curved slightly. "Forgive me for injuring your pride."

"This . . . situation was much easier for me when I could think of you as my enemy."

"Likewise."

They stared at each other for a long moment, each measuring the other, weighing what these admissions cost them.

She folded her arms across her chest, hugging herself. "You could have escaped."

"I'm not a monster, Marika," he said as though she should have figured that out on her own. "I wouldn't leave anyone to be taken like that."

She should have been happy with that, but it was unsettling knowing she had been so wrong about him, and it bothered her that he would have done the same for "anyone."

And if by chance she had died, would he have returned and made a little monument for her? Would he tend her grave three hundred years from now?

She must have damaged her brain when she hit her head earlier. Surely that could be the only reason she would want a vampire to think she was special.

She appeared on his doorstep shortly after midnight. His housekeeper, Floarea, was alarmed to find a young woman at the door—especially when she realized that Marika was Irina Comenescu's granddaughter.

Irina lived not far away, apparently. Was that where Marika had gone after she finished tending to her men, after disposing of the bodies of her attackers? Bishop hadn't been allowed to help her with any of that. Even if the rising sun hadn't stopped him, Marika would have.

It had been her idea for him to leave. He hadn't wanted to leave her unprotected—not that he was much good to her during the day. It had to look as if he had escaped, she said. There was too big a chance of his being discovered if he stayed there, even hidden in the cellar. She didn't want to take the chance of her men discovering him and blaming him for the attack.

And since Bishop hadn't wanted to risk them turning on her either, he had done what she wanted and slunk back to his own house like the useless creature he was.

He would have to ask Floarea about Marika's grandmother and family later. Not only would it assuage his own curiosity, but he wasn't so smitten that he was above collecting information that might prove useful later.

There was only one piece of information he wanted when Marika entered his study a few moments later, and that was the answer to this: "Why do you have a suitcase with you?"

Marika set the battered case on the rug and gave him a surprised glance as he rose to his feet. "Would you have me parade around your house naked?"

Floarea looked appalled by the suggestion and turned her heavily lined face toward him. Stared down by the two of them, Bishop knew he had better answer that question less honestly than his first instinct demanded.

"I wouldn't have you parade around my house at all."

Now she frowned. Poor Floarea didn't looked terribly pleased by this answer either. It was a trifle rude, true, but his housekeeper didn't know who this woman truly was. *What* she truly was. Floarea's employer would not be pleased to have the Huntress stay under this roof.

Bishop was not pleased at the prospect either. In all his years of existence, the only women he had shared a home with had been women he was romantically involved with, and those had been few and far between. He preferred having his own lodgings, his own abode.

One he could sleep in without fear that someone would try to kill him while he was unaware.

When she made no response, he tried a different tactic. "You do not plan to stay here?"

Marika's stance turned defensive. "You said I could."

"I said you needed to find a safe place to stay." Marika was absolutely the last person he wanted as a houseguest. Her blood called to him. He didn't want to worry that one of them might "accidentally" find his way to the other's bedroom. She might kill him for it later, but if he went to her and tasted her again, she would allow it.

Tasting her again would be a mistake, even if she tasted like nothing he had ever experienced before.

"Yes. But," she insisted, "before you left the village, I told you I would come here—you agreed."

This conversation was going to get loud, he could feel it. And Floarea was watching with far too much interest. Bishop smiled at the short woman. "You may go now. I'll ring if we need you."

She gestured at Marika's luggage. "You want me to take that upstairs?"

The smart thing would be to say no, but Marika looked so lost he couldn't do it. "Yes. Take it upstairs."

Marika actually smiled at his capitulation. Her face lit up in such a manner that it literally stole his breath just to look at her.

What the hell was he getting into?

"You won't regret this," she told him as the housekeeper left with her bag.

"I already do." He slumped into the nearest chair. "This is just temporary, you understand, until we figure out our course of action."

Her face fell a little, and he mourned the loss of her smile. "You do not trust me."

She made it sound like such a betrayal. He stared at her. "No, I don't. You kept me in a cellar and tortured me; you'll have to forgive me for doubting your change of heart."

"I thought you were my enemy."

She really was adorable with her dirty face. Nothing threatening about her at all. "I'm not convinced that you aren't mine."

"What about putting our conflict aside to fight a common enemy?"

"I didn't say I wouldn't trust you to fight beside

me. I just don't trust you to be in my house when I'm sleeping."

A sly smile curved her lips. "The big, powerful vampire is afraid of a woman?"

"Afraid, no. Wary, yes. I'd be an idiot not to be."

She rubbed a hand over her forehead—and left a smudge. He had a bathtub upstairs. She could make use of it—God knew she needed a bath. The grime of last night was still on her.

He could offer to scrub her back.

"You do not think that I will lie awake wondering if you plan to take revenge against me for all I did to you?"

Bishop was pulled away from thoughts of her wet and naked by the vulnerability in her tone. "I suppose you would have to be an idiot not to consider that as well."

"And yet I am here."

"Obviously you're an idiot."

To his surprise she laughed at that. "I suppose I am. I am willing to trust you, however. If you are willing to trust me." She lowered herself onto the sofa across from him. Her shoulders sagged and he could see the fatigue in her eyes.

"Why?"

She met his gaze with a frank and level one of her own. "Because I have never backed down from my duty."

"How is living with me a duty?" True, he was no easy man to live with, but she made it sound as though she were sacrificing herself on an altar.

She sighed. "These men are hiding behind my name. You said yourself that your friend believes me responsible for her brother's disappearance."

He noticed she hadn't answered his question. "Yes, all evidence, what little there was, pointed toward you."

"You said this friend was gentle—peace-loving."

"He's a fairy," Bishop replied dryly. "Have you ever heard of a dangerous fae?" Well, there were banshees, but he wasn't about to tell her about *them*.

She swallowed. His gaze went to her neck. He remembered how silky and salty-sweet the skin there was. "I do not want the death of innocents accounted to me."

It was all he could do not to openly sneer. "So now you're concerned about innocents?"

"Yes," was her simple answer.

He didn't know how to respond.

"I do not understand it," she told him, "but aligning myself with you feels right. It feels more right to me than anything has in a long time. I could have gone to my grandmother's but I don't want to endanger her. I could have gone to any one of my men and asked for shelter."

"But you don't want them to know I'm still around."

She pinned him with that black stare of hers, so intense and fathomless. "I feel safer with you."

She did? In truth, she was—at least from the men hunting her.

"Even though I took your blood?" He shouldn't have brought it up. It was a reminder of how she had felt beneath him—on his tongue.

She swallowed, pulling his attention once more to her throat. Saliva moistened his mouth. "You could have killed me, but you didn't."

"Your men stopped me."

"We both know that if you had wanted me dead I would be."

He tilted his head, leaning back in his chair. "I suppose so."

"There is nothing to suppose. I captured you, and you could have killed me for it. You would have been right to do so, but you didn't. That tells me you can be trusted."

He arched a brow, the silent question lingering between them; could he trust her?

"I owe you a debt," she continued, her face tight, as though saying the words caused her pain. "I will not let that go unpaid."

Bishop shook his head. That was undoubtedly the closest to an apology he was going to get out of her. Oddly enough, it appeased that part of him that needed such a gesture from her. She was offering him her trust and asking for his in return.

And damn it, he wanted to give it.

How had this happened? All he had wanted to do was find Nycen. This woman had abducted him, tortured and threatened him. Hell, she had been about to turn him over to people who wanted to kill him. And now she was talking as if she had some code of honor.

Oddly enough, he believed her.

She was right when she said they had a common enemy, and he knew they would be safer and stronger if they fought together instead of against each other. But could he trust her not to betray him in the end? Once that common enemy was defeated, would she try to kill him? If he trusted her, he would be vulnerable to her.

And he was already vulnerable enough where she was concerned. Her blood was in his veins and it called to him, drew him to her. Her strength attracted him, her determination and the defiant way she faced her fear intrigued him. He was becoming increasingly affected by her, to the point where he wanted her as a man wants a woman—and not strictly in a sexual manner.

Given the fact that just a few days ago she had wanted to kill him, this awareness was unsettling to say the least.

Even if she did not want him dead now, there was the issue that she hated the vampire side of her nature—hated that he was a vampire. If they gave in to this attraction between them, it would lead to trouble.

She was looking a little anxious. "Are you going to keep me waiting much longer? Say something."

He said the first thing that came to mind. "You are the strangest woman I have ever met."

She actually smiled a little at that. The effort made her look younger, softened her to the point that she nearly broke his heart, she was so lovely. "Does that mean you're going to let me stay?"

He nodded. He was going to live to regret it, of that there was no doubt. "You can stay."

Chapter 7

"Tell me about Saint."

Bishop sighed and set aside the book he had only just begun to read. He had read Mary Shelley's book about Victor Frankenstein and his creation several times since its publication in 1819, and every time he found something new in it. This time he was caught up in the theme of man's brazen arrogance, and the persecution of that which is frightening and misunderstood.

"How many times must I tell you I do not know where he is?"

"I believe you." Marika's gaze held his. "I want to know about him—what is he like?"

If this was some kind of new ploy on her part, she hid it well. Marika's expression was one of innocent curiosity as they sat together in the little sitting room at the front of his house, waiting for full darkness to descend upon the town.

Once it was dark, they would be able to go out and start searching for answers to all the questions the attack on Marika's home had wrought; until then they strove to find some way to be easy in each other's presence.

"You want to know what he was like before we became vampire or after?"

She thought for a moment. "Both."

Bishop smiled at her hesitancy. He knew that feeling. His father had died when he was but a child. Even though his mother remarried and he had been very close to the man who then raised him, he used to barrage his mother with questions about his father. It had meant so very much to him to know the little details she imparted—little things that made him feel closer to the man who influenced his life even in death.

Most of the time the things his mother told him were good, but sometimes, when Bishop was too stubborn or eager to fight, his mother would tell him—with a flush in her cheeks that betrayed her own temper—just how much like his father he was.

Marika deserved that same candor, if he was going to make her see Saint as a man and not some demon from her nightmares. If her mother was the woman Bishop believed her to have been, Marika deserved no less.

"When I met Saint we were both very young. We were from the same village, and our fathers would hunt together. We were typical boys. I was not as good at being sly as he was—he could talk anyone out of almost anything—and convince others to do his bidding with frightening ease."

She tucked herself into her chair, like a child curling up for a story. "What were you good at?"

He was surprised that she asked. "Fighting. I was good at fighting."

"Obviously not good enough. I captured you."

Such bravado. And was that a little warmth he detected? She wasn't actually teasing him, was she? "With the help of four men and poison. And let's not forget what you did to me with holy water."

"I am sorry for that."

"Are you?" It surprised him. He had not been expecting her to ever apologize. Perhaps he should apologize for punching her, or biting her. Sometime. "Given that I can't scar from it, I will forgive you."

Something passed between them in that moment. Bishop didn't know what it was, but it unsettled him. It obviously unsettled Marika as well, given the paleness of her cheeks.

"So you knew Saint from childhood?"

"Yes, but his name was Adrian du Lac."

"And you became childhood friends?"

"Friends? Perhaps we were merely that, once." Bishop smiled, remembering some of the moments he and Saint shared as boys. It had been so very long ago, yet his mind held on to them. "We were so close, we were more like family. We didn't always get along. We fought, and bullied each other, but in the end, we always knew we could depend on each other. Trust each other."

"And you became vampires together."

"We were soldiers first."

A little frown tightened the flesh of her brow. "You were a soldier?"

"You didn't know?" How had she managed to stay alive so long? "You haven't researched us very well, have you?"

Her little chin came up in defiance. "I knew all I needed to know to hunt your kind."

Resting his elbow on the arm of his chair, he braced thumb and index finger on the side of his face. "Yes, ignorance makes it surprisingly easy to justify taking a life."

"Speaking from experience?"

"Of course, as are you." His voice was still low and calm, despite her attempts to rile him.

"Vampires are soulless, dead things."

Sweet Jesus, she didn't honestly believe that, did she? All those old wives' tales of vampires rising from the grave, of being the undead?

"My heart beats."

"Only because of the blood—the life—you steal from others."

"My God, I cannot believe you have survived this long. I am not dead!" He reached across the scant distance between them and grabbed her hand, forcing her palm against his chest so that she might feel the beating there—the rise and fall of breath.

"It does not need to beat as often as yours, nor

do my lungs need to draw breath as often, but I am alive, Marika. I'm just no longer human."

She stared at him, her long, cool hand pressed against his flesh through the thin lawn of his shirt. His heartbeat picked up.

"I still know the difference between right and wrong," he told her, his thumb caressing the delicate bone of her wrist. "I believe in God, and I believe that my soul is where it has always been."

"Next you'll tell me that when you die you plan to go to Heaven." She mocked him, but she did not try to remove her hand.

He merely smiled. At that moment she reminded him a little of Elisabetta. She'd had some very decided notions about Heaven and who belonged there herself. "What happens to me when this life is over is a matter between me and God."

She opened her mouth—to debate him, no doubt, so he spoke before she could. "Do you want to hear about Saint or do you want to debate religion with me?"

Her jaw set mutinously. "Saint."

Bishop hid a smile. He enjoyed talking with her, even though he vacillated between wanting to kiss her and wanting to shake her. She was so strong and so capable, yet she was almost childlike in her beliefs. It truly was amazing that no one had killed her. Yet.

With that thought turning his blood to ice, he released his hold on her and told her what she wanted to know.

"We were fairly young men when we decided to fulfill our duty to king and country." Could she hear the mockery in his tone? "We thought we would be noble heroes. That our lives would be one big adventure. It wasn't quite that romantic."

"But you were good at what you did?"

He nodded. "We were. It didn't take long before we were introduced to the others. Each of us had traits that doomed us to a special place in the king's forces. His private puppets."

"What was your role in this group?"

"Fighting, of course."

"And Saint's?"

"He was a thief. The finest, most roguish thief I've ever had the pleasure of meeting. No lock existed that he could not open, no treasure he could not procure for his own."

"You say that with a smile, as though you admire those traits."

Bishop shrugged. She didn't understand, but then she was prejudiced—as was he. "Yes, I admired him for his talents. We had many successful adventures because of them."

"Successful kills I imagine as well." There was the faintest hint of a sneer in her tone.

"I would be lying if I denied that sometimes happened as well."

She didn't seem as pleased as he might have thought by the information.

"Becoming vampires didn't make us killers, Marika. Being soldiers did that."

She nodded, taking that in and thinking whatever she would of it. "Did your friendship with Saint change when you became vampires?"

"No. The change affected all of us differently. We became intoxicated with our new abilities, but once the blush wore off, we found we weren't that altered."

"Except that you drank blood."

"Yes." He frowned a little, remembered how wrong it had seemed to want that taste so badly. "That was perhaps the biggest adjustment to make."

"How did it happen?"

She really didn't know much about them. Or maybe she did but wanted to hear it from him. Perhaps she expected him to lie about it. "During a raid on a Templar hold we found a cup that we thought was the Holy Grail. Chapel—he was Severian then—was injured, and he drank from the cup to see if it would cure him."

"Did it?"

The scene played out in his mind as though it had happened only yesterday. He remembered Chapel bleeding and Dreux giving him the cup. Chapel drank and then fell unconscious.

"The wound closed. It was miraculous the way it healed. We thought for sure it was the Holy Grail."

"But it wasn't." Obviously she knew the answer because she hadn't phrased it as a question.

"No. I think we would have drunk from the Blood Grail even if we had known what it truly was. Power and immortality are very tempting regardless. We abused our powers and abilities. We reveled in the debauchery our new natures afforded."

She was watching him, her gaze curious as his bitterness increased. "Then what happened?"

"Then Dreux—the one I told you about who tried to deny what he was—went out one morning to watch the sun rise."

To her credit, horror brightened her gaze. "You saw?"

He nodded. "Yes." He didn't elaborate. No matter how long he lived, he would never forget the sight of Dreux shattering. "We had all grown up Catholic and so we returned to the church for guidance. For penance."

"Is that when you had the cross branded on your back?"

Bishop felt a shadow fall over his face. "The church thought it would be a good way for us to remember our place so they branded us with silver crosses."

"And it left a mark?"

"We burn. We can heal, but fire and blessed silver together . . . You are the last person to whom I should give this information."

He expected her to smile at his admission but she looked a little sad instead—like a child whose hands had been slapped while reaching for a sweet.

"You think I'm going to use any information you give me against you."

"You wouldn't be much of a hunter if you didn't exploit your enemy's weakness."

Marika tilted her head. The braid she wore fell against the side of the chair with a low thud. "You think I regard you as an enemy?"

"Regardless of our present alliance, I have no reason to think your opinion of me and my kind has altered enough for me to believe otherwise.'

"What of your opinion of me?"

He smiled slightly. "I am waiting to see if you give me reason to change it."

She nodded, accepting his response admirably. "What happened after you went to the church? Did you change?"

He shrugged. "Some. We allowed them to mark us, to rename us. We served them for a while. Saint was the first to leave. He said he wasn't going to spend eternity being punished for what he was. He thought the church enjoyed degrading us."

"Did you agree?"

"After a while, yes. By that time Reign had already left as well. By the time I decided to go, Temple was already preparing to take the cup into hiding so no one else would find it."

"Why not give it to the church to hide?"

He sent her a glance that told her what he thought of that question. "Even if we trusted the zealots who had us with the cup, there was always the chance of someone stealing it. After all, that's how we got it in the first place."

"So you left the church and you and Saint went from being practically brothers to almost strangers."

"No. Never strangers." He couldn't explain the nature of his connection to Saint and the others. There was a bond that could never be broken, a loyalty that could never be sundered.

She stared at him for quite some time, no doubt processing all that he had told her. He waited, patiently, for her next question. It wasn't one he expected.

"Do you like it?"

Bishop frowned. "Being a vampire?"

"Drinking blood."

No, not what his first thought for her to ask would have been.

"I do." He raked a hand through his hair. "I suppose that's part of being a vampire."

"I think it's revolting."

She was very quick to give her opinion. He would return the favor—and the boldness. "Is it revolting when a man comes inside a woman?"

"I beg your pardon?" She was flushed, but he didn't sense any virginal indignation.

"It is natural for a man to spill his seed inside a woman. It is natural for lovers to taste each other in many ways. Do you find those things revolting?"

"No, but it is not the same."

He shrugged. "Was it revolting when I did it to you? Did I hurt you, do anything that made you feel dirty?" He needed to know this. Needed to know he hadn't harmed her in a manner beyond the physical.

"No." Her voice was small. Was it possible that she had actually enjoyed it?

"It is strange to you so you loathe and fear it—perhaps you are more human than I first believed."

From the darkness that overshadowed her features, she knew that wasn't a compliment. "You talk of how I should not judge based on the fact that you are a vampire, and yet you judge me because I am human."

"I judge you based on your actions, which, yes, are sometimes very human."

"I told you why I hated vampires. Why do you hate humans?"

"I don't hate humans, I just don't trust those who destroy what they don't understand."

"Because they took your friend?"

"Because they burned my home and raped and killed the woman I loved."

Her face couldn't have gone any whiter if he had drained her of blood himself.

"She died in my arms." Why was he telling her this? It was painful, but three centuries made it more like a tragic tale than his own life. "I begged her to let me change her, even though I knew she didn't want it. I would have done anything to keep her alive. I failed."

"Elisabetta."

"You know her name." She hadn't known he was a soldier, but she knew about Betta. He must be quite the local legend after all.

"I saw her grave."

Marika was no threat to Elisabetta, but it bothered him all the same. "Why were you there?"

"I lost my necklace when we captured you. I went back to retrieve it and I wondered why that place was so special that you had been there that night. I looked around and I found the grave."

"I buried her there after the men had left, I didn't want to leave her alone in the night."

"Some stories say you sacrificed her to save yourself."

That didn't surprise him, but it needled all the same. He would never do such a cowardly thing. That Marika thought he might added to the insult. "She hadn't been feeling well, so I went out that night to feed."

"Normally you fed from her?"

"Yes."

"She allowed it?"

"Yes."

She leaned forward in the chair, regarding him with intense interest. "Did she like it?"

They should be distasteful to him, these questions, but they weren't. Her curiosity intrigued him. Perhaps she had enjoyed his bite after all. "Normally I would tell you that is none of your business but what does it matter? Yes, it was a moment of intimacy between us."

Marika nodded. Bishop could smell her body temperature rise. Obviously she didn't find the idea of being bitten as repulsive as she originally claimed. What he wouldn't give to climb inside her head then and see what she was thinking. Was she thinking about the night he had attacked her? Was she remembering what it was like to have his fangs buried her neck?

God knew he was thinking about it. His fangs ached to lengthen and sink into the sweetness of her flesh. His cock hardened, thickened. He wanted to fill her with every inch of himself, wanted her writhing and whimpering beneath him as he drew her blood into his veins and emptied himself inside her.

He had been too long without a woman if he wanted one who had tried to kill him.

"Do you crave blood?" The question escaped him before he could think to stay silent.

Her whole body jerked as her eyes widened. Her reaction was answer enough.

Interesting. He could crow about it, rub her face in the fact that she was no more "human" than he was, but he didn't. In fact, he felt sorry for her. "For how long?"

Marika turned away. "A few years now. That's why I want to find Saint."

"I thought you wanted to find him to kill him."

"I do. I want to kill him to cure myself."

Bishop didn't say a word, but Marika's heart plummeted all the same. He wasn't deceiving her—there was no way he could force a look of such pity.

Killing Saint would not cure her.

"All the legends . . ." She drew breath to keep her lower lip from trembling. "Are wrong." Killing her "sire" would not save her.

He nodded. "I'm afraid so."

She glanced around the room—at the low fire burning in the hearth, the shadow of flickering flames on the brightly colored carpet. How could she have been so stupid to believe the stories?

Because she had wanted to believe them.

"I thought I could avenge my mother and rid myself of this horrible affliction at the same time. Now I must be content with avenging her death and accept my fate."

"Marika, about your mother . . ."

Her head jerked around, her gaze locking with his. "What about her?"

Bishop shook his head. "Are you certain Saint killed her?"

"That is what my father told me. He attacked my mother and sent her into labor. Loss of blood made her weak, and she died shortly after I was born." Anger eased the pain inside. "Saint took advantage of her situation and killed her."

Her companion didn't respond, but something in his expression gave her pause. "You think my father lied to me."

He shrugged. "What I believe does not signify."

"He would not lie about such a thing."

The vampire met her gaze with a cold one of his own. "Of course not. After all he kept you by his side and loved you all these years."

It was a cold slap. How did he know about her not living with her father? The housekeeper. She knew Marika's grandmother, and obviously Bishop had thought to ask questions about her family.

Did he know where her grandmother lived? Would he hurt her? Her fingers twitched, closing around the blade at her thigh. "If you harm any of my family . . ."

"You will what?" His eyes narrowed threateningly. "You are no match for me alone, little halfling. You should remember that."

Sickening dread rolled in her stomach. He was right.

"You should also remember that if I want to hurt you, I will hurt *you*. I won't use your father or grandmother to do it."

"I am supposed to believe a vampire has honor?" Hadn't she already admitted as much?

"You are still alive, are you not? If I wanted you dead, you would be by now."

"And why aren't I dead?"

"I have no desire to kill you. And since the men who took my friend are very likely the same who are after you, it suits my purpose to keep you alive, doesn't it?"

"I suppose it does. We are of use to each other, then."

The way he looked at her sent a sharp heat spiraling low within her. What was he thinking? Of biting her, or making love to her?

How could she even think of lying with a vampire as "making love"? Regardless, she did. And the thought of his hands on her, of feeling the hard heaviness of his body upon hers once more, was more delicious than she wanted to admit, even to herself.

"Why would my father lie about Saint attacking my mother?"

"Because perhaps he was jealous."

"Jealous? Of the vampire?" She meant it as a joke, but when he didn't laugh, when he simply regarded her with those bright gold-green eyes, the laughter caught in her throat.

"No." Her voice was hoarse, strangled. "My mother would never . . ." She couldn't finish. The thought of it made her head swim, made her stomach churn. No, not her mother. Not with a vampire.

She leapt to her feet, bolting for the door. Faster than she could think, Bishop was there, blocking her way. She was faster than human but he was faster still—a fact that had her heart slamming against her ribs.

"Your mother would never what?" Anger roughened his voice. "Never give herself to a vampire? Never love a vampire? Never make herself a monster's whore?"

He was dangerous now. She had touched something personal. He had lost the woman—the human woman—he had loved. Her horror was an insult to that woman's memory—to Bishop himself.

Even she wasn't so certain of her own abilities

that she wanted to be alone in a room with a very old, very angry vampire.

"Yes," she admitted. It might not be smart, but it was how she truly felt. It wasn't that she thought it was awful to love a vampire—one couldn't always choose whom one gave one's heart to, she knew that—it was simply that she couldn't imagine her mother betraying her father in such a way. She couldn't imagine her *mother* loving a vampire.

"You little hypocrite." His face was inches from hers as he backed her farther into the room. His eyes seemed to glow with a light of their own, and between the firm lines of his lips, she glimpsed a flash of sharp white.

His fangs were growing. The knowledge made her own gums tighten in response. Her senses screamed at his nearness. He was too near. Too warm. Too tempting. She could smell him—so clearly, it was a sweet, spicy taste on her tongue.

"You think I can't smell it?" he demanded. "You think I can't feel your heat? You tell me how disgusting you think vampires are and yet you desire me."

There was no use denying it. She met his gaze instead. Were her eyes glowing like his? Could he see the glimmer of fangs in her mouth? Did he know that he made her feel inhuman and at the same time more a woman than she had ever felt before?

"Yes," she admitted, fingers curving around the back of a chair for support. "I desire you, and yes, part of me is disgusted by it."

He stared at her, his eyes narrowing. He had such long eyelashes, so thick and dark. They would be soft, like the brush of a butterfly's wing against her cheek. His touch would be gentle, his body hard and unyielding. He would take all she offered and more, and give of himself until she could take no more, filled to the brim with his power.

Long, warm fingers touched her throat, where her pulse slammed frantically. "And the other part of you?"

Marika couldn't help it; her gaze fell to his lips. The upper curved slightly upward at the corners—a sensuous bow above a pout that she longed to catch between her teeth.

She longed to bite . . .

Suddenly she was in his arms and those beautiful lips were on hers—firm and demanding, yet so sweet. He tasted of night, of earthy spices that made her head swim. How could she have ever believed vampires to be cold, dead creatures when this one was so hot, so very much *alive*?

She wanted him, and she despised him for it. Her fingers tangled in his hair, pulling at the silken strands hard enough to hurt a mortal man. She wanted to hurt *him*. How could she react this way to him? To a vampire? How could he make her feel these things? He was the very thing she had always hated. The thing she'd hunted. The thing she would rather die than become.

So why did she feel invincible when he was with

her? Why did the thought of sinking her teeth into his flesh excite rather than sicken her?

And when had she decided that he was the most beautiful creature she had ever seen?

It only inflamed Bishop more when she pulled his hair. He ground his lips against hers, teeth scraping together. His hips pressed into hers, sandwiching her between him and the chair. His sex was full and hard, pressing between her legs through the layers of clothing that separated them. Her body answered with a heavy throbbing and a rush of warmth.

His lips tore free of hers and he lifted his head despite her grip. "Do I disgust you now?" he demanded, his breath hot on her face. "Or do you want me?"

She should tell him to let her go, that he sickened her. Instead she met his gaze with a grim smile. "What do you think?"

He didn't reply, but his eyes flashed bright for a second before his head lowered to hers again. This time when he kissed her there was no restraint. His fangs scraped the inside of her mouth, drawing blood. Her own taste in her mouth made Marika's heart pound. Between her legs Bishop thickened even more. His tongue swept against hers, tasting.

He stepped backward, his hands sliding down her back to cup her buttocks. When he lifted her, Marika wrapped her legs around his waist in a tight grip.

She didn't remember releasing his hair. The next

thing she knew there was a loud shearing sound and she had ripped his shirt down the back. He set her down and shrugged out of the ruined linen.

Marika watched him like a hawk watching a mouse. He was so golden and smooth in the lamplight. His muscular chest was broad, his collarbones sharp. A light dusting of hair started at his navel and drifted downward, beneath the trousers that rested low on his lean hips.

His dark hair was mussed—touched with copper in the dim light. His lips were moist and flushed from hers. When he reached for her, Marika stood her ground. He seized the neck of her shirt in both hands and tore it like it was nothing more substantial than tissue. Yanking it down over her shoulders, he held it there for a moment, effectively pinning her arms to her sides as he buried his face in her throat.

His fangs brushed her flesh, and Marika shivered. The undulating heat between her thighs intensified as she waited for the sting of his bite.

It never came. He pulled her shirt off and raised his hands to her breasts, reaching inside her demi-corset to tease her aching nipples into tightened peaks. Gasping, Marika watched as he took one of her nipples into his mouth and suckled—gently biting.

Her trousers came next, followed by his own. His sex stood thick and erect in a nest of coarse, dark hair. She barely had time to admire it before he picked her up again. He slid into her as her legs went around his waist, and Marika cried out at the slick intrusion. Her body was ready for him, willing and wet. He fit as though made to be inside her, and when he thrust, she felt her body clench around him.

Bishop moved, each step sending him deeper inside her until Marika thought there couldn't possibly be any more of him to take. Her back met the wall; the wallpaper was cool and smooth against her flesh, a startling contrast to the scorching heat of the body joined to hers.

Locking her legs around his flanks, she moved with him, raising her hips, grinding her pelvis against his until little sparks of delight shivered through her groin.

Bishop's palms were flat on the wall on either side of her. The muscles in his forearms stood out beneath his flesh as he thrust into her. His lips claimed hers in a demanding, greedy kiss that robbed her of breath as well as reason.

There were no words to describe how he felt inside her except that she thought she might die if he stopped. Need drove her onward, ground her against him as though her very life depended upon the release his body promised.

She didn't just want him. She had to have him. She needed him more than she needed air or food.

The need drove her more than any ambition, more than her desire for revenge, more than her hatred. Bishop could give her something no one else could. Her body recognized it, even if she had no idea what it was.

"Please." The rasp of her voice against his mouth was almost inaudible, yet it echoed in her head.

Bishop knew what she wanted—she saw the acknowledgment in his bright gaze. He stared into her eyes as he shoved himself into her. He withdrew almost all the way and then thrust again, bringing a cry of surrender to her lips. She didn't want to fight him, didn't want to stop him from doing whatever he would with her.

Still holding his gaze, she leaned her head back against the wall, tilting it so that her braid slipped over her shoulder, baring her neck. She offered him her throat, and with it, her trust.

He stilled for just a second, but she felt his hesitation. A faint frown pulled between his brows and was gone just as quickly. Then his mouth was on her neck, his hair tickling her jaw.

Marika closed her eyes. A sharp pinch as his fangs pierced her flesh and she gasped, arching herself into his embrace. The pain quickly gave way to a pleasure so intense, it flooded her body with sensation, sending her over the edge as orgasm tore through her. Her cries filled the room as Bishop slammed her against the wall, his own body stiffening with release. Warmth filled her as he groaned against her neck.

Marika was only vaguely aware as he licked her neck, closing the wound. He carried her to the sofa and gently set her on the soft cushions.

Gently. After all that had just happened, why was it that gentleness that brought hot prickling to the backs of her eyes? She had told him she was disgusted by what she felt for him. Their intimacy was born from distrust and violence and yet he handled her like she was fragile and delicate, not at all his enemy.

Like a woman.

Pushing him away, she jumped to her feet. Between her legs was cool and wet and empty—so very empty.

"Marika?" He didn't move from the sofa, but she felt the concern in his voice as heavily as a hand on her shoulder. "Did I hurt you?"

Hurt her? He had turned her world upside down, made everything right, wrong, and everything despicable, desirable. How could she go back to her old life knowing there might be other vampires out there as incapable of evil as he?

What if the Englishman found him? What if they killed him? Would she be able to live with herself if she didn't warn him?

God, had her mother loved Saint? Had Saint loved her mother? The very idea made her feel so terribly empty inside—taking away everything she ever held as true.

Limbs shaking, she pulled on what remained of her clothing as he watched her silently. Her hands shook as she tied her shirt together in the front. With a jacket covering it, no one would know it had been ripped. She didn't dare look at Bishop, afraid of what she might see in his wide-set eyes.

"Regrets are a horrible thing, halfling." He

made it sound like an endearment—when had that happened?

Tears burned the backs of Marika's eyes. He thought she regretted being with him? She wished that were true. At least then she would have something that made sense to cling to. The ground beneath her feet was ready to give way any second.

She shoved her feet into her boots. "I have to go." Her voice was fragile and she hated it. If only she could hate *him* for it.

He made a sound and she looked at him—even though she knew better. His lips were curved in a hard, cynical smile. Was that pain in his eyes?

"Yes," he agreed, rising to his feet in all his beautiful, naked magnificence. He reached for his trousers and stepped into them with a smooth grace she envied. "Run away from the monster before it attacks again."

She didn't correct him. She pivoted on her heel and ran to the door. She tore through the house and out into the newborn night. She ran until she was certain he wasn't following her and then she stopped, crouching in the corner of a dark alley between two businesses that were closed for the day.

That was where she let the tears finally come. She sobbed into her shirtsleeves, salty tears washing the taste of Bishop from her mouth, but not the scent of him from her skin.

When there were no more tears left, she dried her cheeks and rose to her feet. She alone was responsible for this situation. She alone was in charge of her life and her destiny. Suffering and uncertainty were not new to her, and she knew what she had to do. She had to make certain no one else suffered because of her actions. In particular, that Bishop didn't suffer because of her actions.

She no longer thought of Bishop as just another monster.

God help her, she was starting to think of him as a man.

Chapter 8

Bishop followed her.

Even though he knew she could protect herself, that she was faster and stronger than any mortal man, he felt in his heart that he was the only person who could truly keep her safe. God only knew what kind of trouble she could get herself into in this state. Right now she was a danger not only to herself, but to any unsuspecting fool who had the misfortune to cross her path.

She was his responsibility. If he had kept himself under control this wouldn't have happened. He wouldn't have the smell of her all over him, wouldn't have her taste in his mouth. And she wouldn't have run off in shame after having sex with a vampire.

After having sex with *him*.

It stung his pride knowing that being with him was so appalling to her. One would think he would be used to it. Elisabetta might not have been ashamed of him, but she had thought him less than human in the eyes of God. If he wanted to be accepted as a man, then he had to pretend to be nothing more than one, and those attachments rarely lasted more than a week or two. That was why he usually focused his attentions on shadow-world women; they understood.

He didn't have to pretend with Marika, but she didn't understand him at all.

He watched her sob in the alley with a mixture of anger and helplessness. He wanted to go to her and comfort her, but she would find no such solace in his arms.

He wanted to shake her for being so foolish. It was only sex. It wasn't as though he had turned her into a vampire. What they had done wouldn't change what and who she was—even he wasn't so much an optimist to hope for *that*.

As for the effect being inside her had on him . . . he refused to think of it. It had been amazing. Wonderful even. Parts of him were still trembling.

And other parts of him despised her for it.

After a while, Marika stopped crying, stood up, and took off at a quick run back toward Bishop's house. She didn't go inside, however. She went to the small stables around the back and saddled her horse. When she rode out of town, Bishop followed—running at a fast enough pace to keep up but to avoid being seen.

She rode to a small, dingy tavern at the base of the mountains. It reminded him very much of the one he had gone to after Elisabetta's murder. He had gone there looking for the men who killed her, and he had found them.

He had left none alive.

He watched from the roof as Marika dismounted and went inside. Closing his eyes, he concentrated all his hearing on picking her voice out of the noisy interior. Finally he found her—asking someone if the "Englishman" had been there that evening. She was told that he hadn't been. She thanked him, and that was the extent of the conversation.

This Englishman, was he the one who had hired her in the first place? Did she plan to hand Bishop over to him now that she had played him for a fool?

He would like to see her try. He was prepared now—and he wouldn't allow anyone to get close enough to drug him again.

Crouching by the chimney, Bishop ignored the sting of her possible betrayal and kept himself hidden as Marika approached her horse. More horses entered the yard. One of men riding them hailed her.

It was a man with an unmistakable English accent.

Though there wasn't much of a moon in the cloudy sky, the tavern was well lighted inside, and outside lanterns lit the way for drunken patrons. Bishop had a clear view of Marika, and his keen vision gave him just as good a view of her companion.

The man was medium height, slight and fair. He

wasn't dressed like a local. His coat was too well cut, his hair too artfully styled. He was from London, by way of Paris fashion. What the hell was he doing here?

More importantly, what did this man want with him? He didn't look like the type who liked to get blood on his hands—or his cravat, for that matter. He wasn't a hunter. If he was, he wouldn't have hired Marika. Did he collect exotic creatures? Bishop shuddered at the thought. Perhaps he had no other motivation but hatred of all things nonhuman.

No wonder Marika had agreed to work with him.

Bishop didn't recognize him, but that didn't mean the man's vendetta wasn't personal. Saint might not recognize Marika either, but that wouldn't change what she thought of him.

One thing was clear; he had no need to think of this man as a rival for Marika's charms. There was no hint of the supple seductress who had wrapped herself around him in his den. Her shoulders squared, her spine stiffened. No, she did not like or trust this man at all. Bishop was more pleased by that than he should be.

Marika's fingers went to her thigh, where she normally wore her dagger—the same dagger that was currently on the floor at Bishop's house, where he had tossed it after removing it from her leg.

She was defenseless aside from her reflexes and skill. One exceptional woman against . . . he counted half a dozen men.

"My dear Huntress," the man said as he handed the reins of his horse to one of his men and approached Marika. "I am delighted to see you. When you missed our meeting I worried that you might have met with an accident."

The way he spoke brought a scowl to Bishop's face. "Accident"? Did he know about the attack on Marika's village? Had he orchestrated it? If so, for what purpose? Had the men been there to collect her for this man, or had it been meant as a warning?

Whatever the attack's purpose, it had failed. Bishop wasn't modest enough to not take credit for that. Were it not for him, Marika would have been taken or killed. Even she was no match for so many guns.

"As you can see, I am fine." Marika kept her attention on the blond man, but Bishop knew she watched the others just as carefully.

"Where is my vampire?"

His vampire? As though Bishop were a horse. He had a mind to show this arrogant little worm that he belonged to no one but himself.

"I do not know," Marika replied. It was odd to hear her speak English. She had a good command of the language, which meant she had been taught to speak it. If she'd been brought up in such circumstances, how had she become a hunter? Surely her father would have expected her to make a decent marriage?

Perhaps her father hadn't cared what happened

to his daughter as long as he didn't have to see her.

"Do not know?" the Englishman asked. "Or refuse to tell me?"

"Why would I lie?" Her tone was just a little too defensive, and the Englishman picked up on it.

"I do not know. Perhaps you have gone soft. Perhaps you are foolish enough to attempt deceiving me." The blond man eyed her carefully—with a bit of a leer. "Or perhaps you have developed feelings for the creature."

Marika stiffened. There was little point in trying to discern just what had offended her in his words—there was so much that could have done it. For a second, Bishop allowed himself to believe that she might have started to develop feelings for him—but only for a second.

"He escaped."

The Englishman's eyes narrowed. It was obvious he didn't quite believe her. Bishop wouldn't have either, not knowing Marika as he did. "How?"

She held the man's gaze; he'd give her credit for that. Although it didn't bode well for his own trust of her that she could so directly look into someone's eyes and lie. "I sent most of my people away in preparation for moving the vampire. One of my men got careless and the creature attacked."

Why did it hurt to hear her refer to him as a creature? She had called him much worse than that in their brief acquaintance. He was getting soft and sentimental. One screw and he wanted to be a hero in her mind.

The man stepped closer to Marika, examining her in an almost insolent fashion. Luckily for him he didn't touch her—if he had, he wouldn't be long for this world.

"You don't look like someone who has been in a battle."

She tilted her head, giving him a view of her throat where Bishop had bitten her earlier that evening. The wounds were healing quickly, as they always did, but there were two red dots on her neck, surrounded by bruising that left no question as to what had caused them.

"I'm lucky he didn't drain me," Marika stated coldly, "or worse."

"Yes," the man agreed, seeming satisfied with her evidence. "It very well could have turned you into a creature of the night as well."

It? Bishop might have laughed were it not for the fact that he wanted to kill this fop. Marika was every bit as much a "creature" of the night as he was. The only difference was she could go out during the day and not burst into flames—not that she seemed to spend much time in the sun.

Apparently she had inherited something of vampire weakness along with the strength.

"You realize this negates our agreement?" The Englishman ran a gloved hand down his lapel. "I have no intention of paying you for goods not delivered."

Marika nodded. "The money you already gave us was more than generous."

Pale lips curved into a smile that revealed crooked teeth. If he had never spoken Bishop still could have identified him as English just by his smile. "Enough to keep your ragged little band fed for a few months, eh?"

She nodded sharply. "Yes."

That's why she abducted him—not only to get information about Saint, but for money to care for her people.

Christ, at this rate he'd have her ready for saint-hood soon. Her motives didn't change her actions—didn't change a thing.

"Now, if you'll excuse me?" Marika moved to climb up into the saddle. "I would like to return home. I do not like being out alone with Bish— the vampire running free."

The Englishman's head bobbed in agreement. "Yes, of course. The monster might come back for revenge. Would you like us to escort you?"

"No." Her tone was incredulous and Bishop chuckled softly. She'd do better by herself than with these monkeys.

The blond stopped her with a hand on her arm as she placed her boot in the stirrup. "I sincerely hope you are not playing me for a fool, my dear."

Bishop tensed at the threat in his voice, ready to pounce at any moment.

Marika stared at his hand until the man released her. Then she swung herself up into the saddle and rode away. She didn't even bid him farewell.

The woman had balls, he'd give her that.

"Do you believe her?" one of the man's companions asked.

The blond shrugged. "Either she's telling the truth or she's the vampire's whore. If she's telling the truth we need to prepare."

Bishop raised a brow. Prepare for what?

"And if she's the vampire's whore?" asked another.

Another jagged grin. "Then he's a brave bastard."

The men all laughed and strolled toward the tavern, the blond bringing up the rear.

Silently Bishop dropped from the roof to the grass. He should just leave, but he couldn't. Not yet.

Swiftly he moved up behind the group, stopping his quarry with a hand on his shoulder.

"Touch her again and I'll rip your throat out," he snarled in the man's ear.

By the time the Englishman turned around, pistol in his trembling hand, Bishop was already gone.

Marika had fallen asleep in the stables behind Bishop's house, on a mound of hay with a rough wool blanket covering her.

She woke up in a bed—in Bishop's house—naked beneath crisp sheets and soft blankets.

How could *she* have slept through being carried into a house? How could she have slept through having her clothing removed? Good God, had she slept through anything else?

No, if he had made love to her again she would have woken up, of that she was certain.

Odd how she could think of what had happened as lovemaking. Not long ago she would have called it vampiric seduction. She would have convinced herself that he had *made* her want him. Bishop hadn't done anything to persuade her; she could admit that to herself. It might have started as intimidation—his male need to prove a point—but it hadn't continued that way. If she had told him to stop he would have.

No, she had wanted him to take her—wanted to know what it was like to be joined with a man she didn't have to worry about hurting—a man made for a woman like her.

Her heart jumped. That had to be her heightened emotions talking. She and Bishop had shared something incredibly intimate—of course she would be confused in her thinking of him for a short time. He made her feel wonderful—it was difficult not to attach some kind of romantic notions to that, regardless of who and what they both were.

He was a vampire. She was a vampire killer. He was immortal and she was not. The situation didn't need to be made any more complicated than that.

When they first met he had told her that one of them would not survive their acquaintance. At that time she had been arrogant enough to promise him that it would not be her to meet her end. Now she wasn't so confident. If not for him she would be dead already.

She had been weak and caught unawares. An attack like the one on her village would never have happened before she met Bishop. If she'd held any other vampire—any other man—she would have had men patrolling the boundaries of their settlement. She would have been ready, her mind focused on what had to be done, not on a vampire who made her feel accepted for what she was. Oh, he sometimes used the information to irritate her, but only because he knew it bothered her. He didn't care that she was dhampyr. No one but her grandmother had ever accepted the truth about her.

Not even her father.

Bishop's words came back to haunt her. Could her father have lied to her about her mother? Was it possible that her mother and Saint had a relationship? If it was true, her father wasn't likely to confess to her now. He never wrote to her, rarely asked about her. He had sent her off as a child to bounce between her grandmother and school. Marika used to believe it was so she would have a good upbringing, but that wasn't it. Sometimes she thought maybe he blamed her for her mother's death.

Maybe looking at her was simply a reminder of the woman he had lost.

Or perhaps he looked at her and saw the product of his wife's infidelity with a mon— vampire.

There was one person who could give her answers to these questions—her grandmother.

Tossing back the covers, Marika climbed out of the warm cocoon of the bed and strolled naked toward the wardrobe against the wall. Rays of sunshine streamed through the window, making the carpet beneath her feet toasty and inviting. Sometimes she wished she could stretch in those rays like a cat, let the heat lull her into a lazy sleep. If she did, she would wake up with a headache and a burn so bad she wouldn't be able to think or move for a week.

She hesitated in front of her meager selection of clothing. What she wanted to wear and what she knew she *should* wear did not match.

Her grandmother hated that she wore trousers, and since it was daylight and a Sunday, Marika knew it would garner less attention if she wore a skirt to see the old woman. Out in the country among peasants and Gypsies she could get away with wearing men's clothing and being who she was. Here, in town, she would stand out in a way that might embarrass her grandmother.

She would rather fight Bishop bare-handed than do anything to cause her *bunica* discomfort.

She chose a blue skirt and matching blouse from the closet. She had only one other fancy outfit and it was much better suited for evening—not that she knew much about women's fashion anymore. As a young girl she had read all the books from Paris and constantly begged her grandmother for the latest fashion. Her father had paid for it, of course. He paid for everything. Now she was more concerned with having a coat that didn't restrict her movement.

She had given up one of the most wonderful and frivolous joys of womanhood in her pursuit of monsters.

After washing at the basin, she donned her undergarments and demi-corset. Fashionable ladies in Paris or London would no doubt be appalled at her underwear, but Marika had no maid to help her dress—she needed ease and economy.

The long skirt was a rich blue, not too wide, and it swished prettily when she walked. The matching blouse was snug-fitting and high-collared. The color complemented her fair skin and dark hair—which she brushed, rebraided, and then coiled into a thick bun at the back of her head.

Thankfully the house was quiet as she left. She didn't want them to see her this way—didn't want a certain *him* to see her dressed this way. The housekeeper would be tending to her daily chores, and Bishop be asleep in his room upstairs. Or did he keep a hiding spot? A crypt or a cellar nearby?

Or perhaps he slept in a normal bedroom. No coffin. No dirt. She prided herself on being well versed in the habits of vampires, but he had proven many of her assumptions wrong. Lord only knew what else she had been misinformed about. God, she was lucky to still be alive—lucky that the things she had used against the creatures had worked.

Creatures. It was difficult to think of them—of Bishop anyway—in that manner now. She wasn't convinced that he was correct in his reasoning that most vampires were good and not evil by nature. Perhaps he wasn't, but that was because he'd had awful things happen to him. He had retaliated horribly though, hadn't he? He admitted to killing the men responsible for his wife's death.

Just because he planted a seed of doubt about Saint in her mind didn't mean she had to let it bear fruit. She would believe Saint killed her mother until she heard otherwise.

The vampires she had killed were evil—she had to believe that. She had seen many of them kill. She had found some covered in blood, their kill at their feet. Not even Bishop could deny their guilt.

Vampires killed humans to survive. Bishop was an old one and didn't need to feed like the ones she encountered. Or perhaps vampires were different where he came from, but here, in the land where Bram Stoker had set his now-famous novel, vampires were every bit the monsters the author had written them to be.

It was this thought that kept her world from tilting beneath her.

In the stables she found a sidesaddle and lifted it onto her mare's back. She preferred riding astride as it was her habit, but there was no way she could do that in her skirt. The discomfort would be worth seeing the look on her grandmother's face when the old woman saw her looking like a woman.

When she arrived at the house, her grandmother had company. Two neighbors had accompanied her home from church and were having refreshment in the parlor. *Bunica* had pastries, cheese, and meats on platters for them to enjoy. Marika's stomach growled at the sight.

"Marika!" Her grandmother's handsome face was creased with joy as she held out her arms. "You look so beautiful. Iulia, Marianna, is she not beautiful?"

Blushing as the women dutifully agreed, Marika embraced her grandmother and then took a seat beside her on the sofa. There she sat, eating and making conversation, waiting not so patiently for the other women to finally take their leave.

Almost half an hour passed before they did so. When they were finally alone, her grandmother turned to her with a shrewd look on her face.

"You want something, child. What is it?"

Sometimes Marika swore her grandmother was able to read minds.

She nibbled on a piece of cheese. "I came to visit you, *Bunica*. That is all."

The old woman snorted and selected a small slice of meat from the tray. "You do not lie well, Marika. You never did."

There was no point in pretending. "I do have another reason for visiting besides missing you."

Her grandmother fixed her with a knowing look. "And that is?"

Marika angled herself toward her grandmother and leaned forward, bracing her forearms on her thighs. "I need you to answer some questions for me."

"Oh, dear. Marika, ever since you were an infant I have dreaded hearing those words from you."

She smiled at her grandmother's expression. "I need to know the truth, *Bunica*. I hope you will tell me what you can."

Irina wiped her hands on a napkin and nodded solemnly. "I will answer what I can. What is your question?"

"Did my mother betray my father?"

Ruddy color swept up the old woman's face. "What do you mean asking such a thing?"

"*Bunica*, please. It is important. Was there another man?"

Her grandmother rose to her feet and strode across the room with quick, erect strides to stand in front of the portrait of Marika's mother painted shortly before her death. Marika didn't have to look at it to know that she looked very much like her mother—except for her very dark eyes. Those eyes weren't her father's either.

In fact, she was beginning to suspect that her eyes had come from her vampire "father." If his bite had given her the abilities she had, then it was reasonable that he contributed other traits as well.

Whatever they were, she didn't want to know. She had to take this slowly, otherwise she'd go mad.

"There was . . . another," her grandmother replied finally, still staring at the portrait. "I told her it was wrong, but she was so happy."

Marika's heart twisted. "Was it . . . was it the vampire?"

Bunica glanced over her shoulder at her. "I do not know. She said his name was du Lac. Adrian du Lac."

Eyes closing, Marika drew a deep breath to steady herself. That was the name Bishop had given her as Saint's Christian name.

"She . . . loved him?" She opened her eyes once more and found her grandmother had turned away from the portrait and was watching her closely.

"Yes. You must not judge her, Marika. Her marriage to your father, it was arranged, and he . . . he was not an attentive husband."

"He was not an attentive father," Marika replied more bitingly than she wanted. "Of course I do not judge Mama." But in her heart—*Oh, Mama, how could you? With a vampire?*

She had no right to ask that, no right at all. She had given herself to Bishop without hesitation. She wanted to defend herself and say that sex was different, but it wasn't. She was no better than her mother and her mother was no worse than she. Perhaps it was a defect of the women in her family. Perhaps they were the victims of some kind of vampiric charm.

At least her mother had been in love with Saint. Marika didn't have that excuse. But she thought she had been in love with Grigore when she gave herself to him, and it had been nothing like the desire she felt for Bishop, a man she was supposed to despise.

"Did Adrian du Lac kill my mother?"

Her grandmother shrugged, a pained expression on her face. It was painful for her to speak of her dead daughter, even though more than two and a half decades had passed. It wasn't easy for Marika either.

"I do not know. Your father told me she was attacked by a vampire and that she died after having you, but . . ."

"But what?"

A long, aged hand brushed across Irina's cheek. Even from that distance, Marika could see the tremor in it. "Your mother was planning to leave your father. She and du Lac were going to run away to Paris and raise you together as their own."

Marika could not be any more shocked if her grandmother had told her that her mother had decided to run away with a band of Gypsies.

"If she changed her mind about leaving, he might have killed her out of rage."

Bunica shot her a pitying glance. "Marika, when I went to the house to help care for you, I found luggage in your mother's room. She had been packing. It was the middle of the night and she was preparing to leave."

Oh. She could argue that, could try to think of an excuse, but there was no point. Bishop believed that Saint had loved her mother, and *Bunica* believed that her mother had loved Saint. Apparently they had both loved her. In fact, the only person that didn't seem to be loved, or have it to give, was her father.

"She had been bitten," her grandmother told her softly. "If du Lac was a vampire and took her blood, I do not think he intended to kill her. Her last thoughts were of du Lac, and of you. She wanted both of you to know she loved you."

Was it possible that Saint hadn't been trying to hurt her mother? What if he had been trying to change her—not kill her? But what kind of idiot vampire tried to change a woman in labor?

One who was afraid the woman he loved was going to die, like Bishop trying to change Elisabetta as she lay dying in his arms.

Her stomach clenched and rolled. She took a deep breath to keep the contents of it from coming back up. There was no way she could keep the world from tilting now. It was so slanted, she very much feared she was going fall off.

"Why did you never tell me this before?" She was angry at her grandmother and it felt wrong.

"I never thought that du Lac and the vampire were one and the same," *Bunica* explained, her gaze dull with regret. "And I promised your father I would not speak of it."

"But I've been hunting vampires all these years because I thought he killed her." All that hate that had eaten at her. Had it been for nothing? "You could have stopped me."

"Stopped you? I've never been able to prevent you from doing exactly what you wanted." It wasn't said cruelly, but it stung all the same. "If I had told you your mother had a lover—even if you had known it was the vampire—you would have found a way to hate him because you needed to hate him."

She was right. Marika could admit that. It was only her association with Bishop that made her see things differently. Life would be so much simpler if she could go back to her ignorance!

The things she had done. The things she had justified because she thought Saint a monster. All vampires monsters. Some had been, but what of the others?

Saint hadn't killed her mother.

"There are only two people who can tell you what happened," her grandmother said, her tone gentle. "Adrian du Lac and your father. You will have to ask one of them what really happened."

Marika barely made it to the water closet upstairs before vomiting. It wasn't the idea of talking to either her father or Saint that made her retch, but the truth of what they might tell her.

That the only person responsible for her mother's death was she.

Chapter 9

Victor Armitage did not like disappointment. He particularly did not like to be the one doing the disappointing.

Maxwell was going to be very disappointed when he learned of Victor's meeting with the dhampyr. People who disappointed Maxwell very often met with bad ends. Or simply disappeared.

"Where is the dhampyr, my boy?" the older man asked, not bothering to look up from the papers on his desk as Victor entered the study.

"I do not have her, my lord."

"Why?"

"The men we sent for her failed. I believe they were killed."

Maxwell looked up, surprise clear on his aristocratic features. "By her?"

Victor cleared his throat. He hadn't been told to sit so he stood before the great desk like a schoolboy before the headmaster. "And possibly by the vampire."

The older man's dark brows rose. "Really? That is a surprise. Was he loose?"

"I do not know."

"No, of course you don't. My, but this is unexpected. I assumed he would follow when she was taken because he would realize she wasn't the one responsible for the disappearances. I never dreamed he would defend her."

Victor bit back a sigh. Perhaps he would escape this meeting unscathed after all.

Frowning, Maxwell leaned back in his chair, tapping a pencil against the polished top of his desk. "Are we certain it was the vampire who aided her?"

"Fairly, yes." He was more confident now. "Last evening, after I realized our men had been defeated, I returned to the tavern where the dhampyr and I met. She was there."

"And you did not take her?"

"She claimed to have come looking for me, to tell me of the vampire's escape. I thought it better to let her go so we could watch her—determine if she is planning to betray us, or let her re-collect the vampire for us." In truth, Victor hadn't thought of taking her. She had seemed agitated and a little wild. She had frightened him.

The older man nodded, but he was still frowning. "I see."

"It is a good thing that I did have such care, my

lord. Not a minute after the dhampyr departed, the vampire himself appeared. If we had tried to take her then he surely would have killed all of us."

His announcement was met by a shocked stare. "You lie."

"On my honor, it is true. He told me if I went near the dhampyr again I was a dead man." His mouth went dry at the memory. "I pulled my pistol but when I turned he was gone."

"They're very quick, vampires. Bishop and his brothers are quicker still, given the pureness of their blood." The pencil ceased tapping. "It would seem the vampire and dhampyr have some kind of relationship. Are they fucking, do you reckon?"

Victor's jaw sagged at such vulgarity from such a lofty personage. "I cannot tell you, my lord."

Maxwell waved his pencil. "It is nothing but conjecture, but this is all very interesting, Victor. Very interesting."

Victor preened at what he took for praise. "Thank you, my lord."

The older man rose to his feet. "I have a new task for you, my boy. Follow me."

"A new task, sir?"

"I want you to see something, Victor."

He followed Maxwell to the heavy door, which when opened revealed nothing but darkness.

Victor peered through the opening. He saw nothing but the beginning of a set of stairs in the blackness. A foul odor rose out of the depths on a breath of cool air. It was a cellar—one that stank of violent death and decay.

"What is it?" The question slipped out before he could stop it. He didn't really want to know.

"It's your new home," Maxwell replied, shoving him into the black. "Perhaps you won't be such a disappointment after this."

Victor didn't have time to react. The older man was stronger than he looked, and Victor stumbled. The door slammed behind him as he fell down the stairs.

He screamed as pain, sharp and abrupt, sliced through his ribs. How many were broken? His forearm cracked against the boards, the bone snapping as it bent under the force of his own weight.

Finally he hit bottom, rolling and gasping on the cold dirt floor.

He opened his eyes. Was that a light? Yes, the flicker of flame coming toward him, the sound of muted footsteps.

A face, pale and long, loomed over his, sinisterly shadowed by the light of a small lamp.

"Yes," the man said in a voice that sent a chill through Victor's heart. "You'll do. You'll do indeed."

Then Victor caught a glimpse of the thing behind him and screamed.

"Good God." Bishop stared at Marika as she entered the house just before sunset that evening.

The house was dark with the curtains drawn, but he stepped back from the dying light that poured through the door at her entrance. "Please tell me you didn't put that on for my benefit?"

"Of course I did not." High color flushed her cheeks as she stepped into the artificial light given off by the many lamps. Electric lights had not yet made it to this part of the country. "But if I had, have you been alive so long that you have forgotten that it is customary to compliment a woman when she has taken effort with her appearance?"

Bishop shook his head to clear it. He hadn't meant to embarrass her. "Forgive me. You look lovely."

It was extremely odd to see her wearing something so feminine—something that revealed just how womanly she was. He'd held her practically naked in his arms and yet he was more agog at seeing her fully clothed. Not long ago he had wondered what she would look like in a dress, and now that he saw it. . .

"That blouse."

Her hands went to her trim waist, just below where the fabric hugged her ribs. "What of it?"

It molded to her breasts in a way that made his hands want to do the same. Last night had been too urgent, too rushed. He wanted to take his time with her. "It's nice."

"Thank you."

His arms folded across his chest. There was no point in playing coy—no need to torment that part of him that was slightly annoyed that she hadn't dressed up for his benefit after all. "Where were you?"

She frowned at him, annoyed. "It isn't any of your business, but I went to visit my grandmother."

Like hell it wasn't his business. Until he was certain she wasn't going to kill him, everything she did was his *business*.

"Not that I wish you gone, but why did you not stay there?" It did make more sense that she would want to reside somewhere that made her comfortable and safe.

If she took any offense to his remark she didn't show it. "Because my presence at her home might put her in more danger than she is already in simply by being my relation."

"If your presence could be so dangerous, why did you go see her?" Why did he care? It was unlikely that she would enlist her grandmother's help to kill him. Unlikely, but not impossible.

This wasn't sane, not quite trusting someone yet wanting her so badly.

She hesitated. "I needed to talk to her." Those few, ambivalent words said so much.

So that was the way of it. "Did she absolve you of your sins?" It was the sullen question of a lover discarded like trash.

She shot him a look that would have sent lesser men to their knees begging forgiveness. "I'm the only person who can do that."

"Blasphemy." He couldn't stop the thin smile that came with the accusation.

"Reality," she retorted, brushing past him with a swish of skirts and a haughty lift to her chin. "Excuse me, I need to change."

"I'm going hunting." He followed after her, to the base of the stairs. "Would you like to join me?"

Marika turned to him, brows raised. "Hunting for what?"

"The men who attacked you."

Her eyes narrowed. "Why?"

What a suspicious wench. Of course, he was keeping secrets—secrets he might as well reveal now that she was sniffing for them. "I've received word from an associate of strange happenings in England." He had been surprised by Father Molyneux's missive—and dismayed to see that it had gone to his residence in Spain first. Weeks had already passed.

"Related to the attack on my village?"

"I'm not certain, but a friend of mine has gone missing, and I find that too suspicious to ignore." Suspicious? That was an understatement. How someone had managed to take Temple was beyond him. As a man he had been formidable. As a vampire . . . well, whoever had done it must have had an army with them.

She watched him, searching his face for an answer to a question she obviously wasn't sharing. "Of course I want to go with you."

"There's a little tavern not far from here I thought I might investigate. Rumor has it some Englishmen have been frequenting the place as of late."

All the color leached from her face. "You do not want to go there."

"Why? Because you do not want the men you were going to sell me to knowing that you deceived them?"

He wouldn't have thought it possible, but she went paler still. "How did you know?"

"I followed you last night."

The roof did not lift off the house as he expected—not that she wasn't angry. "Followed me?"

He might have rolled his eyes if he dared to take his attention from her. "You didn't honestly think I would allow you to go off on your own after what happened?"

Marika's jaw was tight, her posture rigid, but she seemed more embarrassed than furious. Was she wondering if he saw her cry? "Did you think I might harm myself?"

"After soiling yourself with a vampire?" He leaned against the banister, arms across his chest. "The thought had crossed my mind, yes."

She flinched, surprised. "I will not lie to you, Bishop. Parts of me are at odds over what . . . happened between us."

"Which parts?" He couldn't help baiting her.

She ignored him. "Whether or not I live to regret it remains to be seen, but that is not why I left."

He might have been irked by her cool boldness were he not so relieved that she hadn't run out on him because she was sickened by what had happened between them. "Why *did* you leave?"

Marika sighed and rested one hand on the top of the banister post, the other on the full curve of her hip. "Because you make me wonder where before I was certain. You make me restless where before I found ease. I do not like doubting myself. I like realizing a vampire might not be wholly evil even less."

He shook his head with an appreciative smile. How much her words pleased him—more than they should have, that was for sure. "Are you always so honest?"

"When I choose to be."

His smile drifted away. That did not bode well for his next question, perhaps. "Why did you go to the tavern?"

"To tell the Englishman that you had escaped and put an end to our arrangement, but you already know that if you were there."

He shrugged. What could he say, that he wanted to hear it from her own mouth, with her looking him in the eye?

"Now it is your turn to be honest. Was it you who took me from the stables?"

He nodded. She would say something about him removing her clothes, surely. Demand to know if he had defiled her again.

"Thank you."

"You are welcome." He regarded her for a moment. She was being so open, it would be a shame to waste this opportunity. "You do not regret last night?"

She met his gaze. "Not yet, no."

He chuckled. "You wound my pride, halfling."

"What is it about you men that makes you so fragile where your prowess is concerned?"

His amusement faded, gave way to something a little more serious, a little more vulnerable. "I think that is the first time you have referred to me as a man and not a monster or a creature."

She looked away. "When you call me halfling now it sounds like an endearment. Perhaps we are both changing more than we like to admit."

"Perhaps."

Her gaze locked with his once more, black and unreadable. "That does not mean I have to like it."

"Nor I."

"And do not expect what happened last night to happen again. It was a moment of weakness, nothing more." If that was true, why was she drawing closer to him now?

"Curiosity got the better of you?" He was amused—and a little insulted.

"Exactly. It was a moment of heightened emotion."

"I was angry." That was an understatement.

Her chin came up defiantly. "You wanted to prove a point."

"That you are attracted to me." He said it to goad her and they both knew it. "I think I proved it."

There was little more than an inch or two between them as she stared him directly in the eye. "Yes. I think we both know our effect on the other."

Bishop didn't quite appreciate being goaded back. "Does it make you feel vulnerable?"

"A little, yes."

"Good." He took a step backward to allow her access to the stairs. "Go change. The night won't last forever."

"No." Marika held up her hand to signal an end to the discussion as she stomped through the night toward the stables. He was like a dog with a bone, worrying her until she was tempted to give in just to shut him up.

Bishop ignored both her hand and her words. "It will be much faster this way."

"I said no!" She whirled on her heel to face him so fast, they almost collided. "Why will you not listen?"

He smiled—just a trace of mockery on his sensual lips. "Scared?"

"As a matter of fact, yes." Ha! He had not seen that bit of honesty coming! "It is not natural for man to fly."

"But it is convenient," he argued. "I can't believe you are actually afraid of something."

He needn't sound so surprised. There were many things that frightened her—but she wasn't about to let him in on any more of her secrets.

Such as that she was terribly afraid of him—and his effect on her. Being near him made her heart speed up, made her lungs struggle to draw breath. Yet despite this discomfort, being with him was becoming far more preferable to being without him.

"Trust me," he said, drawing her into his arms. "I

would never allow anything to happen to you."

Against her better judgment, her own arms locked around his neck. "I want to, but you're everything I've been taught to distrust. My heart tells me you are dangerous."

He grinned. "Your heart is right, but that doesn't mean you cannot trust me."

Before she could protest, they were in the sky. She had felt nothing more than his knees bend slightly and then a strong breeze blowing down on them.

"Oh, my God!" Squeezing her eyes shut, Marika clung to him as the ground retreated.

Bishop's chuckle was warm against her ear. "Do not be afraid, halfling. I have you."

Cautiously, Marika opened one eye and then the other. Bishop held her so that she faced him, and unless she twisted in his arms, all she could see was him. They streaked through the sky like an arrow, but there was nothing but his bright eyes, the shaded outline of his face.

His arms were secure and strong around her, holding her tightly but not painfully. He was so very strong. And he would not drop her, of that she was certain. Slowly she relaxed, and concentrated on the beauty of his face.

He smiled at her as the tension left her muscles. "Better?"

She nodded. "I think so."

"We're almost there."

He hadn't lied. Within minutes they were on the ground again. He was right—it was quicker to fly.

Fortunately he'd had the forethought to set them down just outside the perimeter set by the torches in the village. Her men were there, repairing the damage that had been done. Would they bring their families back here, or would they want a safer home for them now?

Marika hesitated before entering her camp. This was her home and these were her men, but she was bringing an intruder with her. She knew she could trust Bishop not to drop her from the sky, knew she could trust him to find their common enemy, but after that, what happened? She had abducted him, even tortured him. Surely he would want to see that debt repaid.

Her men would not understand why he was there—not when she could not tell them the whole truth. She trusted them with her life but not the truth. How queer that on some levels she trusted Bishop more than her own friends.

She led the way into the center of the village, where a fire burned, fueled with the debris that could not be reused. The sounds of conversation, hammering, crackling fire and even laughter filled the night. She hated to interrupt.

A light hand touched her arm. She half turned, expecting to see one of her men. Instead there was only Bishop, his face shadowed and his eyes bright. There was no mistaking the concern on his face.

How could he be concerned for her well-being after all she had done to him?

She smiled—in a reassuring manner, she hoped—

and waited until he had dropped his hand to call out to her men. It wasn't his touching her that she didn't want them to see—it was how much she appreciated the gesture that she wanted to hide.

He was surprised that she feared things. She feared her men discovering what she was more than anything—feared how they might react, that they might not understand.

What did that fear say about her? About them?

The men put down their tools, left their tasks, and came to her, one by one out of the shadows. She saw them all clearly—better than they could see her.

How was it that none of them had ever noticed that she was more than human? Had they simply not wanted to see?

They called out in happy voices, pleased to see her, until Dimitru noticed her companion.

"What is *that* doing here?" He pointed with his good arm, the other still stiff and bent at his side.

Marika bristled. "*He* is with me."

Dimitru seemed not to notice her annoyance, otherwise he might not have stood before her so defiantly. "Why?"

"Because he has offered his assistance in finding the men who killed Ivan."

The stocky man was bare from the waist up, and the firelight only enhanced the heavy musculature of his torso. In a fair fight he might be a match for Bishop—were Bishop human. "It was because of him that Ivan was killed. We do not need his help."

She would keep her temper. She would stay calm. To show anything but command would be a weakness—one Dimitru might try to abuse and Bishop might try to defend. "Those men were after me, Dimitru. And we do need his help. They would have killed us all were it not for him."

"Bah. We weren't prepared. Now they are dead anyway."

"There will be more."

Her men stared at her in stunned silence. She took advantage of the moment to press her suit. "I do not ask you to stay and help me fight this battle," she told them, her voice ringing through the dark. "It is mine alone to fight, but if you do stay then you will accept Bishop as one of us and earn my eternal gratitude."

Dimitru spat at Bishop's feet, as if his opinion hadn't been clear enough before she spoke.

The vampire didn't move, but Marika felt his presence swell before her, as though he sought to restrain his power. These were not his men, they were hers. She had to regain her leadership, and if that meant having to prove her dominance over Dimitru, she would.

"Do you want to fight me, Dimitru?" She voiced the question softly, but clearly. "Do you challenge me over this?"

Dimitru sneered, but directed his gaze to Bishop. "The vampire cannot be trusted."

Marika could have sagged in relief. No challenge then.

"You have had much to drink tonight," Bishop told the smaller, roughened man. "And you smell of a woman who is not your wife. I have done many things you would not like, but betraying a loved one is not one of them."

They all stared at Dimitru in shock. Marika waited for him to deny the accusation—*willed* him to deny it. But he didn't.

"A Gypsy," Bishop commented, seeming to catch a scent on the breeze. The look he gave the man was dispassionate, almost quizzical. "A virgin. Did you force her?"

Hands fisted, Dimitru took a step forward, but he had not lost all his sense, it seemed, for he stopped abruptly. He knew better than to attack Bishop, but he glared daggers at him regardless.

"Oh, Dimitru." Her disappointment was clear in her voice. And the feeling wasn't directed only at Dimitru, but Bishop as well. She knew he was only defending himself, but to reveal such an awful thing about a man in front of those who respected him was low.

And yet she could not deny that she would have done the same were their situations reversed. He might have revealed the deed, but Dimitru was still the one who had committed it.

Man and vampire stared at each other, one flushed and angry, the other cool and poised. There was a tightness to Bishop's shoulders she did not like. He was like a coiled spring that needed only the right provocation to snap.

"Stop it, both of you. Dimitru, if you cannot fight beside Bishop, then go home to your family, where you belong." She could not resist that last dig. She had known Dimitru's family for years. She had always thought of him as a devoted father and husband. As a devoted friend. Now that one of those beliefs had been called into question, she didn't know how to feel. But she knew that she believed Bishop through and through.

The heavyset Romanian said nothing, but he stepped down from challenging Bishop, rubbing the stubble on top of his head with a dirty hand.

Surprisingly, it was Sergei who stepped forward. Out of all the men there—easily a dozen and a half—he was one of the few who had been there that night to witness Ivan's death.

"I saw the vampire save Marika's life that night," he told the others. "He had his chance to escape and stayed instead to help us. If Marika trusts him, then I will as well."

It took only that one testimonial to convince the others. They talked quietly among themselves for a moment and then came forward, one by one, to pledge their continued allegiance. Dimitru was the last to step up, but step up he did.

Marika hid her sigh of relief behind a smile. "Thank you, Dimitru."

He nodded, but his attention was on Bishop. "But I will kill you myself at the first sign of betrayal."

Bishop nodded—that universal male sign of understanding.

"Did they leave anything useful behind?" she asked Sergei once the rest of the men returned to work. "Anything that might give us a clue to their identity?"

He reached into his pocket and held up something with his dirty fingers. "We found this."

Marika took it from him, holding it up to the firelight. It was a ring—plain and silver, the top of which turned. The metal made her skin itch, but she ignored it. One side depicted a chalice. The other, a hand, palm facing outward.

Marika showed it to Bishop. "Have you ever seen anything like it?"

He did not touch the ring—that itch would be a terrible burn for him—but leaned over her hand to study the design. The action put his head very near to hers, and she could smell the warm, spicy scent of his hair. Her heart knocked heavily in response, and when he raised his gaze to hers, she could see her own uninvited desire there.

How could this have happened?

"No," he replied, straightening.

"I've seen this design somewhere before." Marika peered at the ring, her mind clearing as Bishop drew away. The design swam in her head—a hazy vision from another time. "I wish I could remember where."

"You try to remember," Bishop urged her. "Meanwhile I will ask Molyneux if he is familiar with it when I pen my reply to him."

"Wonderful. Thank you."

They stared at each other a moment, the heat of the fire nothing compared to the heat of their gazes. This attraction was growing out of hand. She wanted him again, wanted to feel him moving inside her. In his arms there was no danger, only safety and pleasure.

How bitter it was that the only place she truly felt as though she belonged was in the arms of a vampire—her sworn enemy.

There was no balance to her world anymore.

She almost went to him. In fact, she had taken two steps in his direction when a horse and rider came galloping into the camp.

Good God, were she and Bishop so caught up in their desire for each other that neither of them paid any attention to their enhanced senses? One of them should have heard this intruder long before he arrived.

It was Andrei, Sergei's oldest son. He was all of eighteen, tall and lanky, but he had his father's strong shoulders and strength. At this moment, however, he looked more like a frightened boy than a young man.

He jumped off his horse and went straight to his father. Then, seeing Marika, he changed course and came at her instead.

"Andrei." She took him by the shoulders. "What is it? Is someone hurt?" Was someone killed? Had there been another attack?

"A village to the east," he told her, his breath

coming in short gasps, "was attacked early this evening. More than half the people there were killed."

Warmth drained from Marika's face and hands, rushing down her body to pool in her feet. "How?"

The boy looked over her shoulder, leveling Bishop with a look of sheer hatred. "Vampires."

Chapter 10

"**T**hank you for not hurting him."

Bishop winced as Marika dabbed at the cut in the corner of his mouth. It was already healing, but had the acute discomfort of a paper cut. They were back at his house, in the quiet of his bedroom. She demanded that he allow her to play doctor and so he indulged it—if for no other reason than the pathetic need to feel her hands on him.

"If I had hurt him it would have turned the others against me as well." Besides, Andrei had hit him only a few times before his father and the others pulled him away. All Bishop had to do was stand there and take it.

He had taken worse.

She gazed down at him. In this light her eyes were like black opals—so bright and yet so dark. Her Cupid's-bow mouth so flush and kissable. She reminded him of a doll—a doll with a dagger concealed in it.

"Could you have killed them all?" She asked it with a hint of awe and certainty that made him frown. If he answered honestly, would she think him more of a monster than she already did?

"Perhaps," he replied. "Your men are skilled fighters and more of a threat than average. It would depend on their weapons and whether or not they have more of that drug you used on me."

She blushed. "They don't."

With her standing this close he could sense the increased heat of her blood. Of all the women in the world, why did it have to be her who could make him want her with just a breath? She could kill him in his sleep, kill him so damn quickly and easily that other vampires would shake their heads and lament his stupidity.

She finished with his cut—it was almost fully healed—and tossed the cloth she'd used into the basin of water on the bedside table.

"You do not have to come with us." She kept her gaze averted as she spoke.

She was going after a murder—a coven—of vampires. Of course he had to go with her. He watched her face, but found no emotion there. "I am not letting you go alone."

"They are your kind and I plan to kill them."

"They are killing innocent people. They deserve to die."

Her gaze turned back to meet his. "Do you truly believe that?"

He nodded. "I do."

"You are not going to betray me in the middle of a fight and join with them?"

Were it not for the real fear he heard in her voice, he might have thought she was joking. "No. Why would I do that?"

Marika hung her head, the thick black braid falling over her shoulder. "Because of what I did to you—abducting you, torturing you. You may harbor a need for revenge."

He shrugged, bringing his fingers up to toy with the velvety tip of braid. "You have already repaid me for that."

She actually jerked in surprise. He had to let go of her braid to avoid pulling her hair. "I have?" Her face changed then, became hard. "By having sex with you, you mean."

The braid had fallen behind her. He had to reach around her waist to find it again. Slowly he wrapped the thick rope of hair around his hand. "When you willingly give me your blood it thrills me more than any vengeance. It means you trust me—whether you want to or not."

She didn't say anything, but he heard her gasp. His other hand went to her hip—soft and full beneath her rough trousers—and pulled her closer. She stood in the vee of his legs, her knees pressed against his mattress, her chest just inches away from his face.

"When you took my cock inside you that first time, I knew your torment was as great as mine."

She shivered, a simple little reflex that brought his fangs out. "The first time? The only time."

"Not if I can help it." He slid his hand down from her hip to her knee, pulling until she half knelt on the bed. "I want you, Marika. I want to be inside you."

She stared down at him, bracing one hand against his shoulder—so he couldn't pull her off-balance, no doubt. "Sexually or as a meal?"

He chuckled. "Both." He let go of her hair to reach for her other knee. When he had her straddling him, he held her there. "If I had to choose I'd take sexually."

"Oh?" Her breathy question sent a bolt of heat streaking through him that ended in his groin. He thickened and tightened, straining against the front of his trousers.

"I can get blood anywhere, but there's no one else in the world who feels like you."

And then he realized he'd said too much. Something in her eyes changed—softened. Darkened.

She lowered herself onto his lap—the warm softness of her settling against his own stiffness. Bishop groaned at the sweet torture.

Marika's hands parted the collar of his shirt, popping the buttons until she had bared his upper chest and shoulders. Her soft fingers ran along the wall of his chest, through the hair and up to his clavicle to finally stroke and curve around the column of his throat.

"What would happen if I bit you?" Her voice had dropped an octave, to a low, throaty growl. The points of her little fangs glinted in the lamplight, and Bishop shuddered at the sight.

To have those teeth pierce his flesh, to feel her take from him as he took from her. . .

Her mouth was on his neck, a subtle scrape that had his cock throbbing in desperation.

"Don't," he managed to gasp. "Marika, I don't know what will happen if you do."

She raised her head, her dark gaze locking with his. She understood what he meant; he could see it. He didn't know what would happen to her and he would never forgive himself if his blood changed her.

Her hand slid down between their bodies, to the tautness between his legs. She stroked and gripped until spots floated before his eyes. "There are other ways to taste you," she murmured against his mouth, and then she was gone, sliding down to the floor to kneel between his legs.

He didn't try to stop her. In fact, he unfastened his trousers, pushing them down so that the full, burning length of him was freed. Bracing himself on his palms, arms rigid behind him, he waited, hips arching as her strong hands circled him. And when her soft lips closed around the head of his cock, he eased back his head and groaned in utter submission.

Her mouth was hot and wet, her tongue like velvet as it stroked him. Every brush of her teeth—the sharpness of those delicate fangs—sent a shudder coiling at the base of his spine. She sucked and licked and swirled until he thought his control would snap.

And then she was gone, leaving him throbbing and pulsing and coolly wet.

Lids heavy, Bishop opened his eyes to see her standing before him. She had removed her boots and was working on the rest of her clothes. Golden light bathed her. Her eyes were black, her lips red and damp. She removed her shirt, revealing the little half corset beneath. It pushed her breasts upward into golden, shadowed hills he wanted to bury his face between. Hell, he'd chew through those laces if it would get her naked faster.

He began removing his own clothes as well, watching as she slowly and methodically stripped. Did she know what her little "show" was doing to him? If he were human he would have already spent himself by now.

Thank God he wasn't a normal man faced with the wonder of this woman.

The last thing she removed was the bit of leather holding her braid. Lifting her arms, she finger-combed the braid as she came to him, gloriously naked. Ribbons of black streamed over her shoulders, flowed over her breasts. Sweet pink nipples peered through the strands that drifted downward toward the moist curls at the apex of her thighs.

"Goddess," he whispered as she joined him on the bed. "You are the most beautiful woman I have ever seen."

She gazed at him with questioning eyes as he positioned her on her back against the mountain of pillows. He knew the question in her mind as surely as if she had said it out loud.

More beautiful than Elisabetta?

"Yes." It was a throaty rasp, an admission he did not want to make even as his heart demanded it. The conflict between head and heart drove him down, filling him with an almost feral sexual aggression. He didn't want this little dhampyr to be more than Elisabetta when it had been people like her who had killed such an innocent woman. But he couldn't deny that he reacted to Marika in a way that he had never reacted to Elisabetta. He did not worry about hurting Marika. Her strong limbs held him, cradled him. There was warmth and safety in her arms.

God help him, but Marika felt as though she had been made especially for him.

He crouched between her splayed thighs, not wanting her to see the charge of emotion in his eyes. His hands slid up the pale flesh to the fragrant valley between. His thumbs parted her—so slick and swollen—and he leaned in, his tongue darting in to brush the sensitive knot of flesh hidden there.

She gasped, hips arching. Grimly, possessively, Bishop gripped her hips and delved into her. He took her with his tongue, licked and stroked mercilessly until she was undulating against his mouth, little cries and sobs breaking incoherently from her throat.

He wanted to take her where no one else ever had. He wanted to make her as vulnerable to him as he was to her. Any man who followed him would forever be compared to the way he had made her feel.

The idea brought a growl to his throat. There would be no other man. No other.

He teased her with soft licks. Her fingers tangled in his hair, pushing on his head, trying to force him deeper between her legs. He slid two fingers inside her welcoming wetness, curving them upward until he felt her respond. He explored until he found the spot that made her gasp and shiver. Smiling to himself, Bishop matched the strokes of his fingers to the stroke of his tongue and was rewarded with the sweet, flooding spasms as her body stiffened and Marika cried out with orgasm.

Rearing up, Bishop grasped her legs in his hands and settled her knees on his shoulders. He guided his cock to the entrance of her body and buried himself to the hilt inside her. She drew a sharp breath, arching upward to accept him. Around him, he could feel the tight walls of her sex still spasming from the release he had given her.

He positioned her so that her bottom rested on his thighs and then he leaned forward, opening her to his thrusts. One hand braced by her head, the other went to her sex, stroking that little ridge that was still stiff and sensitive to his touch.

"No other," he growled, his gaze locking with hers. She was flushed and dewy—heavy-lidded and lips parted. He thrust hard. "No other."

She clutched at his arm with one hand, her fingers biting into his biceps. The other seized his hair, pulling his head down to her breast.

"Never," she panted. "Never like you."

Bishop groaned in agreement as her sex tightened around him, clenching at him with a ferocity that made him grit his teeth in an effort to keep his control. He refused to come until she did. He wanted to know he had sent her over the edge a second time before giving himself up to pleasure.

He teased her nipple with his tongue, feeling the tender pink flesh stiffen and pucker under his attention. He sucked it, nipped it with his teeth, pulling until she writhed beneath him, her heels digging into his back.

Her fingers pushed at his skull. Bishop opened his mouth farther, letting his fangs fully lengthen. He pierced the flesh of her breast and drew her into his mouth, tasting the essence of her. Marika stiffened, arching beneath him as she cried out in climax. His own followed—a mind-numbing torrent of pleasure that had him slamming into her, his mouth fastened on her breast until he exploded inside her.

When his senses returned, he was lying half on top of her, his head on her chest. Somehow he found the strength to lift his head and lick the puncture

marks on her breast. They would close quickly and
be fully healed within a few hours.

"I'm sorry," he murmured, his fingers gingerly
caressing the flesh around the wound. "There may
be a bruise."

Her fingers stroked his hair. "It will fade."

Bishop closed his eyes and pushed his scalp into
her hand. If he could purr he would. "It will last
longer next time, I promise."

"I won't survive it."

He smiled at the humor in her voice.

Her other hand touched his back, embracing him.
"I know I should say that this was the last time and
it will never happen again, but I can't."

Opening his eyes, he turned his head to regard
her. The look of resignation on her face broke his
heart. He wasn't offended, just saddened. And a
little guilty for being the one to have put it there.

"All you have to do is touch me and I am on fire."
She tucked a lock of hair behind his ear. "I should
hate you for it and I cannot. You could leave me
tomorrow and I would not regret knowing you this
way."

He kissed her cheek. "Nor I."

A few moments of silence passed before she
spoke again. "You don't care, do you?"

He kissed her temple. He could spend the rest of
eternity nuzzling this woman. "About what?"

She turned toward him. "That I have . . .
experience?"

He licked the curve of her ear. She shivered. "Sexually?"

"Yes."

"No." He was getting hard again. "In fact, I'm glad for it."

"You are?"

He supposed she was surprised because she had spent some time in a society where an experienced woman would be branded a whore, but he was too old for that foolishness. "Yes. I don't have to worry about hurting you or scaring you."

She tried to pull away. "Ah, so I'm convenient."

He tightened his hold on her, molding his body against hers. "You sound jealous. Is it possible the great Huntress has developed feelings for me, a lowly vampire?" He meant it in jest, but one look at the red in her cheeks made him want to slap himself.

"Marika, I—"

She stopped him with a finger to his lips. "Yes," she replied, her voice harsh. "I am stupid to admit it, but I do feel something for you. I have come to like and respect you, Bishop. I could not be here with you otherwise."

She humbled him. "I know." But really he had no idea just how much it cost her to say those words to him. He could only guess, and even that touched him in ways he wasn't ready to admit.

"Am I wrong to assume you feel the same about me?" There was such raw vulnerability in her voice.

And more. "No. You are not wrong." Now was not the time to tell her that he missed her when she wasn't there, that he feared for her safety. At one time he had wanted to kill her himself, and now here he was, holding her in his arms and thinking of how much life she gave him.

"If things go badly when we hunt the vampires—"

Now it was he who shushed her. "They won't." He would make sure of it. He would not lose her. Not now.

"Don't let them turn me."

He stiffened. "What?"

"If one of the vampires tries to turn me, kill him. Or kill me. Will you promise me?"

What the hell was he supposed to say? She looked at him, so serious and needy that he wanted to give her anything, but she might as well have stuck a stake in his heart.

"You would rather die than be a vampire?" The accusation was thick in his throat.

"I would rather die than have it forced upon me." Her gaze begged him to understand. "I did not ask to be born this way. If I am to become something else I want that decision to be mine."

He understood then, and it pulled the tension from his muscles. A choice. He had been given a choice all those lifetimes ago. He had given a choice to Elisabetta as well, but Marika . . . someone had made the choice for her.

"I promise."

Her smile cracked his heart. "Thank you."

He kissed her, rolled her onto her back, and made love to her again—tenderly this time. It was the only way he could tell her everything he wanted to without actually using words. Words could come back to haunt him. Her touch and taste, the feel of her already did.

If the time ever came that Marika wanted to become vampire, he wanted to be the one to change her.

It hadn't been dark long when Bishop arrived the next night in their camp near Brasov. They were just a few kilometers west of the village Andrei had told them about.

And even though Marika trusted him, a little voice in the back of her mind had questioned whether he would come to help her. She even went so far as to fantasize about returning to Fagaras after this was over—after miraculously defeating the vampires, of course—and finding him long gone.

The thought of having him gone from her life was worse than the thought of dying at the hands of a vampire.

At one time she thought becoming a vampire was the worst thing that could happen to her, but as she watched Bishop approach her, the light of their camp illuminating the sharp, masculine structure of his face, Marika realized that wasn't true.

Losing Bishop would be the worst thing. He had taught her much, and there were still so many more things she could learn. Most importantly he had taught her that not everyone who seemed a monster actually was one.

She rose to her feet as he moved toward her, all fluid grace and sensuality. He was dressed in black, blending seamlessly with the night. His skin shone golden, his eyes bright swirls of green and gold. His hair shone with russet highlights. He was, in her mind, masculine perfection.

She wanted to throw herself into his arms, wrap her legs around his waist and bury her face in his neck. She wanted—oh, God, how she wanted— to pierce him with her fangs and taste the salty warmth of him. It was an act she associated solely with vampires and it should disgust her.

But it didn't; even though she knew what it would do to her, it didn't disgust or frighten her half so much as it should have.

Perhaps Bishop was right. Perhaps she was less human than she wanted to believe. Perhaps the vampire side of her nature was the stronger. It was a revelation that didn't bother her as much as it once would have, and for that reason alone, she resolved to think upon it no longer.

"You came."

He stood before her, loose limbed and at ease. Beneath the smells of the night—forest, dirt, burning wood and restless horse—was the scent of him. It was that spicy sweetness that made her think of warm cinnamon, nutmeg or cloves.

"I told you I would." He offered her a smile, his

eyes reflecting the flames of the fire. "Stop looking at me like that."

Despite the danger they might encounter, she smiled. "Like what?"

"Like you want very much to take a bite out of me."

"Maybe I do."

A low growl rumbled in his chest. "I know just the spot."

"Marika!" It was Dimitru who broke the spell. "We go. Now!"

Sighing, Marika smiled ruefully at Bishop. "Ready?"

"Lead on."

They joined her men and prepared to break camp. Within minutes they were riding toward the next village.

Based on what Andrei had told them—and other accounts they had gleaned during the day—they were fairly certain the vampires would attack again tonight. Their pattern seemed to be every two days, beginning with an attack four nights ago. They were working their way west if they held to habit.

Marika hadn't said anything, but she feared the vampires were working their way toward Fagaras. She had no evidence, but her gut told her they were after her—or Bishop. Since her instinct was rarely wrong, she listened to it when it told her that the village they now rode toward would be the next target. It was the only one for quite some distance, and its isolation made it the perfect hunting ground.

They heard screams as they approached, and Marika raced toward the cries. She saw people running through the village like ducks stalked by wolves. One by one they fell to the hunger of what was easily a dozen vampires.

"So many," she breathed. She'd never seen so many.

"Young ones," Bishop replied, slipping his fingers through the straps of a katar. The blade fit snugly against the top of his hand, the broad hilt against his wrist. No child-vampire would dislodge this blade as he struck with it. "They will be fairly easy to kill."

She took his word for it and sent her men in quickly. Hopefully they would be able to save some of the townspeople.

How had the vampires gotten there so fast? Had they been lying in wait?

Or did they follow us? To anyone else it might sound far-fetched, but the thought gave her pause. What if the vampires had been lying in wait for them? This whole attack could have been orchestrated to get her attention, to bring her out here where she and her men would be vulnerable.

What if she had led them into a trap?

She was stopped from wondering further when a vampire came charging at her. It moved too quickly for her to see it clearly, but there was something wrong with its face. Its eyes and fangs seemed unnaturally large. Reflex took over and she pulled her blade, but before the vampire reached her it exploded in a flash of light. When her vision cleared, she saw Bishop standing before her, his hand was bloody and there was something in his palm . . .

He had driven his hand through the vampire's back and ripped its heart out.

If she doubted his loyalty to her, she never would again.

"Are you all right?" His voice was harsh.

She nodded. The last thing she wanted was for him to be distracted by concern for her. "I am now. Go."

He did, whirling around with feline grace. He bounded toward another vampire. The katar flashed and the vampire fell. Then her attention was taken by her own battle, and Marika lost sight of him.

It felt like hours later when she had a reprieve, though she knew it hadn't been more than a few minutes. Her jaw was sore from a vampire's fist, but it wasn't broken. Her neck was scratched, as were her arms, but nothing too serious. She was lucky. The leather vest she wore provided some protection against claws, but it had been ripped during the fight. If not for the vest she would very likely be the dead one—not the vampire smoldering at her feet.

There was blood on her hands and her face. It was all around her, seeping from the bodies of men and vampires that lay dying not far away. She smelled it and she smelled her own. Fear and aggression rolled through her, surging in her veins. The blood seemed to call to her, strengthen her. Then, on the breeze, another scent. Another's blood.

Bishop.

She ran toward the scent, her keen eyes searching for her lover in the dark. Her heart drummed wildly, without rhythm at the thought of his being injured.

She sped into the center of the village and found him fighting two vampires while three of her men battled one. The vampires were not as strong as Bishop but they had weapons. He was bleeding from cuts on his chest and arms, and from a larger wound she couldn't see, but she knew it was there from the strong scent of his blood. It was that larger wound that worried her.

With her own dagger in hand, Marika bounded toward them. Power spurred her, gave her speed that wasn't normal even for her. Fangs burst from her gums as something deep within her raised its head and roared.

She pounced—that was the only word for it. She caught one of the vampires around the middle and tackled it to the ground, driving her silver dagger into its heart. The air instantly filled with the scent of burning flesh. Marika withdrew the blade and methodically slit the creature's throat, ensuring it would not heal itself and rise again.

She leapt to her feet, wiping her blade on her thigh. She turned to see Bishop dispatch the other vampire just as three more rushed toward them. Her men finished with their own prey and moved to join them.

Marika moved to stand beside Bishop. "Can you

fight?" She demanded, her voice low. Not that it mattered; the vampires could hear her just as well as he. Could smell his blood just as she could.

"I'm fine," he replied, his gaze never leaving their opponents.

"He's weak," one of the vampires cooed. "Take the old one first. Then the men. Then the woman." His cold, bright eyes lit upon Marika, bespeaking a promise of sexual torture.

He thought it would frighten her, but he was wrong. That thing within her laughed at his threat, clawed itself closer to the surface. With a sound of almost pure joy, Marika bared her fangs and lunged. Bishop moved with her.

Her blade flashed and slashed. She moved with a lightning-fast grace she hadn't thought she possessed. Her only thought was Bishop and his survival. She killed to protect him. She killed for him. She lost count of the vampires that came for her. She didn't know how many she killed or how many of her men had died in the fight. Once one vampire was dead she moved to another.

The scent of blood filled the night, driving her onward until finally there was nothing but silence. The vampires were all dead or gone, leaving nothing but smoldering ash where their bodies had been.

Bishop came to her, as tired and bloody as she. Her arms went around his waist as he pulled her to him.

"Are you hurt?" His breath was hot against her cheek.

"Nothing that won't heal," she replied. "And you?"

"A blade between the ribs. I will be fine once I have a taste of you."

He made it sound so seductive, she almost forgot to be concerned. "Now. I want to know you are fine before we return to camp."

He released her and she turned to walk away. She took one step and froze.

What remained of her men—all of them except two—stood looking at her, staring at her as though she were an abomination.

"You are like *him*." It was Dimitru who spoke. His front was spattered with blood and his face was battered, but his voice was strong. "You are vampire."

"No," she told him. "I'm not." As she spoke she shot Bishop a glance that let him know that there was no one in the world like him—no one.

"You have fangs." It was Sergei this time—sounding more anguished than afraid. "I saw them. I saw your eyes."

"You saw me earlier today, all of you." She tried to smile reassuringly at them—not showing her teeth. "I was in the sun."

"Maybe you aren't a vampire," Dimitru amended, "but neither are you human."

It was then, with them staring at her so hollowly, that Marika realized her days of hiding her true self were over. "I am no different than I ever have been. I was born dhampyr and have been my entire life."

Her explanation did not have the desired effect. It should have calmed them, made them see reason, but it did not. They moved toward her as a group, their faces set, their eyes angry.

"*Monstru*," Sergei hissed. "We trusted you with our lives, with our children."

"And I never betrayed you." Bishop had her arm, but she refused to budge. These were her men, damn it! Her family.

"That you live is betrayal enough." Sergei lifted his chin. "When were you and your demon lover planning to kill us? When we returned to the camp?"

"Kill you? Sergei, I would never harm you." She tried to go to him, but Dimitru jumped in front of her, a wicked-looking blade in his hand.

"Hell spawn." He actually sneered at her. "I will send you back to your Maker!"

Were it not for Bishop's quick reflexes, her former friend would have embedded the knife into her chest just as she had seen him to do to the vampires moments ago. Marika stared at him, unable to comprehend even though she was aware of everything going on around her.

Bishop had her around the waist now, as her men converged upon them with cries of hatred and war. A searing pain scorched her leg as they left the ground—Sergei had tried to stab her in the thigh.

The flight back to Fagaras was not as smooth as the last trip Bishop had taken her on. Marika clung to him long after they touched ground again. In the untouched blackness in the garden behind his house, she offered him her neck so that he might heal—and so that she might feel something other than the numbness threatening to overtake even her soul.

Her men thought her a monster. Despite all they had been through together, they no longer trusted her. They thought she was evil. It didn't matter that she had fought beside them, fought for them.

If they ever found her, they would kill her.

Chapter 11

His little house couldn't boast many modern conveniences, but it did have a big bathtub with amazingly hot water—something he took full advantage of when running a bath for Marika. He filled the tub as high as he could, adding oils and herbs he thought might soothe her.

Truth be told, he didn't know what else to do with her. She was cold and trembling and covered in blood. He had fed off her after their return—but only enough to heal the gash in his side, and only then because she seemed to need him to do it even more than he did. If he had known just how deeply the evening had disturbed her, he wouldn't have bitten her at all.

Normally he might have given thought to her feelings, but he was so riled from the fight that he hadn't been thinking clearly. Now that his wits had returned he realized just how devastated she must be.

"Come." Taking her by the hand, he drew her into the bathroom. Her teeth were chattering despite the fire he had built and the blanket around her shoulders.

This reaction unnerved him. He was used to seeing her strong, bold and defiant. Seeing her like this was a terrible reminder of just how human and fragile she truly was. It wasn't the fight that had done this to her, it was the betrayal of those she held dear. If ever he had wanted to know her weakness, he did now.

At least he could relax knowing that her men had no idea where his house was or how to find them. She hadn't told anyone where she was staying, perhaps because she was ashamed or perhaps to protect all involved. He didn't care. He was simply glad for it.

And now he just wanted to take care of her and not think about what might have happened.

He undressed her as he would a child. Her discarded clothes he tossed in a heap near the door to be burned. The blood might come out but they would be a constant reminder of her men's betrayal—something he would spare her if he could.

If only vampires truly had some of the powers Mr. Stoker and others had given them. If only he could enter her mind and take this horrible night away.

And then he might take it from his own mind as well.

He scooped her into his arms and carried her the short distance to the tub. She shivered, her eyes unfocused as he lowered her into the warm water. She sighed as the heat met her skin, and he knew she wasn't completely lost to him.

When she was settled he unbound her braid and unraveled the sticky strands. He would wash the blood out of it for her later. Then he removed his own clothes, adding them to the pile of hers and climbed into the tub behind her, positioning her so that she reclined against his chest. This way he could be certain she was warm.

And safe.

Bishop sat there for some time, his arms wrapped around her as the hot water seeped into both of them. Slowly she relaxed against him.

"Am I hurting you?" She twisted to look over her shoulder. It was the first thing she'd said since they'd arrived home. "Your wound . . ."

"Forget it." She resisted as he tried to draw her to him. "It is fine."

"I don't want to hurt you." Why she was obsessing over it, he didn't know, but it obviously meant something to her.

"Marika, I am fine."

Her dark eyes were wide with . . . fear?

"You're not going to die are you?"

Bishop frowned. "Die? Of course not." Why would she think he was going to die?

She smiled. It was shaky at best. "Good." Finally she leaned back once more. Her flesh was cool against his chest but had lost its earlier chill.

"I'm glad you are all right," she told him, resting her head on his shoulder. "I'm glad you are here with me."

So that was it. Abandoned by her mother, Saint and her father as a child and now by the men she took as her adopted family, she was vulnerable, totally alone and terrified that he would leave her as well. He didn't doubt for a minute that she was mentally and physically capable of being on her own, but that wounded part of her, that part that cried out for acceptance, needed someone to lean on right now.

"I'm not going anywhere," he told her and pressed his lips against the damp curve of her shoulder.

Gathering up the soap and cloth from the side of the tub, Bishop worked the two together until a thick lather coated them both. Then he gingerly began scrubbing the blood, sweat and dirt of the night away from her pale skin.

She was bruised and cut, but otherwise physically unharmed. The gash in her thigh was already starting to heal—one of the more positive aspects of her dual nature.

Her own fingers touched the puckering wound. "It itches."

"Leave it alone. It will heal soon." Christ, he sounded like a mother!

She didn't scratch, but her fingers continued to

trace the raw, reddened flesh. "Sergei tried to kill me." She uttered the words in the same dispassionate tone she had used to describe her wound.

"Do not think about it." He rinsed and relathered the cloth, moving it over her torso and stomach. If he slid his hand between her thighs, would she want it? Would she forget all this if he brought her pleasure? Was there anything he could fucking do to take this betrayal away and bring his Huntress back?

"They are afraid of me. They hate me."

"Ignorant peasants."

A moment's silence passed. Her hands came up to her head. "My hair. I need to wash my hair."

Pushing aside his fear that this night had forever scarred her in some manner, Bishop finished bathing her and himself and then repositioned himself to help her wash her hair. He filled a bowl with warm, fresh water to rinse the suds away. By the time he was done the bathwater was deep pink tinted with brown. He grimaced.

Pulling the stopper on the tub, he helped Marika to her feet and turned on the water again. This time he used the showerbath to rinse them both, sending any remaining traces of the ordeal down the drain.

He wrapped a towel around his waist and briskly dried Marika before bundling her in a robe and carrying her to bed.

She curled against him under the blankets, and he was delighted to discover that she was no longer cold or shaking.

"You must think I'm a weakling," she commented, her voice muffled against his chest. Her breath sent little tremors through him.

"Of course. Anyone who can single-handedly kill three vampires is nothing but a spleeny wretch."

She twirled the tip of her finger in the damp hair on his chest. "I did not react well when Sergei and the others came after me."

He responded to her touch like a needy tomcat. If he were capable of purring the bed would shake with it. "I don't think anyone in that situation would react *well*."

"I could not think. I was too shocked. Too afraid." She chuckled self-deprecatingly.

He had been afraid too. Seeing those men come for her had reminded him of the night Elisabetta had been killed. There was nothing more determined than a group of frightened men against a common enemy. "You thought you could trust them. They were your friends."

She raised her head. "I am sorry I ever doubted you. I should have realized I hid my true self from them for a reason. Deep inside I knew they would turn against me."

There was nothing he could say in response, so he kissed her forehead instead.

Her head went back to his chest. After a while she stopped playing with his chest and was still. So still that he thought she might have fallen asleep. He brushed the hair back from her face so he could see her and was surprised when she lifted her very awake and very alert gaze to his.

He knew just from looking at her that it hadn't been sleep that made her quiet. She had been reliving the night in her head.

"That first vampire." She frowned, bringing the high, black arches of her brows together. "There was something wrong with it."

So she had noticed. "Nosferatu."

"I have heard the term before. I always thought it was another word for vampire made popular by gothic romances."

Sometimes he forgot that not all of her life had been spent in rural Romania. She had been schooled and was well read. Unfortunately some of what she had learned regarding vampires was false—something he would have to rectify if he wanted to keep her alive.

And he wanted to keep her alive for a *very* long time.

"It comes from a Greek word, *nosophoros*, meaning 'plague bearer.' Some have taken it to mean any vampire, but it refers to what we call a vampire who had riddled himself or herself with disease."

She looked confused. "But I thought vampires were immune to sickness."

"It is true that we cannot contract the normal human afflictions, but a diet of diseased blood will take its toll on a vampire's system."

Marika propped herself up on her elbows. He tried to ignore how her towel slipped, revealing the tops of her breasts. "Why would a vampire drink diseased blood?"

"Usually we can tell if a person is sick, and stay away. But sometimes the disease is in its early stages and is undetectable, even to us."

Her dark eyes lit with understanding. "And sometimes, like animals, weakened humans make easier prey."

Bishop grimaced. She made it sound very base, but it was true. "Yes. And then there are vampires who are so reviled by their own nature that they feed only from those who are criminals, prostitutes, insane. Some think what they're doing is merciful, not realizing that they are poisoning themselves."

"How do you know this?"

"Many of us figured it out during the plague years when so many Nosferatu began appearing. Unfortunately by then it was too late."

"How did you manage to avoid it?"

He couldn't quite meet her gaze. "I avoided areas where the plague was. Just because I couldn't stand to see all that death. And I had seen what drinking diseased blood could do. I did not want to risk it."

The back of her knuckles brushed his cheek. It was an oddly comforting gesture, one that warmed his heart. "Your friend? The one you told me about?"

Bishop nodded. Thinking about Dreux was painful. "It took him a while to realize what he had done to himself. The change was slow in coming."

"Could he not be cured? Surely once he began drinking healthy blood again . . . ?"

How easily she discussed the drinking of

blood—as though it was not nearly as repulsive, as *evil* as she had once believed. "Earlier on, perhaps. But once a vampire becomes Nosferatu, there is no going back. Not that I know of."

She stilled, paling a little in the lamplight. "What happened to him?"

"One morning he walked out to greet the dawn. He said he could not bear to become more of a monster than he already was." Christ, it still hurt to think about. As annoying as Dreux could be, as trying and sometimes judgmental, he was still his friend, his brother. One moment Dreux was there and the next he was nothing more than sparks— shards of glorious light and then gone.

"Had he become a monster?"

Bishop nodded. "He was on his way. Like the vampire I killed last night, he had begun to look different, his features distorted along with his body and soul. He was the softest of all of us, but he became a creature that would feed from—and kill— a child if the urge struck. Thank God there was enough remorse left in him to put an end to it."

She watched him closely, the sympathy in her eyes disconcerting. "Still, it must have hurt you to watch him die."

She knew him better than he would have thought—than he liked. "It is not something I will ever forget."

"And then you turned yourselves over to the church."

He nodded. "It didn't take long to see that the church wasn't the answer to our salvation. I remember Saint saying he was going to drain the next priest that tried to 'save' him with a vial of holy water and a whip."

She winced. "Good Lord."

"Yes. After I left I kept in touch, sometimes to help with church-related matters. Temple remained connected as well. Only Chapel remained behind— bound by guilt to be the church's servant."

"You said the cup was cursed?"

"Yes—by Lilith, a demoness. Whether or not there is any truth in that I cannot tell you. Chapel is the lore keeper, not I."

She smiled at him—a little proudly, he thought. "You are the warrior."

Laughing, Bishop twisted a lock of her damp hair around his finger. "The others might argue that title, but I won't, not if that is how you wish to perceive me."

She sobered, her eyes narrowing thoughtfully. "I have been so very wrong about you. I've been awful to you, and for that I am sorry."

He held her gaze. "It's had its pleasant moments."

A faint blush blossomed in her cheeks, but she didn't look away. "Has it?"

He tugged her hair in response. "Yes. If it weren't for you kidnapping me, I might still think you responsible for the disappearance of my friend, and now I know you are innocent of that."

"For his disappearance, yes, but there have been others who died at my hand." Her face contorted, as though in pain. "Bishop, I cannot give back the innocent lives I may have taken—"

He stopped her with a finger to her lips. "Don't. Do not punish yourself any further. Regret it and do what you can to atone for it. Penance will always be rewarded."

"Do you believe that?"

"I have to. Otherwise I'm damned for past mistakes as well."

A look of wonder softened her features, parted the soft pink curves of her lips. "How could I ever have thought you a monster?"

He shrugged. "That's what you needed to believe."

"Do you know what I need now?" A devilish glow brightened her eyes as she asked.

"What?"

The next thing Bishop knew his towel was yanked open and he was on his back with her straddling him, the warmth of her naked groin pressed against his.

"You."

Straddling him, Marika lowered her head to the warm crook of Bishop's shoulder. After all they had been through she needed to feel him, needed to feel his strength all around her—inside her.

"I could bite you here," she murmured against the sweetness of his skin. "Bury myself in you as you do in me."

He shivered beneath her, and she knew it was because her words excited him. "Don't. My blood—"

She nipped his neck with her teeth to quiet him. "I said I could, *not* that I would." She straightened her back to gaze down at him. "Although someday I just might take you anyway."

"Tease." But her words affected him, she could tell.

She stroked his chest. The springy curls there tickled her palms. He was so solid, so strong. "Has anyone ever bitten you?"

His eyes darkened to a rich golden olive. "No."

Marika smiled as that part of him pressed against her thickened. "You seem to like the idea very much."

"I like the idea of it being you very much."

His words thrilled her, warmed her. When he reached for her breasts, she guided his hands to her chest and caressed his forearms as he squeezed her already aching nipples. Her hips rotated against his, and she could feel moisture building between them. She could take him inside right now and not feel any discomfort.

But she wasn't going to do that. Not just yet.

She gazed down upon the masculine beauty of his face. "I have never known a man like you."

His eyes widened at her use of the word man. It humbled her that he would be so surprised that she thought of him as such. "I wouldn't think so."

"I would have thought you the least deserving of my trust and yet you have saved me—twice."

"You owe me a large debt." He arched his hips against her. "Slide my cock inside you and repay it."

Marika chuckled at his crudeness, her laughter turning to a gasp of delight as he pinched her nipples. "I do trust you, Bishop. With my life. With my blood."

He stilled. All his attention seemed focused on her through the heat of his eyes. "I accept that honor, and offer you my trust in return."

They were only words, but they swelled her heart to the point where she thought it might burst. "I am so sorry for all the pain and trouble I have brought you."

"I thought I was going to lose you like I lost Elisabetta."

At the hands of angry humans. It was amazing to her that he managed to keep from attacking them all. He must have felt such anger and pain and yet his first thought had been of her safety, not of vengeance for the past.

She rubbed her palms against the satiny warmth of his skin. "You are not going to lose me unless you want to."

She stopped him from replying with a kiss—claiming his mouth as her own. They had talked enough—said and revealed and promised enough. She didn't want any more words. She slipped her tongue between his lips, stroking his tongue, tasting him.

She wanted to bite him. Wanted his warmth filling her mouth. It wasn't just the blood she wanted, it was him. She wanted to possess him, claim him for her very own.

If she were immortal as well, would he spend forever with her?

Would he love her as she was coming to love him?

What was she thinking? *Why* was she thinking? They could very well be dead tomorrow, and here she was contemplating forever? *Idiot*. All that mattered was now.

Reaching between their bodies, she lifted herself so that she could curl her fingers around the stiff, smooth length of him. She stroked and pumped until his hands left her breasts and slid down to capture her hips instead, urging her to take him inside.

Slowly she guided him to the entrance of her body. Fitting him to her, she rocked back and down, gasping as the broad head slid inside. Her body stretched and gripped around his, accepting his thick heat with slick ease.

Beneath her Bishop groaned. His fingers tightened on her hips, trying to push her all the way down onto his lap, but she resisted. She straightened, covered his hands once more with hers, and held them tightly as she spread her knees and lowered herself fully onto him inch by inch.

They were both trembling with tension when she took him completely inside. His heavy-lidded gaze never wavered from hers as she began to move, slowly churning against him, pressing against him so that not only did he fill her, but the friction of their bodies moving together started a delicious hum low within her.

Her hair fell around them and Marika leaned forward, tickling Bishop's torso with the ends.

His hands moved back to her breasts, cupping from underneath so that he supported her while exquisitely torturing her at the same time. His thumbs stroked her nipples, tightening them, teasing them into taut, aching peaks.

The things he did to her inside. He brought such turmoil to her life and yet so much peace. Everything she thought she knew—she thought true—had been destroyed at his hands, and yet she could not despise him for it. It was as though a veil had been lifted from her eyes and now she saw clearly—thanks to Bishop.

She didn't like some of the things he had shown her—most recently she disliked seeing the darkness inside her own men. They had pledged loyalty to her—claimed to be her friends and then turned against her so quickly, so completely.

Bishop, the one who had reason to turn on her, had instead saved her. Saved her in so many ways.

He hadn't been able to save Elisabetta. He compared the two of them in that way. Did he compare them in others?

Riding him, moving her body up and down on his with a rhythm that left both of them flushed and breathing heavily, Marika gazed down into his hawklike eyes and spoke the words her tongue could not hold. "I'm not her."

His eyes widened, some of the glaze of lust fading. "Who?"

She kept moving, not giving him the chance to leave her. "Elisabetta."

"I know." His back arched. "Believe me, I know."

"Good."

He grinned. "Halfling, I could never mistake you for anyone but your maddening, beautiful self. Are you done talking?"

She nodded, returning the smile. "I am."

"Thank Christ." He rolled so fast, she didn't even sense it coming. She barely had time to squeal in surprise before she was on her back and he was braced above her, pumping himself into her with a desperate rhythm that had her gasping and arching against him.

His head was buried in her neck, his breath hot against her skin. His bite was a brief pinch followed by a wave of intense pleasure as he drew her into himself. Mindless, Marika clung to him, jerking her hips against his as the tension within her grew and grew and . . .

Exploded.

Through the waves of her own release she was dimly aware of Bishop stiffening and shuddering on top of her. Her own body was still rocking, little sparks of prolonged, intense pleasure still popping.

Mine. The word echoed in her mind, unspoken but just as clear as though someone had said it directly into her ear. Bishop had told her he had no powers concerning the mind, but it wasn't her own voice. Or rather, there was another voice with hers.

It was almost as if they had claimed each other at the exact same time. It might be her imagination, perhaps even her heart's wish, but she didn't think so.

He was hers, she thought, as his arms wrapped tightly around her. Her body replied to his, with an unyielding embrace of its own.

Chapter 12

"**Y**ou are certain you never told any of the men the location of my house?" Bishop asked, propping himself up on his elbow in the large bed. It would be dawn soon and he was feeling the fatigue of their earlier battle—not to mention their enthusiastic lovemaking. Sleep would be most welcome, especially since Marika would be snuggled against him.

"I am. I didn't want any of them to come hunting you and find me here." Her lips tightened. "They would not have understood."

He patted her hand. "Given where the rest went after the human attack it's unlikely that they followed you here."

"They would assume a trip to Fagaras would mean staying with my *bunica*."

He smiled at the term. He and Marika shifted between talking English and Romanian and sometimes she did both in one sentence. "Does your grandmother know where you are?"

"Of course not. I would not put her in danger. The men might hunt me, but they will leave her alone out of respect for her age and social standing."

"Good. Then I think we are safe here for the time being."

"What of the servants? Can you trust them not to talk?"

"They have ties with the shadow world, as does the owner of this house. They will not betray me, no."

He heard her gentle sigh of relief and was compelled to add, "But your former companions will hunt us, Marika. Eventually they will find us."

She nodded. "I know. Once we discover what happened to your friend you will be able to leave."

"I'm not leaving Romania until I'm certain you are safe."

A sweet smile curved her little lips. "That could take a while."

"Then you had better grow accustomed to my face."

The shift in her features was subtle, but he saw it. Unfortunately, he couldn't tell if it was for the better or the worse—and he wasn't going to ask. If he didn't ask he wouldn't hear something he might not like, or wasn't ready to hear. He changed the subject instead.

"We need to prepare. We fought off the vampires but that was with help. If we are going to fight more—possibly Nosferatu—we need to fight as one."

She ran her fingers through the hair on his chest—she was fascinated by the unruly stuff. "Yes. We will have to train. Where?"

"There is a sparring room in the cellar beneath this house."

"My Lord, Bishop." She was totally amazed, and it showed. "Who owns this place?"

He smiled. "A friend."

"A woman?"

The suspicious and, yes, jealous glint in her eye might be worth a chuckle were he not naked and she so close. "As a matter of fact, yes."

"Is she your lover?"

Jealous or not, that pricked his pride. "Do you honestly believe I would be here with you if that were true?"

"I am sorry." She looked so abashed, he forgave her instantly. "That was petty and foolish of me."

"And jealous." He just had to say it.

"That too." She scowled at him. Damn, but she could look fierce when she wanted. "I do not like it."

Bishop, on the other hand, was pleased by her admission. He liked knowing she was possessive of him.

"I do not ask about your lovers."

"I've only had one other. My fiancé."

That struck him like a cold wave. Fiancé. She had never mentioned a betrothed before. He understood that she had been with someone in the past, didn't care who had come before, but the idea that there was someone else in her life—someone who would still be there long after he was gone, filled him with a sensation that could only be described as rage.

Murderous. Rage.

"You're engaged?"

She smiled just a little. "Jealous?"

He growled. "Don't tease me, Marika."

"I was engaged, yes." She picked at a speck of lint on the quilt, avoiding his gaze. "But Grigore changed his mind about marrying me after I killed his father."

Bishop had heard and seen many strange things in his years, but even he had to express his surprise at that. "You what?"

"The old man rose from his grave a vampire. He attacked a child. I killed him."

The scenario left a bad taste in his mouth. "A new vampire needs to feed. Waking up in a box and having to claw your way out is enough to make some of them insane—and they go for the first prey they see."

"Prey. You do not see humans as such, do you?"

"No, but I need human blood to survive, Marika. Nothing will ever change that. Either accept it or don't."

Anger flashed in her black, black eyes. "Until you, I thought all vampires soulless monsters. I cannot 'accept' all of this at once, no matter how much you might wish me to."

Sighing, Bishop pulled her closer, lowering himself fully onto the bed once more so that her head was on his shoulder. "I'm sorry. There were things I couldn't accept at first either."

"You talk as though I am a vampire. I am not."

He stiffened. "You are half."

"But that is not the same. There are things about you that I do not understand."

"What about your precious humans? Are there things about them that you do not understand?"

She pushed away, levering herself upward so that now she gazed down at him. "Why are you being like this?"

"Do you think your human blood makes you superior to me in some way?"

"Of course not." She stared at him. "I know you believe humans hate what they do not understand, Bishop. I do not hate you, nor do I completely understand you. Do not be so quick to compare me to those who had no wish to know you as you truly are."

Her words humbled yet pleased him. Telling her that seemed inadequate, so he kissed her instead. Kissed her until they were both breathless and all ill feelings melted away.

When she opened her eyes, she gazed up at him with an expression of total amazement. "I remember where I saw a ring like the one Sergei found before."

He shook his head. "You were thinking about that damn ring while I was kissing you. Where did you see it?"

The expression on her face was one of fear—and hurt. "Marika? Who has a ring like that?"

Her gaze was bright with unshed tears. "My father."

Bishop did not want her visiting her father by herself; he had made himself very clear on that point.

It was for that reason Marika waited until just after dawn, when Bishop was asleep, to slip out of the house to the stables.

Foolish she might be to go on her own, especially if her father was in league with the men who had tried to abduct her, but stupid she wasn't. She left Bishop a note telling him where she had gone, just in case she failed to return. She didn't want him thinking she had simply left him. She'd rather face his wrath at her defying his wishes than have him believe she'd deserted him.

The house she was born in was nestled in the mountains, surrounded by rich, dark grass and lush forest. As far as castles went, it wasn't terribly big or grand, nor was it imposing and frightening. Dark beams stood out against whitewashed outer walls. The steepled, uneven rooftops were tiled in shades of russet and brown. And though the round-top windows were small, there were many of them.

One of the few memories she had of this house was that it was filled with light.

If she was right about her father, that light hadn't

been enough to save him from the darkness in his soul.

As she rode up the long, winding lane she refused to feel guilty for what she was. The choice had not been hers and so neither was the blame. She would not take any hatred her father might have for vampires—or for her for being half vampire—upon her own shoulders.

A young groom met her as she reached the open courtyard. He obviously didn't know who she was because he simply smiled and offered to take her horse to the stable. She thanked him, advised him that she might not be staying long, and gave him the reins.

Her boot heels echoed on the stones as she crossed to the front entrance of the house. Every step drove her heart farther up into her throat. She hadn't been in this house in years—hadn't felt as though she was wanted. It wasn't her home and yet she had every right to walk in as though she owned the place.

Of course, now that there was a boy, he technically owned the place, which was fine. She didn't want it.

Regardless of her rights, she stood on the step and lifted the heavy iron knocker. It hit the door with a loud thud that reverberated throughout the yard.

The housekeeper, a woman named Ana who was in her sixties if she was a day, opened the door after a few moments. She looked every bit as mean and miserable as Marika remembered. Only now Marika was older, taller—and a bit of a legend in these parts.

Ana stared at her as though the devil himself stood before her. "You."

"Good morning, Ana. Is my father home?" She placed her foot on the threshold, waiting for the woman to let her in.

"What do you mean by coming here? Go away."

Marika's jaw tightened. "Is he home?"

The old woman's face was a mask of hatred. "You cannot come in here unless I invite you, and you are not invited, *vampir* spawn!"

Everyone in the house knew what she was—and yet they didn't tell for fear of their employer. While the rest of the area treated her like a hero, in her own home she was treated like a monster.

"This is my house, old woman," Marika informed her, pushing past her to enter the hall. "I do not need your permission to enter it." She didn't need permission to enter any place, but let the housekeeper keep her ignorance.

She was halfway across the hall when the door shut. Scurrying footsteps raced to catch up with her. The ugly old woman could chase all she wanted—she would not get to her father before Marika did. The entire house was filled with his scent—and she was nowhere near the tracker that Bishop was. Instead she latched on to a newer, fresher scent and followed it.

Her brother.

The happy little family was in the front parlor, seated around a small table by a set of French doors that hadn't been there when Marika lived there. In fact, there had been many changes in the interior of the house. It was more modern—more . . . French. Her stepmother was a disciple of fashion, it would seem.

They looked up as she entered the room. She didn't knock, just strode in. If she'd stopped to knock she would have been too afraid to continue.

Her father's wife looked up first. She was an attractive young woman with blond hair and green eyes. Her fair skin grew even paler when she realized who their unannounced guest was. "Constantin," she whispered.

He lifted his head. Marika's heart stopped cold in her chest, waiting for his reaction to her.

His dark hair was grayer than she remembered, his lean face more lined, but other than that her father was the same elegant, handsome man he had always been.

Only now there was a contentment to him that wasn't familiar to his daughter at all.

His gray eyes widened. He set aside his napkin and rose to his feet, slowly. Was he afraid she might pounce and rip his throat out if he moved too quickly?

"Marika? My God, Marika!"

She had expected surprise, possibly even aggression. She hadn't expected him to come to her with his arms outstretched. She hadn't expected him to embrace her as though he loved her. Apparently neither had Ana, because the sturdy housekeeper gasped as she finally huffed into the room.

Closing her eyes, Marika allowed herself to savor the moment—and just for a moment—before pulling free of his grasp. She kept herself rigid, her tone cool. "Hello, Papa. I am sorry to interrupt your breakfast."

"Do not apologize. Have you eaten? Would you like some eggs? Coffee?"

Why was he being so cordial? And why wasn't she better steeled against it? "I do not want to impose—"

"You are not." He turned to the stunned housekeeper. "Ana, bring a cup for Marika."

The old woman was obviously loath to leave, but duty won out and she shuffled from the room—after shooting Marika a look that could only be described as threatening.

Her father took her arm. He might be older but his grip was still firm. "Come meet your brother."

Though she had followed the infant's scent to this room, she hadn't noticed the bassinet beneath the scowling portrait of her great-great-grandfather.

There, in pristine white and swaddled as though he was the Messiah, was her brother. He was long and fat and perfect in all his folds and roundness. Gossamer hair the color of coal covered his head, and eyes the color of the stormy Black Sea gazed about the room as though trying to take it all in at once.

She fell in love with him right then. Never mind that he was only half her blood—less if she included Saint in her parentage—she knew now she would not feel any differently if she and this child had the same parents.

"What a handsome boy." The smile that curved her lips as she glanced at her father could not be stopped.

Constantin's brow twitched, pulling into a faint frown that was gone as quickly as it came, replaced by a proud smile. "Yes he is. Would you like to hold him?"

"Constantin—"

Was that all the woman was capable of saying? Marika didn't glance at her. Didn't want to see the rejection, the fear or repulsion in her gaze. "I do not want to disturb him."

"You won't." Her father cast a sharp glance at his wife. "Our son will know his sister."

This was all so unexpected. Where were the pitchforks, the torches? She had expected a cold reception, not this.

A cold reception wouldn't make her so uneasy. A cold reception wouldn't have thrown her off-balance. Perhaps that was her father's intention—befuddle her so much, she wouldn't know reality from fiction.

Her father scooped the baby up into his arms, gazing down at him with such love, it brought tears to Marika's eyes. He hadn't looked at her that way, of that she was certain. He offered the bundle to her.

Her bitterness and regret faded when she took the child into her arms. Waving his chubby little arms, her brother made a cooing noise, looked Marika right in the eye and smiled—revealing a tiny pink tongue and toothless gums. Cooing gave way to a loud squeal that shook his entire little body and sent his legs squirming beneath his blankets.

Marika smiled back. Oh, yes, there was no coming back from the love she felt for this baby. *Her* brother. There was nothing duplicitous about him. He was the one person in this house she could trust.

Her father looked strangely pleased. His wife looked dismayed.

"He likes you," she commented hoarsely.

Marika shot a look at the woman who wasn't much older than she. "Are you relieved or appalled?"

Her father made a scoffing noise. "Do not be foolish, Marika. I'm overjoyed!"

Marika didn't take her eyes off the woman across from her, whose frightened gazed remained fixed on her son in Marika's arms. "Do you believe that I would never hurt him?"

The woman—Marika didn't even know her father's wife's name!—looked at her. Marika didn't know what she saw, but it was enough to take some of the tension out of her shoulders. "Yes," she replied.

Marika believed her.

Ana returned with a cup. The old woman looked

as though she might drop dead of shock when she saw Marika holding the baby. Marika flashed her a sweet smile and reluctantly gave her brother to his mother. She had come here for a reason, and right now it was more important than enjoying breakfast with this family or scaring the help.

Seating herself at the table, Marika allowed her stepmother to fix her coffee for her. She took a sip and declared it perfect before turning to her father.

"I did not expect this warm a reception from you, Papa."

He actually seemed humbled by her words. She wanted to believe the reaction to be genuine, but she hardened herself against it. She would go along with whatever he offered, but she would remember that this man had discarded her like trash once, and people did not like having their refuse resurface.

"I'm sure you did not," he replied, his voice low. "For that I can only apologize and hope someday you might forgive me for all my sins."

Pretty words. Marika wanted to believe they were true—her heart ached to do just that. She nodded and said nothing.

There was no delicate way to do this, so she simply took the ring from her pocket and offered it to him. "What can you tell me of this?"

He blinked at the ring. Was that a tremor she detected in his fingers as he reached for it? "Iona, leave us."

It was the harshest his voice had been since her

arrival. Marika turned to the other woman, wanting to put her at ease—as foolish as the sentiment
was. "I am sorry, but it is very important."

Iona actually smiled. "It is all right. I will take
Jakob upstairs for his nap."

"You do not have a nurse?"

The smile grew. "I have a woman who helps me,
but my mother took care of me and all my brothers
and sisters. I will do the same with my children."

Marika smiled back. She didn't want to like this
woman who had taken her mother's place, who had
given her father a wholly human child, but she did.

Her father walked his wife to the exit, kissed
both her and Jakob, and then firmly shut the door.
Marika drank her coffee and watched as he came
back to sit beside her. He did not speak until then.

"Where did you get this?"

"It came off a man who was trying to either abduct me or kill me; I am not quite convinced of the
former."

Her father took a drink from his own cup. There
was no denying the tremor in his fingers as the
china rattled against its saucer.

"It is like yours, is it not? You know something of
the man who wore this?"

He shook his head violently. "I know only of the
order to which he belonged." He held up his hand,
displaying the ring on his own finger. "For I was a
member as well."

Disappointment and elation combined. At last
she would have information as to who was after

her, but the idea that her father was aligned with them left her feeling somewhat ill.

"Tell me about them."

"They are the Order of the Silver Palm, an ancient and powerful order that spans across all of Europe."

"What do they want?"

Dark arched brows drew together over Constantin's regal nose. "Power. Influence. When I joined them I thought they could help me destroy the monster that killed your mother."

"And now?" Feeling sorry for him was a luxury she could not afford, not when the blood of that "monster" ran in her veins and they both knew it. Had the order offered to destroy her as well?

Had her father asked them to?

He shrugged and handed the ring back to her. "I find there is little room in my life for vengeance these days."

What a coincidence. It seemed she and her father had more in common than she would have thought—or that was what he wanted her to believe. "Why did you think they could lead you to Saint?"

Another frown—deeper this time. "You know his name?"

She nodded. "I do. And I know that Mama planned to run away with him."

Her father's shoulders sagged. "I had hoped you would never learn the truth about that."

"He wasn't trying to kill her, was he?"

Constantin's face hardened. "She might have lived. Who knows what might have happened if he hadn't . . ."

Marika hesitated, allowed the silence to stretch for a moment, waiting for him to elaborate. He didn't.

"Tell me what led you to this order."

Her father ran a hand over his face. "They are old, very old. And they have ties to the occult and dark magicks. They were able to tell me much of this Saint and his brethren. In turn all I had to do was lend them access to my connections and social influence."

Marika leaned forward, clutching her father's hand in hers. It was strange to touch him, but the need was too great to deny. "You do not practice these magicks, do you, Papa?"

"Once, a long time ago. It left a bad taste in my mouth." He took another drink of coffee as though trying now to wash it away. "I have not been an active member for some time, but there are advantages to keeping my connection to them."

She didn't want to know what those connections were. She didn't want to care about him or what he did. "Why would they be after me?"

"Certain members have an interest in vampires, particularly those associated with this Saint. They recently captured one of his brethren in England. Temple, I believe they said it was."

Marika was too astounded to correct his use

of "it." This order was interested in Saint and his friends. That meant they were interested in Bishop. Was the Englishman who hired her a member of this order? Had he come after Bishop thinking she would not give him over? Or had it been another group?

And if they had been after Bishop, why did the men who attacked her village seem more interested in abducting her?

"What would they want with me?" Even as she asked, the realization was dawning with sickening clarity in her soul.

Her father looked pained. "I would imagine the fact that you are a rarity would make you of interest to them. The fact that it is Saint's blood in your veins only makes them want you more."

Damn it all to hell. What was she going to do? How could she stand against an order that had factions across the continent? Even with Bishop's help it was only a matter of time until they caught her.

She would not let them take her without a fight.

"Did you lead them to me?" she demanded. Father or no, she would treat him like any other threat.

He seemed hurt by her question. "Of course not."

If only she could believe that. Instinct told her that he was being truthful, but she couldn't trust her instincts where he was involved.

"Do they know about *Bunica*?"

Constantin shook his head, the wounded expression still creasing his face. "I would never put your grandmother in danger."

"You had better mean that." She meant the threat in her tone, and he heard it.

"I am sorry, Marika." He was old and pale as he stared at her. "I really am."

She nodded absently. "Thank you, Papa."

"If there is anything I can do to help you, do not hesitate to ask. If you need help leaving the country I can ensure total secrecy."

Her head jerked up. "You would do that for me?"

"Of course. You are my daughter."

Since when had that mattered? "You have a wife and new baby. Won't helping me endanger them?"

"The order will never know. I have friends that are outside their reach. It is the least I can do for you after all the pain I have brought you."

Damn right it was. And who the hell were these friends? Marika couldn't even think of that right now. She had to get back to Bishop. She had to tell him what she had found out. They had to make plans. Yes, once she had talked to Bishop they would decide together what to do.

She tried to look positive as she squeezed her father's hand. "Thank you. I just might ask for your help in the near future. Right now I must go. I have much to do."

"Where are you staying?" he asked, rising as she did. "I can come to you."

"It is safer for you if you do not know." Safer for

her as well. Plus the servants might be listening, and she couldn't trust that one of them might not tell her former companions where she was. "I will come to you."

She was halfway across the room before she stopped and pivoted on her heel. Her father looked startled as she strode back to him, even more so when she hugged him. "Thank you, Papa." He squeezed her, and for a moment she let herself be nothing more than his daughter, and not someone he might want to see dead. Let him think he had her trust, that she would be so easily duped. If he was telling the truth there was no harm, and if he wasn't. . .

She would tear his heart out herself.

She gave him a smile and the promise to return and took her leave.

She rode hard and fast back to Fagaras, making certain no one followed her. Back at Bishop's she quickly took care of her horse before slipping quietly into the house. She managed to make it upstairs without Floarea seeing her and crept into Bishop's bedroom.

The room was dark as she stepped inside and quietly closed the door. Only her keen eyesight made it possible for her to pick her way to the bed without bumping anything.

She slipped out of her boots and her clothes and carefully peeled back the blankets.

"Ahh!" She jumped back and almost tripped over her own boots.

Bishop looked mad enough to kill her, sitting there in the bed naked and scowling.

"Just where the hell have you been?"

Constantin stood at the window for a long time after his daughter left, a mixture of emotions seething within him.

He stared at the ring on his finger, turning the face of it so that it was palm side up. It had been such an honor to be given this ring, to be allowed to wear it. Where was that honor now?

When the creature called Saint had come to Marta's bedside, he had told Constantin he could save her and the child. Like a fool, he had believed the vampire. He pretended ignorance as to how the "saving" would occur, but in his heart he had known. He had known and he hadn't cared.

He had so wanted his child to be born healthy. He had wanted his son—and he had been convinced that's what Marta carried—to live.

So he had watched as the monster violated his wife, took her blood and then fed her his own. He had heard the words of love and devotion on his wife's lips, spoken to another man.

Not even a man.

When the deed was done, the vampire hadn't wanted to leave. The thing actually thought he had a right to be there for the birth—as though he had some claim to the child. The vampire could have Marta, but the babe would be his!

It had taken a great deal of silver and holy water

to force the creature away. He fled into the night smoking and stinking of burnt flesh—almost unrecognizable. Constantin might have admired the thing's determination to stay by Marta's side if he hadn't been so filled with rage and fear.

And then Marta had delivered him a girl. She screamed the whole time while Constantin paced the halls. She called out for her lover—not once asking for her husband.

He remembered praying that she would shut up. She did. She died shortly after Marika was born.

When the vampire came back, Constantin told him the child had died as well. In hindsight, perhaps it would have been better to give the girl to the vampire, but anger and grief made him hang on to a child he didn't even want. He could have accepted a dhampyr child had it been male.

Having Marika came in handy when he joined the order. She had them to thank for her life. He might have given her away if not for them.

More's the pity that he hadn't. The order would have ignored them both if only he had done the right thing.

The sound of footsteps roused him from his regrets. Raising his head, he turned toward the door, only to have his heart sink at the sight of his visitor.

"Maxwell."

The Englishman smiled, a predator in every sense of the word. "Hello, old friend."

Chapter 13

Did she not trust him, or was she afraid of him? The question burned in the back of Bishop's mind as he waited for Marika to answer his question.

Her chin lifted. "I went to see my father."

Spots danced before Bishop's eyes. Of all the things he had imagined happening to her, of all the places she could have been, her father's house was not one of them, because he had expressly asked her not to go there. Not without him.

Asked. Not demanded. He had *asked*—and rather nicely too. "Why?"

She was still holding the sheets—they shielded some of her body from his view, but he was totally bare before her. Yet she was acting like the vulnerable one. The one who had something to hide.

When he thought of what could have happened to her. . .

"I had to talk to him alone. You know he would never trust you because of your association with Saint."

And she knew he would never trust her father because of how he had cast his own daughter aside like an unwanted dog. "You could have been attacked."

"Even if my men knew where to find us, they would not be able to mount an attack this soon. They would never suppose I would go to my father."

She said it so nonchalantly, so unconcernedly. He had been helplessly waiting for her to return, knowing that even if she needed his help he would not be able to give it to her.

"Your father could have been the one to attack you. You have no idea how deeply he is involved with the order."

"If he intended to hand me to the order he could have done it much easier and earlier than this." Her blasé attitude needled him. She was so certain she could protect herself, with no regard as to how worried he might have been. "I wasn't in any physical danger from him."

No, the danger presented by her father was more emotional, more damaging. That was *exactly* the kind of danger he wanted to protect her from.

"I didn't want him to know the extent of my relationship with you," she explained. "As you said, we have no idea how deep his involvement with the order runs."

She was right, damn it.

When he said nothing, she smiled slightly at him. "I did not mean to make you angry. I left you a note."

"You said you were meeting your father. You did not say where—not that it mattered. I was terrified. Now I'm angry."

Marika stared at him, an expression of pleasure lighting her dark eyes, curving her little bow lips. "Terrified? For me?"

A growl rumbled low in his chest, so soft even he could barely hear it. "Come here."

She hesitated. He grabbed the blankets and yanked, sending her tumbling onto the bed. He was on her in a second, a hawk on a mouse. She didn't struggle—she wouldn't have even if she had time. She knew what he wanted, and from the way she welcomed him, he knew she wanted it too. He pinned her on the mattress and pushed her thighs apart, setting himself between them.

"Next time," he rumbled, "wait until dark."

He took her with his mouth first, licking and stroking her with his tongue until she was panting, teetering on the brink of climax. Then he rose above her and shoved his cock as deep as it would go inside her. Her legs locked around his back as he reached down between them and jerked his thumb against the slick ridge between the lips of her sex.

Later he would pass this off as a fuck—base and crude—but he knew better. He had been scared. And now he was hurt and angry. Taking her like this was a claim on her—the only one he could make that gave him any peace.

He both loved and hated that she could take care of herself, that she was so independent of his strength and protection. When would she realize that she could trust him? That he wanted to fight *with* her, not against her?

When would she realize that she was his? And God, he prayed that she would never realize just how much she meant to him—how much power she had over him.

She wanted him, he knew that much. Marika matched his thrusts with little cries of encouragement. After feeling powerless the entire time she was gone, he could finally regain some sense of control by taking hers away.

They came together in a loud, shuddering embrace that left them both unable to speak for some time.

"You realize," she told him later, her lips nuzzling the side of his neck, "that I do not consider what you just did to me punishment?"

"I don't want to punish you," he replied gruffly. "I want you to trust me."

Raising her head, she looked at him—looked deep into his eyes. He stared back, hiding nothing. Finally she nodded, a sheepish expression falling over her face. "I'm sorry for worrying you. I will not do it again."

"Good."

She continued to watch him. It was obvious that there was something else she wanted to say. "No one has ever worried about me before—except for *Bunica*."

"I cannot protect you during the day, not like I want to." He didn't tell her how helpless he'd felt, how he had been tempted to risk the sunlight to find her. He needed to end this conversation. Worrying, protecting . . . these were all things one did when one cared deeply about a person—when one feared life without that person in it.

But rather than push the conversation as many women might have, instead of becoming defensive, Marika simply took what he offered and was satisfied. Oddly enough, Bishop was a little disappointed that she didn't push him to admit deeper feelings. She merely leaned over and kissed him lightly on the lips.

"I do not need your worry or your protection, Bishop, but I like knowing I have it all the same. As you have mine."

There was nothing to argue, because she hadn't told him that she didn't *want* it. And as much as he wanted to deny it, he liked knowing that she felt the same for him. So he simply kissed her back, and allowed this new development to ease what was left of the discord within him.

Braced on his elbow with her mirroring his posture, he played with the ends of her hair, rubbing the soft strands between his fingers. "Tell me what happened with your father."

She did. If she left anything out he couldn't tell and didn't care. He could not believe what she told him.

"This order has Temple?"

Marika nodded. "According to my father, yes. I have no reason to doubt him."

What kind of power did these men wield that they could take Temple? He had been the fiercest of them all. His closest rival in strength had been Chapel; in speed, Bishop himself. Saint might have been a little more sly, Reign a little more sophisticated, but Temple was their leader. They followed him without question and he never let them down.

The thought of someone—no matter how many of them there had been—taking him down left Bishop feeling hollow and more than a little uneasy.

If they had taken Temple, they could take any of them.

Did Molyneux know all this? Did Chapel? What were they doing about it?

Marika's soft fingers caressed his hip. He closed his eyes, centering himself on her touch. Magically, the torment inside him lessened. "I understand if you need to go find your friend."

He scowled at her for suggesting he might abandon her. "Thank you, but I'm not leaving you to go chasing after Temple. For all we know that could be what they want me to do. I'm not going anywhere until I hear from someone I trust that Temple needs my help."

"But my father—"

"Is part of the order," he reminded her roughly. "He might very well be involved with the men who attacked you. I'm not about to take any advice your father offers."

She actually looked a little hurt. "He might have been telling the truth."

"If you need to believe that, go ahead." He tried to soften his tone, but didn't succeed. "I'll distrust him enough for both of us and maybe I can keep us alive."

"He offered me information." Now she was frowning as well. "Why are you so suspicious?"

Sighing, Bishop reached out and twined a strand of her hair around his finger. He hated having to point out the obvious to her. "Marika, be reasonable. If this was anyone but your father, would you trust him?"

She looked away, but the slight pout to her lower lip gave away her thoughts.

"I know you want his approval, halfling, but don't let that need overwhelm your instinct."

She nodded, still not meeting his gaze.

Gently he pushed on. "What does your instinct tell you?"

Several heartbeats went by before she shot him an angry, grudging glance. "That he accepted me into his life too quickly for a man who has never wanted me in it before."

He fought the urge to smile. He didn't want her to think the pain she obviously felt was amusing. "Smart girl."

"My father also said that the order wanted me because of Saint's blood." Her tone was clipped, agitated. "They want me for the same reason they want Temple. Should I disregard that as well?"

If words were blows she would have laid him out flat with that remark. "No. Of course not." The words came out stiff, as his tongue had difficulty forming them.

While there was blood in his veins, he would tear out the throat of any man who dared try to harm Marika. "They will not have you," he promised.

It was one thing to think that the order wanted her dead, or that they were "collecting" shadow creatures. But they were focusing on the five of them who found the Blood Grail and drank the essence of Lilith herself. It was personal, and mere killing was not going to give them the vengeance they wanted.

Christ, Temple was the keeper of the Grail. Had the order taken it as well? What would these men do with that kind of power? Their predecessors had lost the cup to the Templars, who protected it for years until Bishop and his friends stumbled upon it. What would they do to have it back? And what would they have planned for those who stole it from them?

He was going to have to send word to Molyneux; Molyneux would tell Chapel. Molyneux would contact Reign and Saint as well. And then Bishop would write to Anara and tell her that he hadn't found her brother—and that this situation was deeper and far more sinister than they had first thought.

Marika's hand came up to cup his cheek. Her fingers were light and soft, yet they placed a heavy weight upon his heart. "Do you understand now why I thought I had to see him alone? He would not have told me all of that if you were with me."

"Of course. I'm sorry." It was easier to say what she wanted to hear than tell her that he realized now her father would have known him regardless of what they told him. He would have known because his associates had already told him that his daughter was in league with Bishop.

They were trying to draw him into their game, trying to bend him to their will.

They would soon learn that he did not bend.

Marika didn't have to hold back with Bishop. She could give him all of herself and he took it—demanding more.

"Harder!" he commanded. He wasn't even sweating, the lout.

Marika, on the other hand, was damp beneath the arms and in other places, and her breath was coming in gasps.

"No more, please." Her palms were braced on her thighs as she bent forward, breath coming in harsh, hard gasps. "I surrender."

He was in her face before she could blink. "No. You do not. Harder. *Now*."

She straightened and swung, but he dodged the blow with graceful ease. "What the hell was that? Your grandmother could do better than that."

"Go fight her then." She was sick of this cellar— as modern and clean as it was. She wanted a bath and she was hungry. Most of all she wanted Bishop

to be quiet and stop torturing her. This was his revenge for all she had done to him. He was going to
provoke her to death.

He poked her in the chest. She ignored it even
though she wanted to kick him. "We've only been
doing this for three hours, Marika." He slapped her—
lightly—on the cheek. "Can't you go any longer?"

She knew what he was doing. He was baiting her.
She didn't care. She swatted his hand away. "Leave
me alone."

"Ten more minutes." He put himself between her
and the stairs out. "Put all you have into ten more
minutes and we'll stop."

God, if she thought she could render him unconscious she would use all that was left of her
strength to do it. "I am done *now*."

He scowled. "You think the order will stop when
you're tired? No. You think other vampires or your
former friends will stop when you're *done*? You'll
stop when *I* say you're done, and I say that's in ten
more minutes."

God, he was good. Her fists itched to connect
with that smug mouth of his, just to shut him up. "I
will say when I'm done and I. Am. Done."

"I'll take you to Saint."

Her head snapped up—so fast her neck cracked.
"What?"

Bishop was grinning now, not even trying to conceal his intent. "Fight me like your life depends on
it and I will contact Saint and tell him you want to
meet him."

She stared dumbly at him. Her search—her quest—to find Saint had taken second place to simply staying alive. She had almost allowed herself to believe that she might never find him. She had even started to entertain the idea that Bishop was truly ignorant as to his location. "You will?"

He nodded, too self-satisfied for words. "Now fight me."

Marika lunged for him, swinging with both fists and feet. "You told me you didn't know where he was, you bastard!"

"I don't." He ducked as she swung. "But I know how to contact him. Makes you angry, doesn't it?"

Damn right it did. He dodged many of her blows but she managed to kick him once in the head— hard enough to knock him backward—and she punched him in the mouth hard enough to draw blood.

He grinned at her, pressing the back of his hand to his lip. "Is that all you have?"

Snarling, she attacked again. He wasn't fighting back with all his strength, but this session wasn't about him. It was about her and seeing how far she could push herself before her strength gave out.

It didn't matter that he trusted her enough now to bring her closer to Saint, what mattered was that he would have taken that information to the grave with him. He would have let her torture him, hand him over to Armitage, all to protect his friend.

She was angry—what was the expression?— *pissed* that Saint had that much of his loyalty.

No, not pissed. She was jealous. Jealous of a vampire who had known her mother while she was never given that chance, and whom Bishop would die to protect. What had Saint ever done to deserve that kind of loyalty? If he was so wonderful, why had he never come for her?

The more he swept her aside, the angrier she became. The rage fueled her, heating her blood. Soon her fists were a blur, even to her, and Bishop had lost his smug smile. She was making him work at deflecting her. He had to defend himself now.

Now it was her turn to be smug. She managed to keep that thought for about two seconds. When her knee came up into Bishop's groin for the finishing strike, he doubled over and retaliated with a punch that knocked her halfway across the cellar. She landed hard on her back, her head striking the floor with a solid thunk that left her seeing stars.

So much for smug.

Bishop was there in a second, crouched over her with a frightened expression on his face. "Marika? Sweetheart, I'm so sorry. Marika? Say something."

She smiled at him, little colored dots dancing before her eyes. "I like Sweetheart better than Halfling."

And then there was nothing but blackness.

She woke up in bed. They spent far too much of their time in bed—not that Marika minded, but Bishop was right when he told her earlier that she needed to keep her wits about her and not allow her emotions to affect her judgment. And where Bishop was concerned, her emotions could not be trusted.

Neither, she thought, gingerly touching her throbbing jaw, could his reflexes.

It had been her possessiveness of him—her want of some connection with her mother—that had kept her from focusing on the fight. She couldn't blame this on him; all he had done was react to what essentially was a dirty strike.

"Put this on it."

She peered up at him with one eye. The other one didn't want to open much. He was pale and strained-looking—an expression she was beginning to recognize as guilt. It wasn't a look he wore well, although she thought he looked rather boyish when he tucked his lips in like that.

She took the bundle from him. It was cold—ice wrapped in cloth. It stung a little when she held it to her face, but it would help. "Thank you." Like every other injury she'd ever sustained, this one would heal quickly.

Out of the corner of her good eye she noticed a plate with a sandwich and a glass of milk on the bed stand. It must have been Floarea's doing. Like her grandmother, the housekeeper thought food could fix anything. Her stomach rumbled in response. Once she was certain she could open her mouth, she was going to shove that sandwich in it.

He sat on the edge of the bed. He wore the same trousers and shirt they had fought in—nothing fashionable. His hair had been pushed back from his face with anxious fingers, and his lips were pressed together as he watched her. He looked almost . . . fretful.

"I like looking at you even with one eye," she told him with a small smile.

His lips curved in response, his features taking on an expression she found much more appealing. "I am so sorry I hurt you."

She shrugged, and then winced as the movement pushed the sack of ice into her bruised flesh. "I will heal soon. I have been hit by a vampire before. I do not remember it hurting quite this much but I suppose that is because you are so old."

He arched a brow. "Was that a compliment? Because it was a horrible one."

Marika chuckled. That hurt too, damn it. "I meant only that you are very strong."

"I am and I should have been more careful."

"I shouldn't have hit you . . . where I did. It wasn't fair."

His smile actually grew. "But effective."

"Have you . . . has it . . . recovered?"

A chuckle escaped him. He was so lovely when he laughed. "Fully, thank you."

That was a relief. "Why are you so much stronger than normal vampires?"

"My blood," was his simple answer. "We drank from the Blood Grail. The vampire essence that entered us was pure, not filtered through human veins. Other than Lilith herself, who was banished when the angels fell, we're the purest-blooded vampires in existence—or so I'm told."

That was an awe-inspiring inheritance. "Do you ever use your abilities to their full extent?"

He shook his head. "As far as I know that only happens when we're feral—like I became when I attacked you. You can understand why we don't allow that to happen very often."

Yes, she could.

Bishop continued, "Everything we know about ourselves came from old texts and what we learned on our own. There may be things I can do that I don't know of, but I doubt it."

And she was second generation, with some human mixed in. No wonder she could fight a newborn vampire with ease. "Do you ever wish you hadn't found it?"

His laugh was harsh. "Of course. Not so much as of late, however."

Heat flooded her cheeks at the light in his eyes. How he could look at her that way when her face was bruised and swollen was a mystery, but she loved him for it all the same.

"Marika? Are you in pain?"

She shook her head, willing her heart and lungs to resume their functions. "No, no. It is nothing, Bishop, honestly." *Only that I've just realized that I love you.*

It was fairly obvious that he didn't believe her. She changed the subject. "Will you contact Saint now?"

He nodded. "I gave my word and I will keep it."

"Thank you." She set aside the ice—her face was so cold it was starting to hurt more—and picked up the sandwich. She set the plate in her lap and pulled small bites of bread and meat to pop into her mouth. It didn't hurt much at all to chew. Perhaps she was starting to heal a bit already.

"Do you think he will like me?" she asked. Her throat tightened as she asked. This meant so much to her—more than any thoughts of revenge ever had. Her mother had loved him. He could tell her things about her mother that she didn't know.

He could tell her about Bishop—about what he was like when he was human.

"He will love you." He sounded so certain that Marika's heart jumped. Did Bishop love her? Maybe just a little? Or had her running off to see her father damaged the trust he had for her? Did he wonder if she was in league with her father to capture him?

"Do you trust me?" There was no point in wondering when she could simply ask.

He frowned. "I thought we already established that I did."

"I know, but you do not trust my father and I thought—"

One dark brow lazily arched. "That I would suspect you of conspiring against me?"

She nodded.

"Sweetheart, you are far too honest to convincingly carry off subterfuge like that. You would simply kill me at the earliest convenience and be done with it."

He was right. And she really did like it when he called her sweetheart. "Hesitation and patience are two luxuries I have never been able to afford."

His smile faded. "I wish I could take all this away from you."

"Away?" She tore a larger chunk off her sandwich and offered it to him. He shook his head and she shoved it into her mouth instead. "How? Why?"

"If I had my way you would have grown up with a mother and father who would never leave you. Never abandon you. You would think vampires the stuff of stories and you would spend every day in a pretty dress with hundreds of admirers vying for your affection."

Surprising tears prickled the backs of her eyes. "That sounds lovely." He hadn't mentioned where he fit into that vision.

He shrugged. "I would give it to you if I could."

"But then we would never have met."

The smile was all but gone. "And you would be safe—not sitting here with half your face black and blue."

She set the sandwich on the table once more, her appetite gone. "But I would not know you."

The curve of his lips was self-deprecating at best. "I don't think that would be such a bad thing given the circumstances, do you?"

"Yes."

"Marika—" He looked away.

"Would you wish me out of your life, Bishop? If you want me gone, simply say it." Her throat spasmed around the words, trying to keep them in. "I will go and you needn't worry about me again."

He lurched to his feet without his usual grace. He grabbed her arms and hauled her up onto her knees on the bed, pulling her against him with an expression that stole her breath and warmed her in places that made her tingle inside.

"You leave me and I will hunt you down." His jaw was clenched as growled the vow. "There's not a place on this earth you can go where I won't find you."

Oh, God. He might as well tell her he owned her. She should fight that claim. She was used to answering to no one but herself, and she should remind him of that.

She looked him straight in the eye. "I'm not going anywhere."

His lips came down on hers, crushing them. She whimpered.

Bishop pulled back. "Did I hurt you?"

"Yes," she murmured against his mouth, her arms winding around his neck. "Do it again."

Victor Armitage was fading. Fading so quickly there was very little left of him.

Would that the fall down the stairs had killed him. It had only broken him in places.

Was this punishment for failing to bring in the dhampyr? Would they torture him until there was nothing left of him to destroy and then kill him? How much longer would it take? How much longer could he hold on to some semblance of himself? More importantly, how soon before he could just let go and make this all be over? All he wanted was for this to be over. He even prayed for it. He prayed hard. The vampires guarding him laughed whenever they heard him talk to God. He did it in his head now, although some of the things he said weren't as Christian as they should be.

He hadn't seen Maxwell since the old bastard kicked him down the stairs. That was one throat he was going to enjoy tearing into if he ever got out of this prison. He was going to kill him slowly, taking pleasure in every little snap and pop.

And then he was going to go after that dhampyr—the little bitch. If not for her and his involvement with her, he wouldn't be suffering now. He wouldn't be slipping away as he was.

Yes, there was very little left of him, and what was taking over scared the hell out of him. They weren't killing him. They were doing something far, far worse.

Chapter 14

The following evening found Marika and Bishop preparing to dine with Marika's grandmother. Marika had been to visit the aging woman earlier that day, hoping to persuade her to leave town for a few days—at least until Marika was certain her life wasn't in danger.

Her grandmother maintained that she was not afraid of death and didn't want to go, but she told Marika she would consider it if she brought Bishop to dinner. Marika didn't ask questions; she simply said yes.

"Do you really believe she'll leave?" Bishop asked as he tucked his shirt into his trousers.

Marika sat at the mirror putting the finishing touches on her hair and enjoyed watching him dress. She liked seeing him in fancy dress. Of course, she preferred him naked. "If she does not agree to go willingly I am prepared to use force."

He flashed her a grin from across the room. "Why doesn't that surprise me? You look lovely."

Three simple words and she was blushing like a girl. It was foolish and she loved it. For the first time in her life she felt normal. With Bishop she could be just a woman and not worry about whether she might hurt him or whether he would be repulsed by her true nature. He accepted her—flaws and all. It was a wonderful feeling.

And though she preened under his words, she did not doubt them. She knew she looked nice— and she saw the truth of it in his eyes. She wore the one gown she owned suitable for evening—a simple dark blue silk in the Empire style that she had been given by a wealthy—and very grateful— French woman. The woman and her husband had been traveling through Transylvania on their way east, looking for the spots Bram Stoker wrote about. They were looking for vampires and a vampire found them. A very hungry vampire.

The woman had been so thankful that Marika saved them from "that poor wretched creature"— she hadn't realized he was a vampire, but merely thought he was trying to rob them—that she gave Marika the gown. At first Marika planned to give it to Roxana, but when she got it home, she couldn't part with it. Her grandmother took her to the dressmaker in town to have it altered and that was that. It fit beautifully, accentuating her bosom, the strong curve of her shoulders. And it made her feel not just like a woman, but like the lady she could have been if only she had been born wholly human.

No. If she hadn't decided to hunt monsters rather than dance at parties and flirt with suitable young men. Her birth—her nature—could have been forever concealed. She had made the choice.

Until now she hadn't ever thought that it might have been the wrong one. But it wasn't her choice that was wrong—it was all the things that had led her to make it.

"You are too quiet," he remarked. "What are you planning?"

Marika smiled at him in the mirror. He had finished dressing and was standing in the center of the room in a gray suit and cravat with a snowy white shirt and shiny black shoes. His thick, dark brown hair was combed back from his face, and he was freshly shaven.

"I was thinking how I wouldn't change anything that has happened in my life because everything that happened contributed to bringing you to me."

He arched a dark brow. "Perhaps you might change the bit about poisoning me and chaining me to a wall?"

She rose to her feet and walked toward him with a smile. "And have you escape from my clutches? I think not."

His lips curved as he reached out and wrapped around his finger a long curl that had slipped loose from the bun on top of her head. "I suppose the end result was worth the pain."

Hawkish eyes glittered with warmth as he let her hair spring free. Heat crept up her stomach, flushing outward.

"If we do not leave right now I'm going to force myself upon you," she informed him.

Amusement lighted his face as he took a step closer, bringing the scent and warmth of him so close, her head swam. "I think you only keep me around for your own pleasure."

Marika grinned. "Mine and mine alone."

Bishop shook his head. "You are right, we need to leave. I do not want to be the one to tell your *bunica* we were late because we had to screw first." He moved around her toward the dresser where his weapons were.

"*Screw*." It wasn't a term she was familiar with, but she understood his meaning perfectly. "Is that what we do?"

He looked up from slipping a blade into the arm-sheath beneath his shirt. "Would you prefer I called it making love?"

"I would prefer you found a term that did not make me feel as though I should ask you for money afterward."

Color leached from his face, followed by a look of indignation. "Are you implying that I think you're a whore?"

Hands on her hips, she stared him right in the eye. "I'm implying that I find what we do together a little more wonderful than simply slapping body parts together!"

He stared at her for a moment before bursting into laughter. The bastard actually laughed!

"Making love it is then." He refastened his cuff. "Ah, Marika, you never fail to amaze me."

Much of her anger faded at that. "Thank you." She walked over to him and lifted her skirts. "Now I need you to adjust my thigh sheath for me. I can't bend properly in this cursed corset."

Ten minutes later they were on the roof of Bishop's house—courtesy of a secret stairwell hidden behind the wall of his bedroom.

"It's an escape route," he informed her as he led the way up the darkened staircase. "Remember it in case our location is discovered."

She would. "You could have told me about it before this."

He glanced over his shoulder at her. "You will not be pleased tonight, will you?"

He was right. She was irritable and anxious but it wasn't his fault. She was out of her element, involved in things she didn't understand and worried about the people she loved as well as herself. "I am sorry, Bishop. I suppose I am not as strong as I thought I was. This whole situation scares me, and I am scared for the people I care about as well."

The smile he offered her was reassuring. "I will do everything in my power to protect you and your family. Understood?"

She nodded. "And I will protect you."

He brushed his knuckles against her cheek. "I would expect no less." Then he turned and started climbing once more.

Marika sighed and hiked her skirts to follow him the rest of the way. He was amused by her. She could argue about it or simply accept that his laughter didn't necessarily mean he was laughing *at* her. She chose the latter. In her heart she knew that was the truth.

At the top of the stairs was an angled door that led out onto the roof. Bishop stepped over the threshold and then offered her his hand. It was a charming, very sweet gesture that affected her more than it probably should have.

She covered the burning in her eyes by making a great show of inspecting her gown and cape for dirt or cobwebs from the stairwell. There were none.

"I cleaned it earlier," he told her, as though reading her mind. "While you were in the bath."

Again her heart seized. At this rate she would be dead before ever reaching her *bunica*'s. "You are too nice to me. You are so thoughtful and I have been so mean to you . . ." She trailed off, choking on a sob.

"Marika. Sweetheart." He drew her into his arms. "You need to stop this. I know you are afraid, but do not let it make you weak. Use your fear as a source of strength and it will serve you much greater that way."

Sniffing, she nodded. "You are right. I have never feared an enemy before and I refuse to now."

"Beautiful." He kissed her forehead and wrapped

his arms around her waist. "Now, hold on."

The flight—she still had trouble realizing they were actually flying!—to her grandmother's house was mere minutes. They touched ground in the back garden, protected by darkness and the thick foliage there.

"Why do you think she wanted to meet me?" Bishop asked as they approached the back door.

"Perhaps to make sure you are good enough for me," Marika quipped.

Bishop chuckled. "Of course. I should have thought of that."

Marika knocked, and a few seconds later heard her grandmother's shuffling footsteps. *Bunica* opened the door, and their usual greeting followed, only this time she introduced her grandmother to Bishop—the only man she had ever brought home. Not even her fiancé had been presented in this manner, having been selected by her father.

It wasn't until they were fully inside the house, the door shut behind them, that Marika noticed there was something odd about her grandmother. She realized this at the same moment Bishop clamped a strong hand around her arm.

"Someone is here," he whispered, close to her ear.

Fear, then anger washed over her. Her gums ached as the emotions tore through her. If this person was using her grandmother to get to her, he would be very sorry.

"*Bunica*," she murmured, "do you have another guest?"

Irina turned, wringing her hands in that guilt-stricken way only a grandmother could. "He said he had to see you, Mari. He said your life was in danger."

As they turned the corner into the little parlor, Marika saw the man sitting on the sofa, his hand braced against his thighs. Bishop saw him too—and growled.

It was her father.

Bishop stepped in front of Marika, shielding her with his body just in case his suspicions about her father were correct.

Many emotions played across Constantin Korzha's face, but duplicity wasn't one of them. Bishop saw—and sensed—fear and uncertainty, and a deep sorrow, but no anger. No hatred.

Marika pushed her way around him, shooting daggers at him with her black eyes. What a little snipe she was tonight. He might as well give up trying—nothing he was going to do this evening was going to be right.

God, he adored her.

"Papa," she said, crossing the distance between them. Bishop followed. "What are you doing here?"

Constantin nodded at Irina. "I wanted to see you so I came to your grandmother and asked her to arrange it."

Bishop wasn't surprised, but Marika was. She gaped at her grandmother. "You invited us to dinner knowing he would be here?"

The old woman nodded, tight-lipped with guilt. And rightfully so, Bishop thought without sympathy. She had no idea what she might have brought Marika into.

"Do not be angry at your grandmother, Marika. I told her how important it was that I speak to you."

Bishop never took his gaze off the other man. "You told her Marika's life was in danger?"

Constantin nodded, holding his gaze surprisingly well for a human about to have his neck snapped. "I did."

"Did you happen to mention that *you* were the danger?"

Irina gasped, but both Bishop and Marika's father ignored her. They were staring at each other, the way two predators did when they prepared for battle.

"No. I think the less Irina knows the safer she will be."

"How noble." He couldn't keep the sneer from his face. "You didn't want her to know that you are in league with the men who attacked Marika's village."

A soft sob met his ears. Irina was getting quite a few surprises tonight.

"No," Constantin replied. "I did not, but now you have done that for me. You are quite the noble creature yourself, are you not?"

Bishop took a step forward, clenching his fists as he moved. He would not kill this man in Irina's house, not in front of Marika. He wouldn't, no matter how much he thought he should do just that. "Do not talk to me as though I'm the villain here. You knew those men were after Marika. Did you tell them where to find her?"

"Bishop!" Marika sounded ready to box his ears, but he didn't dare glance at her. She moved closer to her father—out of Bishop's reach.

Constantin watched his daughter approach with a guilty expression that ground Bishop's teeth together. "I did."

Marika made the smallest of sounds, but it was filled with such anguish, Bishop's heart fractured at it. "You bastard." His fingers reached for the release on his wrist sheath.

"Why?" Marika's voice was strong if a little tight. "Do you hate me that much?"

Her father turned to face her, aging twenty years in the space of time it took to meet her gaze. "I thought I did, until I saw you."

Frowning, Bishop eased forward. He wasn't ready to trust this man, but his words sounded sincere. Now was the time for patience and caution rather than rash violence. "I think you need to explain yourself, Korzha."

The gray-haired man nodded. "Yes, you are right." He looked only at his daughter as he began, "Marika, when I learned your mother had a lover I wasn't terribly upset. She was pregnant with my child, and as long as she was discreet, what did it matter?"

"But then she stopped being discreet," Bishop offered.

No one acknowledged him.

"People began to talk," Constantin continued. "She was seen in public with this man—and in her condition! I demanded that she stop seeing him. That was when she told me she was going to leave me for him. She was going to take my child and leave."

Bishop sneered. "And there was no way you were going to allow another man to raise what might be your heir."

"Bishop!" Marika scowled at him.

Sighing, Constantin finally afforded him a brief glance. "I wasn't letting another man raise my child." His attention returned to Marika, who was hanging on his every word. "We fought and she went into labor. By the time I sent for the doctor she was already experiencing difficulty. Your grandmother knows I speak the truth."

Bishop didn't look at the old woman, but he heard her soft agreement.

"She wanted me to send for her lover, but I refused. She must have gotten one of the maids to go, however because he showed up within the hour. Imagine the nerve of the man, barging into my house and demanding to be given access to the birthing chamber."

Bishop pursed his lips. He could easily imagine Saint doing just such a thing. In fact, Constantin was lucky Saint even paid the courtesy of using the front door.

"Somehow he got into the room. The doctor had already told me there wasn't much hope for either of you." There was a tear in the old bastard's eye. "I went in to say good-bye and found him with her. I saw what he was. Your mother had enough strength to tell me that he was going to change her and save both her and the baby." He stopped, raising a shaking hand to smooth back his hair.

"Then what?" Bishop finally prompted when no one else would. Marika shot him another foul look but he ignored her. It was his duty to protect her; let her get as miffed as she wanted with him, but he wasn't going to accept everything her father said as the truth until he had heard it all.

"It was too late. She had lost too much blood and was so weak. The vampire gave her his blood and she seemed strengthened by it. She was determined to have the child and called for the doctor. I told the vampire to leave. He didn't want to but I . . . forced him."

"How?" He couldn't imagine this man forcing Saint to do anything he didn't want to do, and his old friend wasn't the kind to walk away from someone who needed him.

Constantin swallowed. He didn't look so much regretful as he did bitter. "Holy water. I doused him with holy water so badly he had no choice but to flee."

Bishop swallowed against the taste rising from his throat. "You burned him."

"Yes."

"Bastard."

Marika's father shot him a defiant glare. "If I had known how to kill him I would have, even though Marta would have hated me for it. She was so happy thinking she could be with him forever."

"Did you kill her?" Bishop asked bluntly.

Both Marika and her father looked shocked that he would ask the question, but that didn't change that it had to be asked.

"Of course not," Constantin replied.

"Oh that's right, she hadn't had the baby yet. You wanted your heir first."

"I did not kill my wife." Constantin turned his attention to his white-faced daughter. "You have to believe me, I did not hurt Marta. Giving birth took all of her strength, and she died before the vampire's blood could take effect. I hid you, and when the vampire came back I told it you had died along with your mother." His brow pinched. "There was such grief in his face."

"Of course there was," Bishop almost snarled. "Everything he loved had just been taken from him." And Constantin could have spared Saint some of that pain. "If you hadn't driven him off he could have given her more blood. He could have saved them both."

"And taken both of them away from me," Constantin's voice was little more than a hiss. "He took my wife. He would not take my child."

Bishop could cheerfully kill this man. "The child you didn't want."

"Did you blame me for her death?" The plaintive tone of Marika's voice had Bishop glaring at her—not because he was angry but because he couldn't stand that she thought so lowly of herself. If her father said yes he'd kill him right there.

Constantin looked just as horrified as Bishop felt. "No, my dear. I blamed the vampire. I blamed myself, but not you. It wasn't until I saw that you were more his than mine that I started harboring resentment. I sent you to live with your grandmother so the servants wouldn't treat you like a monster. Sent you to school abroad so you didn't have to listen to the rumors. I wanted you to have the kind of upbringing a gentlewoman should have."

Bishop snorted. Maybe the old man could convince himself that was true, but it surely hadn't been at the time. "So long as you didn't have to look at her."

This time when Marika looked at him there wasn't any anger. He had said exactly what she had been thinking; he knew it. She was surprised that he knew her so well.

Constantin rubbed the back of his neck. "That too. I had no idea what to do with a girl child, let alone one who seemed to be more than merely human. I resented the vampire for taking my wife and child from me. One night I was too deep in my cups and I told a stranger what had happened, but I didn't tell him about Marika's unique abilities. He invited me to a meeting of a secret 'club 'he belonged to."

"The Order of the Silver Palm?" If words were acid, Bishop would have burned a hole clear through the floor.

"Yes. They told me what I wanted to hear, made me believe revenge was possible. Later, when they found out about Marika, they thought she might be valuable to the cause."

Finally he was getting to the information Bishop was interested in. Unfortunately this information also turned his blood to ice and made him want to do serious violence. "How so?"

Constantin shook his head. "I do not know all the details."

"Tell me what you do know." It was quietly spoken, amiable even, but the threat in the words was obvious. If Korzha didn't speak, Bishop would tear the words from his throat.

Surprisingly, Marika's father faced him with little fear. "I know that the order wants the Grail you and your friends stole from them."

"It belonged to the Templars."

"The order was once part of the Knights Templar. They left after some differences of opinion could not be rectified."

Bishop didn't care and didn't want to know. "They want the Blood Grail. What is the reason for the abductions? Why do they want us? Why Marika?"

"You are children of Lilith, the mother of all vampires. Your blood is the most pure, therefore the most powerful. Marika shares that blood. That makes her powerful as well, especially if she were to become a full-blood."

Marika met his gaze with a horrified one of her own. Was it the mention of blood that made her look so, or the thought of becoming a vampire?

Having Korzha confirm his suspicions did nothing to comfort him. "What do they want our blood for? Do they simply want us dead? Where is Temple and what are they doing to him? How did they manage to take him?"

Constantin held up his hand. "I will tell you what I can, Mr. Bishop. They took your friend Temple because there were many of them and they used a more potent version of the poison that Marika used on you to subdue him."

So he knew about that, did he? "You knew they hired her."

"Yes."

"You son of a bitch." There were so many ways he could kill him. The danger he had put Marika in—using his own daughter as a pawn. "The order set all of this up."

"They did. They don't want you dead, they need you alive. Why, I do not know. I suspect that is a secret kept among the higher ranks, of which I am not a part. All I know is that they want the five of you and they want you alive."

"So what was their plan? That Marika catch me and then hand me over, at which point they'd grab her too?"

"They knew you were looking for the Huntress because of your friend. They took him, by the way."

Bishop's eyes narrowed. "Is he dead?"

"No. He is with the others."

"What others? Where?"

"I only know that there are others. Where, I don't know. Rome maybe, or perhaps Spain or Greece."

"You are not telling me anything useful, Korzha."

"They knew you would find Marika or she would find you. What they hoped was that she would be able to bring you to them. When it became apparent that she wasn't going to hand you over—"

Bishop's head jerked around to Marika. "You weren't going to hand me over?"

She shook her head. "You hadn't told me where to find Saint. I wasn't about to let that go." She shook her head. "I'm sorry."

Ah, so it wasn't that she had had any tender feelings for him then. Well, what had he expected? At that point she thought him a soulless killer. Still, it stung.

"The order then decided that perhaps if Marika disappeared, you would realize she wasn't the quarry you sought, and assume that she had been taken like your friend."

"They wanted me to track her. They were going to use her as bait."

Constantin nodded. "But the two of you changed all that." He sounded almost proud—and more than a little awed as he regarded his daughter. "The order arranged the vampire attacks on local villages to flush you out, hoping that your zealous companions would turn against you when they realized you had aligned yourself with Bishop. That part went better than they had hoped."

"So they had a new plan." Bishop wagered he could fill in the rest on his own.

"Yes. That is when they came to me. They thought Marika would take my offer of help to leave the country, or perhaps tell me where the two of you were hiding." He smiled at her. "But of course, she is too smart for that."

Marika perked up under the praise. God, she was so *young* at times. "So, when we leave here tonight will there be members of the order waiting for us?"

"No. I told them I would try to get your location out of Irina."

"After all these years you expect us—you expect Marika to believe that you suddenly have her best interests at heart and wish to betray the order?"

"Yes."

Bishop sneered. "You're an idiot."

Constantin ignored him and turned his attention back to Marika. "I thought I could do what they wanted. I told myself it was for the best. I could almost convince myself you were a monster."

"What changed your mind?" At least she sounded like herself again, not some frightened child.

"I saw you with my son. And when you smiled, you reminded me of my mother, even though you look so much like your own. I saw you as family,

as my child, and I could not turn on you again."
His hand closed over hers. "I do not want the order
to have you. And you are the only person who can
keep them from Jakob."

Marika's eyes widened. "But you—"

"I am a sick old man whose time on this earth, I
fear, is nearing its end. Even if I live another twenty
years, the order will still be there, waiting for Jakob
to fall into their clutches. Who knows, I might die at
the hands of a vampire—the perfect tragedy to fuel
a son's lust for revenge, don't you think?"

Finally Bishop understood and believed. Korzha
was telling the truth. If the order decided he was
no longer of use, they would arrange to have him
killed and in such a way that might bring his son
into their clutches at a later date. He wasn't trying to make himself a hero and he didn't expect
Marika to fall into his arms, but he wanted to keep
her alive because she was his child and because she
could protect her brother better than anyone else
ever could.

And he didn't doubt for a minute that if Marika's
father did die as the result of a vampire attack, the
order would have arranged it.

Thank God Molyneux, who was in Hungary, had
expressed an interest in meeting to discuss matters. This was too much to put in a telegram. And
Molyneux would be able to get information to Chapel and possibly the others. If the order was trying to take them one by one, his friends had to be
warned.

"The order will not get your son," he promised, drawing startled gazes from both Marika and her father. "They will not get Marika, and if they think they can capture my friends . . . well, then the Silver Palm's about to get one hell of a surprise."

After Marika's father left, she and Bishop sat down with her grandmother and had dinner. Oddly enough, having some knowledge of what was planned for her eased the fear she'd been experiencing, and Marika managed to eat a decent meal. Bishop ate as well, but it wasn't as though food had any effect on him other than taste. Even her grandmother filled her plate—after finally promising Marika that she would go stay with her brother and his wife for a few days.

As they were leaving, Irina took Bishop by the hand. "Thank you for looking after my granddaughter. You will keep her safe for me?"

Marika's heart swelled as she watched Bishop curve his other hand around her grandmother's. His fingers were so big and dark next to the old woman's. "I will. You have my word."

Irina smiled, wrinkling her face. "I will give you some slips from my garden to plant on your wife's grave."

Bishop looked just as shocked by the offer as Marika was. Her grandmother was only being kind, but Bishop looked as though she had thrown cold water in his face. He had forgotten about Elisabetta. No, not forgotten, but Marika and all that had happened had pushed her to the back of his mind. Marika could tell from his expression that he wasn't quite sure how to feel about that.

Nor was she certain how to feel about the fact that she had to let him reconcile his past by himself.

Bishop thanked Irina and helped Marika with her cape, even though she was more than capable of doing it herself.

They left the way they came, through the back. Bishop wanted to go first to make certain there was no one waiting for them.

Marika stopped him. "Earlier you told me I had to be strong. I cannot do that with you always putting yourself between me and any possible danger."

"Fine." He didn't like it, that was obvious, but he didn't fight her.

She took his hand. "Let us go together." Somewhere during their brief time together, she had come to realize that they were stronger when they worked together.

As soon as they walked out into the garden, she sensed that someone was with them. Bishop sensed it as well; she felt him tense beside her. A slight shadow moved near a rosebush—a familiar shape. A familiar scent.

"Roxana?" Letting go of Bishop, she stepped forward. "What are you doing here?"

The girl ran toward her. Marika opened her arms to accept her.

"Who is it?" Bishop asked, his voice low.

"Dimitru's daughter," she replied, sparing him a brief glance.

"Dimitru? One of your men?"

Marika nodded. It was then, as Roxana flew into her embrace, that she realized the danger where she hadn't thought there would be any.

It happened so quickly. It happened so slowly. One minute she was gazing into the girl's dark eyes, so happy to see her, and then she saw the hatred there, and felt the pain that came with it—sharp, piercing pain. Bishop's hand brushed her shoulder and then shoved, but even he wasn't fast enough. Marika stumbled back, but it was too late.

Roxana had already stabbed her.

Chapter 15

Bishop grabbed the girl by the throat and lifted her out to the side. Little feet kicked at his hip and ribs, as skinny fingers clawed at his fingers. He wasn't strangling her—not yet—but he squeezed hard enough that she couldn't scream.

"Marika." He could smell her blood. "How badly are you hurt?"

The sound of fabric shearing sliced through the night. "The blade did not puncture me, but she took off a good deal of flesh." Pain was evident in her voice as she wrapped the torn hem from her gown around her midriff. "This won't stop the blood for long."

Gratitude washed over him. He glanced at the girl dangling from his hand. "Do you want me to kill it?"

The girl's eyes widened and she renewed her efforts to escape.

A soft groan issued from Marika's lips as she rose to her feet. "Stop trying to scare her."

Scowling, Bishop turned his head to her. Scare her? He was serious, goddamn it. "She tried to kill you."

Marika nodded, pressing her hand to her side. Her posture was a little awkward, but at least she could stand. "Put her down."

Was she joking? "No."

"Bishop, put her down. Please."

How could he deny her anything? If she asked him to let the girl stab him too, he just might do it to please her.

Slowly he lowered the girl to the grass. She tried to run when he released his grip on her throat, so he grabbed her by the arm instead.

"Stop struggling," he snarled, "or I'll rip it from its socket."

The girl pivoted toward him. He seized her free hand just as she raised it—just as Marika cried out in warning. There was a stake in it—a crude but effective weapon, given that anything would die once its heart was pierced.

"Do you know how much strength it takes to drive a stake into a body? More than you have, you scrawny little chicken." He pried the wood from her fingers and tucked it into his coat pocket.

This almost felt like the old days when he and the boys would go out to the theater or club, spoiling for a fight. Damn difficult to fight in evening clothes, though. Thankfully this child was more annoyance than threat.

The girl cursed them both in rapid Romanian. The obscenities coming from her mouth would make even the most common man raise a brow. When she called him a *poula*, however, Bishop had to chuckle.

Marika looked at him questioningly. "You find this amusing?"

"I find the fact that she just called me a penis amusing, yes. If you remember correctly I was sufficiently unamused by her attempt to kill you. You told me not to hurt her."

"And I meant it. Roxana, why did you do this?"

"You're a *monstru*, like him. You deserve to die."

The pain that crossed Marika's face was so acute, Bishop felt it himself. "Do I look like a monster?"

"You look the same, but you told me not all monsters look evil."

"No they don't. Have I done anything evil?"

The girl glared at her. "You lied to us. I believed in you. I cannot believe I ever wanted to be like you. Yes, you are evil."

Bishop could stay silent no longer, not when Marika was so visibly pained. "You tried to kill her. To me, you are the evil one, little girl."

The girl spat on his shoe. "You aren't even human."

"Looking at you, I do not think that is a bad thing."

"How did you know where to find us?" Marika demanded. She was pale, but she hid her pain well.

Roxana sneered at her. "I knew you would come to your grandmother eventually. Traitor to her own kind, she helps you."

Marika moved so fast, Bishop was amazed. Her fingers closed around the girl's jaw, lifting her chin and holding it so Roxana had no choice but to meet her gaze.

"I have always thought of and treated you as a younger sister," she told the girl, her voice so low and dangerous, Bishop felt it along his spine. "But if you harm my grandmother I will make you suffer for it."

Bishop almost cheered. His Huntress had returned.

"You cannot hurt me." The girl was all bravado. "I am not afraid to die."

"I never said I would hurt *you*."

It was the darkest threat he had ever heard Marika utter and he knew she meant it. The girl did too. There was real fear in her eyes now.

Marika released her and stepped back. "Now leave here and do not ever come back." She nodded at Bishop to let Roxana go. He didn't think it was a good idea, but this was her decision, not his.

Once free, the girl didn't hesitate. She didn't say anything, she simply turned and bolted for the garden gate. Bishop waited until he was certain she was gone before scooping Marika up into his arms.

"Can you fly with me like this?" she asked, leaning into his shoulder.

"Yes." The cloth around her wound was soaked with blood. He had to get her out of here before they left behind a scent for other vampires to track. He ripped off his coat and wrapped it around her shoulders. That would help. He'd fly blind if it meant getting her home where he could take care of her.

It took a little longer to get back to his house than it had taken when they departed, but he managed it. He took her into the house through the door in the roof. Once they were inside the bedroom, he stripped the gown and ruined corset from her and placed her gently on the bed with a towel beneath her.

He cleaned the wound—a nasty gash that went from the front of her ribs—just below her breast—around to the side, widening and deepening as it went. It wasn't terribly deep, but the flesh was gone and she was still bleeding. It seemed that Roxana's blade had been deflected by the boning in Marika's corset, turned and plowed through her side until it caught on more boning.

It was ugly, regardless of how it happened. The girl had obviously been aiming for Marika's heart.

"You should have let me kill her," he admonished dryly as he sat down on the bed beside her, medical supplies in hand.

"I couldn't, and you wouldn't have."

He shrugged. She was right to an extent. Morality kept him from hurting young girls, but his feelings for Marika were strong enough to threaten his moral code.

"This is going to hurt, but I need you to lie still for me."

Grim-faced, she nodded.

Bishop cleaned the wound with soap and water, flinching the first few times Marika hissed in pain. He worked quickly and efficiently, wanting this over as quickly as she did.

After it was cleaned, he pulled the ragged ends of the flesh together and stitched it closed. He then covered the entire area with an ointment made from natural oils and herbs and—he neglected to tell Marika—his own saliva, which had healing properties of its own.

Only when the wound was bandaged did he dare look at Marika. Her face was as white as the pillow she lay on, and her mouth and brow were tight and beaded with sweat.

"I'm done," he told her softly.

One thickly lashed lid opened, revealing a weary gaze, and then closed again. "Good. Your doctoring hurt more than the actual stabbing."

"But now you will not get infection, nor will you scar." Those things seemed more important before he actually said them aloud.

Eyes still closed, she raised a brow. "What sort of miracle cure did you use on me?"

"You do not want to know, trust me."

She actually smiled a little. "I believe you." Her brow furrowed. "My poor beautiful gown."

"I'll get you another gown, Sweetheart."

Marika smiled at his pet name for her. "A silk one?"

"Of course. Any color you want."

She fell silent after that, and Bishop drew the blanket up over her partially naked body so she wouldn't be cold. His hands shook as he tucked the soft quilt around her shoulders and smoothed a few escaped curls off her cheek. If that girl had been more skilled with a blade ... If Marika had been wholly human ... There was no speculation about it, Marika would be dead, or at the least dying.

The idea of life without his bold little halfling filled him with a dread he had never known possible. He wouldn't think on it any longer.

He stood. He would go downstairs and drink one of the bottles of blood Floarea had procured for him and then he would sit and think long and hard about what had to be done.

"Bishop?" The sleepy voice called to him as he put the medical supplies away. "Where are you going?"

"Downstairs. You get some rest."

"You won't leave me?"

Thank God she had her eyes shut so she couldn't see the tightness of his mouth or how he struggled to swallow past the lump in his throat. "No, I won't leave you."

But he was terrified that someday he might lose her anyway.

So Constantin had gone to the grandmother. While Maxwell supposed the news could be considered interesting by some, he was more concerned with the nature of said visit. Had Constantin gone in search of the dhampyr's whereabouts, or had he decided to betray his fellows out of some newfound sense of fatherly devotion?

Regardless, it hardly signified. Maxwell wanted Bishop to know that the order had Temple. If Constantin gave him additional information as well, so be it. If not Bishop, then one of the others would come for Temple. Their very nature demanded it.

For vampires, the Brotherhood of Blood, as they were called, were very honorable, particularly when it came to one another. Even Saint, that dirty thief, would rally to save one of his own.

All that mattered was that the five end up where they were supposed to—in the hands of the order. To ensure that happening, Maxwell had a plan. He always had a plan. It was the only way to escape disappointment when another plan failed. His current plan involved the dhampyr and the newly completed creation in the cellar.

Unfortunately this new plan required that the dhampyr be sacrificed, but it was a price he was willing to pay if it ensured that Bishop would come to him.

Revenge, Maxwell knew from experience, was a great motivator.

Opening the door, Maxwell carefully descended the narrow, shallow staircase he had pushed Armitage down a few nights ago. The scent of blood and death and evil clung to the air like a thick fog, and he held a linen handkerchief soaked with lavender water to his nose to overpower the stench. He would have to change his clothes when he came back up; the smell was that bad. A bath would be good as well.

Various cells were set into the far wall of the cellar. Maxwell ignored the cries, grunts and other unpleasant sounds issuing from them and continued toward the laboratory in the center.

Three men stood beneath a skeletal chandelier that gave off more light than the electric lights Maxwell's London estate boasted. One of the men was Mikael, his Russian doctor/scientist. The other two were vampires—young, strong and dumb as dogs. They did what they were told in exchange for blood, money and the odd wench. Neither of them possessed the sense to realize they could simply take what they wanted. Thanks to Mikael, they never would.

On the table directly beneath the light was a pale, muscular half-naked young man. Or rather, *former* young man. He snarled when he saw Maxwell.

Maxwell smiled and turned his attention to the stocky Russian.

"Mikael, you have outdone yourself."

"Thank you, sir."

"Whoever would have thought that Armitage— that pathetic fool—could become such an extraordinary creature?"

"Bastard." The voice of the thing on the table was low and harsh but still so very precisely British. The sheer oddity of it made Maxwell smile.

"Is that any way to talk to the man who has given you immortality?" he asked, coming to stand at the foot of the table. He wasn't foolish enough to go any closer. The silver should hold him, but he wasn't a man who had gotten where he had by taking stupid chances.

He smiled at Mikael's creation as he might any other gentleman with whom he hoped to do business. "Tell me, old man, do you remember the dhampyr?"

Armitage hissed. "Bitch."

Maxwell took that as an affirmation. "I have a gift for you, Victor. I'm going to *give* you the dhampyr. You can tear her throat out with your teeth, bathe in her blood, do whatever you want to her. All I ask is that you kill her sometime during your entertainment. What do you say to that?"

Armitage grinned, teeth gleaming white and sharp in the light. And for a moment, Maxwell himself was frightened.

"I'm not going anywhere," Marika informed Bishop two nights after being stabbed. "You cannot make me."

He followed her from the bathroom. She was still damp from the bath and clad in nothing more than one of his shirts. He had waited until she was healed, vulnerable and unarmed to tell her he wanted her to leave the village before the order launched another assault against them.

Her grandmother had left the day before—Marika

had taken her to the train herself. It was a huge burden off her heart knowing her *bunica* would be safe. Now Bishop wanted her gone as well.

"Marika, I want you safe."

She whirled on him, hair flipping around her shoulders like a mass of wet whips. "Do not treat me like a weak human. I am not!"

"I know you're not, but I don't want to have to worry about you."

"But it is all right if I have to worry about you, is that it?"

He scowled. "That is different."

Hands fisted on her hips. "How?"

"You are not immortal."

"Neither are you!"

Muscular forearms folded across his broad chest, stretching his shirt tight across his shoulders. "I'm less prone to death than you are."

She laughed humorlessly at his pathetic excuse. "No. I am not going."

"Please?"

"No!" Finger pointing, she took several steps toward him. "We face them together, Bishop, or not at all. I will not leave you here to fight alone. If I am to die, it will be by your side."

He stared at her, looking a little surprised. "That is quite the declaration."

Good God, he was right, it was. Should she tell him how she felt about him, or should she wait until she was more certain of his feelings? What if he tried to use her love against her to make her leave?

Her men—her former men—had constantly cajoled their wives into doing what they wanted by playing on the women's emotions. "Call it what you want. It is the truth."

"I would expect no less from you." His hands came up to comb through her hair. "What am I going to do with you?"

Her arms wound around his neck as she pressed her body against the length of his. He felt so good, so strong and right. "Accept that you are not going to get rid of me, and screw me."

Sharp brows arched as he laughed. "Screw. Is that what we do?"

Marika smiled coyly as he gave her own words back to her. "Would you prefer I call it making love?"

Warm hands slid down to her backside, cupping the bare flesh beneath the hem of the shirt she wore. "That depends. Which one will get me money when we're done?"

She laughed as he picked her up, wrapping her legs around his waist. "Screwing."

He walked them to the bed. "And what will making love get me?"

Her smile faded as he set her on her back on the bed, hovering over her with his beautiful eyes so full of warmth.

"Me," she replied huskily. "It gets you me."

Gone was his mirth, replaced with a softness that twisted her heart. Was it wonder? Sadness? Love? She couldn't tell, and God help her she was too afraid to ask. Even she could be only so bold before self-preservation took over.

"Making love it is then." His voice was rough. "I'll take priceless over mere gold any day."

And then his lips were on hers and she was lost. He tasted her, stroked her tongue with his own. He nipped at her lips and flicked them with his tongue until she was breathless, her hands cupping his face as she gave her mouth willingly to his plunder.

She felt the loss of his mouth as he lifted his head, but he soon put those soft, warm lips to work kissing her cheek, nibbling at her earlobe, tracing a burning trail down her neck and down to her breast.

He lightly bit her nipples through the thin lawn, dampening the fine material with his tongue and mouth until her nipples stood taut and dark rose beneath a translucent veil. Every stroke of his tongue, every powerful pull of his lips sent a ripple of aching want coursing down to between her legs where it blossomed into pure, carnal heat.

Her hips arched against his thigh, seeking out the sweet pressure his body promised. His erection was hard against her hip, so hard she thought she might bruise from it, as his fingers caressed the inside of her spread thighs. She spread them wider.

"Inside," she half begged, half commanded. "Put your fingers inside me."

Bishop groaned against her breast and bit her tender flesh hard enough that she gasped and arched at the acute pain/pleasure of it. But he did not immediately give in to her. His hot fingers continued tracing light designs on her flesh, ignoring the dampening spot that screamed for his touch. Marika arched her hips and reached down with her own hand to capture his, directing it to the apex of her thighs.

He lifted his head from her breast. "Unbutton your shirt."

She did, fingers clumsy with desire, but she managed to do as he asked, spreading the linen around herself so that her entire body was bare to his touch and gaze.

Finally, with a seductive, triumphant laugh, he gave her what she craved. His mouth went back to her breast, sucking one tight, sensitive nipple into his mouth and tonguing it until she moaned out loud. As he teased and tormented her naked flesh, he slipped one long finger inside her. She was so wet he slid in easily, and she sighed in delight at the intrusion. His finger moved inside her, curving until it found a spot that sparked the most intense sensation of pleasure. She spread her legs farther and he repositioned himself so that he knelt between them. Bending her knees, she raised them to her chest to allow him deeper access to her body. The sensations aroused by his finger increased to a delirious degree.

Just when Marika thought he couldn't give her any more pleasure, Bishop's thumb slipped between the soaked cleft of her sex, to find that one spot that throbbed for his touch. Marika gasped, lifting her hips as he stroked her inside and out. The pleasure was almost unbearable.

Desperate to touch him, Marika slid her own hand down to the front of his trousers. She fumbled for a few seconds and then succeeded in freeing the hot, satiny length of him. He was thick and heavy in her hand, the round head slick with moisture. Her thumb spread that moisture around the tiny cleft, down to the heavy ridge she ached to wrap her body around.

He raised his head for a moment and she met the bright, feral intensity of his gaze. His lips were moist, his cheeks flushed. "Stroke it," he rasped, thrusting himself into the tight vise of her fist.

Marika did. Anxious to please him, eager to find her power to make him want her as much as she wanted him, she stroked him. It was awkward at first until instinct took over and she learned to adjust to the rhythm of his hips and the fingers stroking her. When he increased tempo, so did she, until she thought for certain they were both going to climax in each other's hands.

Then he was gone. Gone from her breast, gone from her hand and gone from between her legs. For a moment, Marika was confused, then something brushed the inside of her thigh and she realized it was his hair. She had but one sweet second to realize what torture he was about to bestow on her next before the wet, hard thrust of his tongue brought her hips off the bed, her back arching in a deep bow. His mouth was on her, his tongue sliding between the swollen lips to stroke the tight little knot of flesh with determined pressure.

Her fingers caught in his hair as her hips undulated under his assault. She had always felt as though there was some part of her that was more animal than human. That was why she could never live in the world her father had tried to fashion for her. Bishop made that part of her come alive with a roar and matched it with one of his own.

He was her perfect match. She had wondered at how he could forgive her for what she had done to him, but now it was all so clear. Whether he was aware of it or not, his soul recognized hers as its mate. He forgave her because he accepted her completely for what she was. He had changed her world with just his presence because her world hadn't been right until he entered it.

This was love and she was never going to let it go.

And then her body did just that—let go with a torrent of rippling, shuddering pleasure that took her breath with its sudden assault.

She was still twitching inside when he reared up over her and shoved the full, hard length of himself into her. Marika gasped at the intrusion, her body so incredibly sensitive. But he felt so good inside her, her body so tight around his that she pulled her knees up to allow him deeper access. He pushed between her internal walls with slick, blunt thrusts that sent shocks rippling throughout her body. He withdrew and plunged, withdrew and plunged, bringing her that much closer to a second orgasm.

And then it happened. She hadn't recovered from the first when another sharp release claimed her, bringing a cry of triumph to her lips.

Bishop's hips pistoned, thrusting himself into her with increasing urgency until he suddenly stiffened. He shuddered, his back arched, head tossed back, and groaned—a long, gravelly, soulful sound that made her shiver inside. She had done this. She had made him spill himself inside her with nothing more than the pleasure of her body. The thought awakened something purely possessive within her and Marika wrapped her legs tight around his hips, holding him deep within her as he came.

"Mine," she told him as he lowered himself on top of her. "You are mine."

"And you are mine," he growled against her neck before piercing her with his fangs.

She thought it wasn't possible to climax again, but his bite, the feel of him sucking at her neck while his body was still joined with hers, made it happen. When he licked her neck to close the wound and eased out of her, Marika thought she might never move again.

They did not get a chance to enjoy a moment in each other's arms. Suddenly the sounds of shouting arose outside. Women and children screamed. And there was laughter. Terrible laughter.

Bishop and Marika shared a horrified look as

they bolted off the bed to the window. There, on the street below, men fought with what appeared to be other men and. . .

Vampires.

"Shit!" Bishop ran back to the bed and grabbed his trousers. Marika grabbed her own from the dresser, remembering to grab a pair of drawers first. Bishop was already dressed by the time she was struggling into her corset. He stopped long enough to assist her. She knew then that he considered her a true partner.

"Dhampyr!" a familiar yet odd voice shouted from below. "Come out and face me!"

Marika returned to the window as she quickly buttoned her shirt. In the street lamps she saw a man standing in the middle of the street. He lifted his face and looked up—right at her.

She gasped. "Oh, my God."

"What is it?" Bishop demanded, shoving her boots into her arms as he came to stand beside her. He looked out the window. "Oh, Christ."

"It's the man who hired me to find you," she replied hollowly, pulling on her boots with numb fingers. "But he's changed. He's become—"

Bishop finished for her. "Nosferatu." His expression was grim. "And a pretty damn deadly one at that."

Chapter 16

The Nosferatu was one of the most far gone Bishop had ever seen. He would never admit it to Marika, but he was worried. It was one thing for the two of them to take on a few young ones and some humans, but a Nosferatu this advanced ... Even Dreux hadn't gotten this twisted and ugly.

Dreux had retained his conscience. Dreux chose to destroy himself rather than become a creature of evil. This ... thing in the street was pure malice with no trace of humanity left in him.

"He wasn't a vampire when he hired you, was he?" he asked with a frown as he turned from the window. Weapons. They were going to need more weapons.

"No." Marika was struggling into her boots.

What the hell? He glanced out the window again, to confirm his earlier assessment of the creature. How had this man managed to become so corrupted in so short a time? It usually took months—even years to become half that tainted.

The order.

He didn't know how they had done it, but the Silver Palm had devised some way to make a Nosferatu in a frighteningly short space of time.

"Do you have a gun?"

She stilled, looking up at him with real fear on her face. "Is it that bad?"

He could lie, but she needed to be prepared. This fight was going to get nasty—nastier than he wanted to admit. "Yes. That thing is vile and poisonous and just might be stronger than both of us."

Her face went white as she swallowed. "How is that possible?"

At any other time he might have puffed up that she thought him so difficult to defeat, but not today. "Vampires are demon kin. Diseased blood corrupts and sometimes it heightens the powers that demon blood brings with it."

She closed her eyes as she straightened. "I don't have a rifle."

Bishop stifled the string of epithets that sprang to his lips. "I have one. I'll ask Floarea if there is another. She and her husband can use the silver shot in those. Load up on weapons. We're going to need them."

Before he left the room, he grabbed her by the back of the head and kissed her so hard, he was sure his lips left an imprint on hers. "Do not leave this room until I come back."

She must have realized his concern to some extent, because she did as he asked. When he returned to the room a few minutes later Marika was fully dressed and strapping her blade around her thigh.

"Did you find another rifle?"

He nodded. "Floarea and her husband have a small arsenal. They're well prepared for this kind of attack." Thank God they were. He and Marika were going to need all the help they could get.

"What is our plan?" she asked, pulling a long, wicked-looking katana from the small armory in his wardrobe. It was the perfect weapon for her—slender, fast and deadly.

"Thinning the ranks," he replied. "The townspeople can match the human men attacking, but not the vampires. Floarea and her husband will help you with the vampires—they are your primary concern."

"While you go after the Nosferatu?"

He nodded, noting the concern on her face. "I need you to watch my back as well. Take the vampires out of the fight as quickly as you can and then come to my side. I may need you." He wasn't about to pretend bravado at a time like this. Their lives were not the only ones at stake. These situations were rarely that simple; if they were, it would be just the two of them and the Nosferatu out there.

"We'll go out through the roof and approach the street from the back. The Nosferatu won't be expecting that." He palmed a heavy broadsword and started for the secret stairwell.

"Bishop?"

Her voice stopped him, and he turned. She stood there, his little warrior, ready but strangely hesitant. "What's wrong?"

She shook her head. "Nothing. Just be careful."

That wasn't what she had wanted to say but he wasn't going to ponder too closely on that, not when he needed his mind focused on the coming fight. "You too."

They went out through the stairwell, across the roof, and jumped down to the back garden. Screams rent the night, and Bishop was glad Marika's grandmother was gone. Marika might have trusted her men not to harm the old woman, but Bishop wouldn't put it past them to lead the vampires to her. The vampires would have surely used Irina in their desire to get to Marika. And Marika would have played right into their hands by going after them in a reckless rage.

He felt her behind him, a warm shadow as they moved, swift and silent through the night. People ran in the street, chased by vampires. Men fought and children cried. Women tried to save them both. If enough townsfolk were roused they would stand a better chance of winning this fight. He hoped Floarea's husband had done what he asked and told the grooms to do just that. Of course, the screaming would bring many people.

Just before stepping into the street where the Nosferatu patiently waited, as still as a statue, Bishop turned to Marika. He needed to kiss her, and so he did. One last kiss before going into battle. One last kiss in case he never got the chance to taste her lips again. The Nosferatu was waiting for her and Bishop was prepared to die to keep it from having her.

She clung to him with her arms and lips. There was desperation and fear and hope in her kiss.

"We are going to kill this thing," he informed her as they separated. "Go for the heart or the head, the same as you would any other vampire. If you get a chance, take its head off. Avoid its blood; it may burn you."

"Vampires first, then the Nosferatu. Avoid its blood." Her face was white but her gaze was steady and focused. "Anything else?"

"Yes, I want you to come back to me at the end of this, so stay alive."

Marika glanced up at him, a faint smile dancing on her lips. "You too."

Around them chaos reigned and yet it seemed as though there was some kind of invisible barrier around them that kept them separate from the thick of the fight. There were only the two of them.

And the monster.

With the light on its face the Nosferatu was a frightening creature. The man it had been was average in height and build and the demon couldn't change that, but it was stronger and faster than any human, and the face had been altered to suit its corrupted blood.

High cheekbones gleamed, the flesh stretched tautly over the bone. Bright yellow eyes were almost too big for the face beneath heavy, arched brows. But it was the mouth that was the most disturbing. Bloodred lips peeled back from fangs that no longer retracted and were roughly the size of a bear's.

But it wasn't the fangs that concerned Bishop—it was Nosferatu's blood. Worse than silver and holy water combined, it could burn through his flesh like acid, marking and corrupting him. If he didn't get it off him in time, too much of it would turn him Nosferatu as well.

And if that happened no one but the remainder of his brethren would be able to stop him—and only if they united.

That was why he didn't want Marika near the thing unless it was necessary. He wanted to keep her away from it and its corruption.

"Give me the dhampyr, Lilith spawn." The creature's voice was cultured English from the very bowels of hell.

Bishop raised the sword—two-handed and steady. "No." And then he charged.

The Nosferatu wasn't prepared and was unarmed, but it was fast. Bishop managed to slice open its arm before it slipped out of his reach, but he had been aiming for something a little more life-threatening.

"I will destroy you first then," the creature remarked casually, batting the sword away as if it were a mere annoyance. Only Bishop's tight grip on the hilt kept it from flying out of his hands.

Suddenly there were four vampires behind the Nosferatu. Where the hell had they come from? Risking a glance to the side, Bishop saw Marika had heeded him and was fighting other vampires alongside townsfolk. She was still alive, her blade flashing crimson in the lights. That gave him strength.

"Kill him," the creature told his minions as he turned away. "I want the dhampyr."

Goddamn it. If he chased the Nosferatu the vampires would attack his back. If he didn't chase the creature it would kill Marika.

He would have to kill these vampires quickly. There was no margin for error. Marika's life depended on it and he was not about to lose her, not when she had given his heart such fullness.

Bishop poised to strike, working out in his head the moves that would bring down the vampires as quickly and efficiently as possible.

Then he struck, gutting one of the vampires with a lightning-fast swipe of his blade.

A shot rang out from behind him, hitting one of the vampires in the chest. It fell back hard, writhing and screeching as silver death ripped it apart from the inside out.

The Nosferatu looked surprised. "Interesting," it commented. Then to the remaining vampires, "Now kill him."

Another shot. This time it only winged one of the vampires. It was all Bishop needed. He swung hard and fast, cleaving the vampire's head from his body. He moved after the Nosferatu, keeping it on one flank and an encroaching vampire on the other.

The Nosferatu ignored him as though he were as inconsequential as a child, moving with smooth strides toward Marika.

The clatter of approaching hooves reached Bishop through the cries of terrified people and blood-thirsty vampires. A man ran by him, and he recognized him as one of Marika's former companions.

Two horses tore into the center of town. Their riders leapt to the ground and ran toward him. The horses turned and trotted off—not far, but far enough away to be out of the chaos.

Palming a throwing blade, Bishop drew back and sent the silver dagger hurtling toward the Nosfera-tu's back. He didn't stop to see if it hit or not before turning to meet another vampire.

As the men drew closer, Bishop risked a side-ways glance at them. He recognized one of them as he ran his vampire attacker through. It had been many years since he last saw Father Francis Moly-neux, and how much the man had aged surprised him, but he would know that determined face anywhere.

He had a pistol in one hand, a bottle of holy water in the other and a dagger in his belt. His companion, a young dark-haired man, had a machete with a silver-inlaid blade.

Lifting his foot, Bishop braced his boot against the vampire's chest and pushed. "Molyneux, I am so damn happy to see you."

"I wish I could say the same, my son," the priest replied in heavily accented English. "Behind you."

Bishop whirled just in time to duck and avoid the Nosferatu's razorlike claws. "You annoy me, vampire," it growled.

"Likewise." At least it wasn't after Marika. Not yet.

With Molyneux and the other man there to deal with the remaining vampires, Bishop could concentrate on the Nosferatu. He swung the sword and met only air as the Nosferatu danced just inches out of the way. The dagger he had thrown was still stuck in the thing's back.

"You fight to protect the dhampyr after all she did to you?" There was real confusion in the seared voice. "I think she must mean something to you. Perhaps you mean something to her as well."

Shit. Why couldn't this thing be stupid? "She owes me money," Bishop quipped, nicking its side. "Plus I wagered her that I'd slay your ugly ass. I want to make sure she pays up."

To his surprise the creature chuckled as it swung its claws at him again. Bishop dodged, but felt the wind of the attempt against his cheek. It was close. Too close.

"Then you won't care if I fuck her before I kill her?"

Bishop's blood ignited. His own demonic nature flared to life, rising to the surface with a sigh of violent satisfaction. The Nosferatu laughed again.

"So you do care about her. Do not worry yourself,

vampire. I have no desire for the bitch other than to bleed her dry." It struck and raked its talons across Bishop's shoulder, slicing through the muscle, almost to the bone. Bishop grunted, but he ground his teeth together against the burning agony that followed. He would not acknowledge it. The pain did not exist. He kept telling himself that, even as his head swam and his shoulder throbbed.

He retaliated with a swift swoop and lunge. The Nosferatu fended off his attack, but not without injury. It was bleeding—all the more reason for Bishop to be more cautious with his blade.

"Enough," the creature growled. "You keep me from my prey." He pulled a sword from the back of a slain human and licked the blade before leveling it at Bishop. "I am afraid I must end this, vampire."

Bishop seized the moment, swinging the broadsword with all the control and strength he could muster with his shoulder torn open. The blade pierced the Nosferatu's side, causing the creature to grunt in pain. Triumph buoyed Bishop, and then a blunt pain blossomed in his gut. He didn't have to look down to know that the creature's sword had passed through him completely.

His legs went numb and he stumbled, collapsing to his knees on the stony street. He had to get the blade out. Had to get to Marika.

The Nosferatu didn't finish him as he expected. No longer seeing Bishop as a threat, apparently, it turned its focus on Marika, who was crossing swords with Dimitru. Her men either thought she was in league with the Nosferatu or were merely taking advantage of the chance to kill her. She was blurry in Bishop's eyes, but his heart would know her anywhere.

"*Mon Dieu*." Molyneux was suddenly on his knees beside him. "Bishop?"

"Get it out," he growled, grinding his teeth. His own hands were slippery with blood and couldn't grip the blade properly. "Get it out now. I have to stop it before it gets Marika."

The old priest nodded and turned to his companion, whose youthful face was streaked with blood. "Marcus, can you remove the blade? Bishop, *mon ami*, this will hurt."

"Just do it." He sagged backward, bowing his chest outward so that the young man could brace his boot against him as he gripped the sword hilt. The guard was pressing into his flesh—the sword had gone all the way through.

Marcus Grey proved to be a very strong lad. He gripped the sword with both hands and pulled— quickly and smoothly. It still hurt like hell. As the blade slid free, Bishop fell forward, gasping and almost retching on his hands and knees as pain swamped him.

Molyneux thrust a vial in his face. "Drink this."

It was blood. Snatching the vial, Bishop downed it in one gulp. Immediately he was flooded with power. His stomach itched as the torn tissues began their amazing healing process.

"Vampire?"

Molyneux shook his head. "Werewolf. I procured it from an old friend on the way here. I thought it might come in handy."

Bishop staggered to his feet. "You were right. Christ, that's amazing." He had heard about weres and their healing abilities before, but this was unexpected.

The wound was still sore, still open, but not bleeding as much. His head was clearing as he turned to track the Nosferatu's movements.

His gaze found the Nosferatu simply by following a trail of bodies, and he saw the creature stalking an oblivious Marika. It was going to kill her.

The silvered steel of Marika's blade clashed with Dimitru's heavier weapon. "I do not want to hurt you, Dimitru."

"Bah," the stocky man sneered. "I will finish what my daughter failed to accomplish."

Her chest squeezed but she would not let her guard down even for a second. "You should be ashamed of yourself sending Roxana after me."

He smiled—a black and evil smile that Marika had never seen before. "She would have killed you were it not for your demon lover." He struck again with his sword and Marika parried, punching him in the face with the hilt of her weapon as she moved to the side.

"And Bishop would have killed her were it not for me."

He shrugged—actually *shrugged*—and spat blood onto the street. "Hers would have been an honorable death."

Was this how her father once thought of her? As his means to a higher end?

She postured once more. "Does our past friendship mean nothing?"

"No. You are not human and therefore must be destroyed."

Their swords slid together again. Had she been so deluded in her thinking? Was it her own fault that he thought this way? No, he had thought such things long before aligning with her. It was only now that she knew the true meaning of "monster" that she could see just how very wrong he was.

See how monstrous he was in his own way.

A dark shape swept up to them. One moment Dimitru's blade was against hers and the next her former friend was on the ground, wide-eyed and sightless, his throat a huge gaping wound. Blood soaked the dirt and stone beneath him, black and oily in the night.

Marika gasped. It had happened so fast. Her gaze jerked up, dry and wide with terror.

The Nosferatu licked its fingers as it stood before her, intently watching her face with its unnaturally huge yellow eyes. "I do not know why you didn't do that yourself a long time ago," it said convivially. "Such arrogance from a minion shouldn't be tolerated."

Marika swallowed against the tightness gripping her throat. She held fast to her sword with palms that were beginning to sweat.

"Armitage," she called him by name, hoping to appeal to what little of his former self was still in there. "Who did this to you?"

"You did." He licked the last of Dimitru's blood from his thumb. "Oh, not precisely, but the fault is yours. If you hadn't betrayed our bargain Maxwell never would have tossed me in that cellar."

Maxwell. If she survived this encounter long enough to speak to Bishop again, she would make certain he knew that name. "I am sorry."

"It's too late for that now, little Huntress." He took one slow, deceptively human step toward her. "The only way to repay what you owe me is with blood. Your blood."

In her chest, Marika's heart thrashed wildly, awakening the part of her that would survive at any cost. She used to think that part was her vampire nature, but it wasn't. It was the same part of her that wanted to protect her loved ones. The same part of her that loved Bishop. It had nothing to do with being human or vampire or in between. It was her soul, and she was not about to let this *monster* take it from her.

She stared at it down the edge of her blade. "I will not give it willingly."

The Nosferatu grinned, red lips opening far wider than was humanly possible, revealing its terrifyingly sharp fangs. There was blood around its gums, glistening under the street lamps. "I will take it then."

Around her, people were fighting and dying and running and crying and Marika was numb to it. There was nothing but her and this creature and the certainty of her death if she could not find the strength she needed. She didn't know where Bishop was, didn't know if he was dead or alive and could not count on him to come to her rescue this time.

Her fingers tightened on the hilt of her sword. "You will try."

It lunged for her and she sliced its face open, jumping back in time to avoid its claws. Obviously stunned, it raised its fingers to the gash on its gaunt cheek. "I underestimated you, Huntress. My apologies."

She braced herself for its attack, legs spread, weight distributed so that she could dodge or duck without upsetting herself.

And then the sword was gone from her hand and she was pulled fast and hard against the Nosferatu's chest. Faster than she could think, it had relieved her of her weapon and held her in a grip tighter than any restraint.

The creature that had been Armitage smelled of soap and cologne beneath the blood. It had bathed before coming there. Why? Was there some human left inside? Or had it thought to mask its scent from herself and Bishop? It had worked.

"Armitage," she wheezed as it crushed her to it. "Do not do this."

It smiled at her, and a drop of its blood fell on her cheek. It burned. It burned like a hot poker through her flesh.

The Nosferatu wiped her face, removing the blood. "Isn't that interesting. I wonder what would happen if you took my blood inside?"

Oh, God.

It yanked on her braid, pulling her head back, baring her throat to its mouth. Hot breath seared her neck, and she shuddered in revulsion.

The Nosferatu's bite was nothing like Bishop's. There was no pleasure, only excruciating fire as huge fangs tore though her skin and muscle, opening her to the night and its vicious embrace. She didn't even try not to scream. Pain tore through her, the agony of it forcing its way out of her mouth into the night.

The creature took her to the ground and pinned her there, driving her shoulders into the stone, grinding her bones. She could feel her life draining from her body and she didn't care. She was too weak. Too numb.

The Nosferatu lifted its head. "I have a gift for you, Huntress." It bit its wrist and forced it over her mouth. Its vile blood filled her, acrid and hot. She refused to swallow, even as it burned her mouth.

"Swallow it," the Nosferatu hissed near her ear.

She shook her head desperately, the torn flesh of her neck stinging as she did so.

"Swallow or I'll have that little brother of yours before dawn."

Calm slammed Marika hard. If she swallowed, God only knew what the monster's blood would do to her, but it might give her the strength to kill it. And she would kill it. She would not let it have Jakob.

Blindly, she groped for the dagger strapped to her thigh. She kept her gaze locked on the Nosferatu's and she slowly nodded.

It removed its wrist with a pleased smile. "Do it."

She did. It burned, but not as much as it did in her mouth. The heat of it filled her, but it did not kill her. In fact, she felt her strength start to return.

Above her she heard a roar of rage that made her heart thump in response. *Bishop.* He wasn't dead.

The Nosferatu lifted its head and Marika seized her opportunity. Her dagger pulled free of the sheath. She aimed it upward and shoved with all her strength. It pierced flesh, slid between ribs, and lodged in the blackened heart just as the heavy blade of a sword swept past her face and severed the creature's head from its shoulders. Bishop kicked the body away, the headless neck smoking from the silver's cauterization.

Marika smiled at him as he fell to his knees beside her. He was so pale, so frightened and beaten. "Marika, sweetheart? Are you all right?"

She nodded gingerly. "Did we win?"

He looked around them. The night was quiet

now. There were soft sobs and voices, but none of the violence there had been before. He dropped his gaze to hers once more. "Yes."

"Good. I think I'm going to need some of your salve for my neck."

He smiled, his eyes surprisingly bright. Were those tears she saw? "I think I can arrange that."

Reaching up, she took his hand. "Bishop, how harmful is Nosferatu blood if you drink it?"

Sheer horror washed over his face, and Marika wished she hadn't said a word. She saw in his eyes what it meant.

She understood Armitage's "gift."

He had made her Nosferatu.

Chapter 17

Bishop looked up from the book in his lap to cast a worried glance across the room to where Marika lay on the sofa. After spending a fitful day drifting in and out of slumber, she was now talking to Marcus about being a dhampyr. The young man hung on her every word as he scribbled madly in his journal. Bishop didn't like it. Marcus was like a vulture, picking at things that were already raw. What did it matter what it was like being a dhampyr when she was about to become something infinitely more terrible?

He said so to Molyneux.

The priest smiled patiently, bent over an old leather-bound tome that smelled of dust. "He distracts her, *mon ami*. When talking to Marcus she cannot think of the fate before her."

Bishop only grunted in response. Distraction was good. Would that someone might distract him from the growing gauntness of her pretty face, the widening of her almond-shaped eyes. Her face was changing. Her demeanor was changing. An hour ago she had thrown a glass across the room because she no longer wanted it.

He was losing her.

Pain, intrusive and uninvited, pushed upward from the depths of his soul. Marika had faced so many battles and won. She had lived her entire life as a fighter and now it didn't matter how much she fought. The corruption in her blood was stronger than she was.

"Haven't you found anything yet?" he demanded, working his lips together. "You've been poring over those damn books for hours."

Molyneux consulted his watch. "Two, actually, and no, I have not found anything yet."

Bishop cursed under his breath and slammed shut the book he had been reading. Nothing there either.

"Have faith, Bishop. We will find the cure in time to save her." The old priest was convinced there was a way to stop the poison from taking Marika over—and that the answer was in one of the old books he carted around with him.

"I should have gone looking for this Maxwell the Nosferatu mentioned to Marika."

"Not by day you could not. And even if you could, would you have wanted to leave her?"

There was something knowing in the priest's tone that had Bishop regarding him through narrowed eyes. "What are you implying? That I couldn't bear to be without her?"

"No."

"Good." Such devotion was for lovesick boys—not creatures such as he who knew firsthand the fragility of human life. He knew better than to put his own feelings ahead of what had to be done.

"I meant to imply that you would not *want* to be without her."

He said nothing, just glared at the priest. What could he say? In his heart he knew it was true. He could go if he had to, but he would not want to. He wanted to be with her in case anything happened. In case she needed anything.

In case she needed him.

When he first saw her, he thought her attractive, but he would have killed her for his own freedom, just as she would have done whatever was necessary to get what she wanted from him. But over the short course of their relationship, attraction had given way to deeper emotions. He respected her honesty. There was no duplicity in her, no caprice. She opened her mouth and out came the truth, even if he didn't want to hear it. She could admit to being wrong and say she was sorry. And even though it must have been so difficult for her, she offered him her trust. She put aside her feelings so they could fight a common enemy.

He knew all these things had happened, but if he looked back on it, he could not pinpoint exact dates or times that marked the changes in his own feelings. One day he wanted to kill her, another he wanted to possess her. Now he would give anything—even his own life—to save her from this fate.

And save himself from having to end her life.

There would be nothing left of her when the corruption was complete. She would be an evil, feral creature that thought only of feeding and violence. First and foremost he was a hunter and it was his job to destroy evil. The Huntress knew that.

"You have not fed." Molyneux's voice interrupted his melancholy thoughts. "Do you have blood here or shall I send Marcus to get some?"

Bishop turned to him. "I have some here. Floarea knows where it is." Thank God for his housekeeper. She and her husband had shot three vampires and several humans during the attack. If not for them, things would have been much worse. Despite the violence, the two of them were still in the house, going about their business as usual.

"Can I get you anything else?"

"Marika needs food." Bishop rubbed a hand over his face. "And you and Marcus should dine as well. I'll sit with her."

Molyneux nodded as though he understood even what Bishop left unsaid. He wanted to be alone with her, even if it was for just a few moments.

"Marcus, come. It is time for supper."

The young man looked up from his journal, the lamplight reflecting on the little glasses perched on his perfect nose. He removed the spectacles and let his bright blue gaze drift from priest to vampire and back again. "Of course."

Bishop had no idea what was going through Grey's head and he didn't care, but if he upset Marika, the next thing that went through the young man's head would be Bishop's fist.

"Perhaps," Molyneux murmured so that only Bishop could hear, "you would like my young friend more if you knew he is descended from your friend Dreux."

Bishop recoiled. He hadn't seen that coming—hadn't suspected at all. No wonder he was so interested in vampires—in the five of them in particular.

"Does he know Dreux was becoming Nosferatu when he killed himself?" he asked in an equally soft voice.

Molyneux shook his head. "Perhaps you might tell him that yourself. He would like to know the reason for Dreux's suicide, I believe."

No doubt he would. "Perhaps I will tell him, but not now."

There was that damn priest smile again. "Of course."

"Oh, Father Francis?"

The priest turned, his face betraying his shock at Bishop using his Christian name. "Yes, Blaise?"

"Someone should contact Marika's father." *Just in case.*

Molyneux nodded—sadly. "Of course."

The priest and his companion left the room together, leaving Bishop and Marika quietly alone.

"Will you sit with me?" she asked, her voice low and husky. "I won't be so afraid of what I might do if you are near."

The request broke his heart. "What do you think you might do, little halfling?"

She smiled thinly. "I'm not a halfling, Bishop. Not anymore. I feel the violence inside me, the anger. I want to break things. Break people. Five minutes ago I thought about driving Mr. Grey's pencil through his eye."

"I had that same thought myself." He strode across the room to take the chair Grey had vacated. "Fortunately I do not have a pencil, so I think I'm safe in your presence."

She held out her hand and he took it. Her skin was warm. Too warm. "I do not like having such thoughts and feelings."

"I know."

She played with his fingers, stroking them with her thumb. "When I start enjoying having them, you will kill me, yes?"

Bishop swallowed. The lump in his throat didn't budge. "When you act on them, yes."

She actually sighed. "Good. I do not want to become a monster, Bishop. You won't let that happen to me, will you?"

He shook his head, throat tight, eyes burning. "I will not."

Her hand squeezed his. "Thank you."

"How is it that you are so calm?" he demanded.

"Why are you not angry? Why do you not fight?"

Marika's already unnaturally large eyes widened. Bishop hid a flinch at the sight. "I cannot fight it, can I? He told me to drink and I drank because he threatened my brother. I am calm because I am not afraid of death, and you will not allow what I am afraid of to happen. And I am not angry, my dear Bishop, because anger feeds the monster inside me and you are angry enough for both of us."

Well, he sure as hell was angry. He didn't know if he could kill her and be able to face the next dawn himself.

"You told me when we first met that one of us was going to die." She laughed dryly. "I was determined it wasn't going to be me."

"It won't be." But he might as well have been talking to the wall for all she acknowledged his remark.

"I do have two regrets," she told him, her strange gaze boring into his. "The first is that I will never meet Saint and know for myself the man my mother loved."

"You'll meet that rotten bastard, I promise you."

Her lips curved slightly. "The other is that I do not have more time with you. Wherever I go, I will miss you, Bishop."

Tears brimmed to her lashes. She blinked, but they spilled over anyway. Bishop reached out with his free hand and wiped them away. They were pink—tinged with blood. She would be gone soon.

"You're not going anywhere," he informed her hoarsely. "I am not going to lose you."

Wearily she opened her eyes and smiled at him. "I love you too."

He couldn't stop the tear that rolled down his cheek. Joy, sorrow and rage all combined within him. Even the loss of Elisabetta hadn't affected him like this. There had been anger and vengeance, but not this hollow, scraping grief. He hadn't felt as though he were dying too.

"If you love me, you'd better fight this." He swiped at his cheek with the back of the same hand that had wiped hers. Their tears mixed, wet and salt and indistinguishable now from each other. "Because I fell in love with a woman that would fight the sun itself if the thought took her, and I don't plan on letting her go."

"Tell me how to fight it and I will."

For the first time since all this happened, a true smile curved his lips. "Do not let it take you. When you feel the rage, fight it. You are stronger than this. You just need to hold on, sweetheart. We'll find the cure." He would believe that. He had to.

"The cure."

"Yes. After that the only thing you'll ever have to fight again is me."

She smiled, leaning back against the cushions. "That sounds nice."

"I love you," he whispered.

"I know. That's why I'm going to fight."

He kissed her. Her lips felt as sweet and soft as they always had, but beneath them were teeth that were slowly growing into monstrous fangs. The woman brave enough to love him was slowly being taken from him.

Bishop prayed.

"Is this what Dreux went through?" Marcus asked Bishop as they sat together in the parlor much later that evening, digging through books and watching Marika sleep. The changes in her had worsened, but sleep seemed to slow them, so Molyneux had given her a mild sedative to keep her calm. It would wear off soon as her body adjusted to it, but for now she was quiet.

"No. Dreux's condition never became this advanced." After discovering that Grey was a descendant of Dreux's, Bishop made the decision to tell him the truth about Dreux's suicide. Even though six centuries had dulled the familial connection between them, Grey seemed relieved to hear his ancestor's death had been for reasons more noble than he originally thought.

Bishop didn't bother to mention that Dreux had killed more often than the rest of them because of his "nobility." If the fool had fed like he was supposed to, he never would have started to become what he had.

But then, Dreux had never taken to being a vampire. Bishop suspected he had been wanting to kill himself for some time. Maybe he had hoped one of the others would do it for him, and then when he realized what was happening to him, it was just a convenient excuse to finally end it all.

Perhaps he assumed that sacrificing himself would get him into heaven. Odd, but Bishop just assumed that's where he ended up anyway—provided there was such a place. Sometimes, given all he had seen, he had his doubts.

He was religious enough to pray for Marika's cure, but not so much that he believed her condition punishment for the way he had killed the men who hurt Elisabetta—that was Chapel's way, not his.

"These Silver Palm acolytes, they are dangerous." Grey ran a hand through his thick black hair. "The poison they used on Temple almost killed Prudence Ryland."

"Chapel's woman?" They had done a lot of talking these last few hours, most of which was done by Grey and occasionally Molyneux as they told him of the recent happenings in England.

Grey made a face at his base comment. "I suppose you could call her that. She's his *wife*. They were married recently in London and left for France the same time we left for Hungary."

"Chapel made her a vampire to save her?"

"No, he drew the poison from her into himself. He didn't make her a vampire until she was about to die."

Bishop frowned. "From the poison?"

"Cancer."

"And Chapel willingly passed on our 'curse'? He must have changed since I last saw him."

He wasn't sure when it had happened, but many

years ago Chapel had started feeling sorry for himself where being a vampire was concerned. He had himself convinced they had been cursed by God. It annoyed the hell out of Bishop and Saint.

"I think he sees his situation differently now that he has Pru in his life."

"He's in love then?"

"Undoubtedly."

What a coincidence that it should happen to them both at similar times in their lives. He had not spoken to Chapel—Severian—in some time, but their lives were connected nevertheless. Bishop was glad his friend had found love—and violently envious that he was able to hold on to it. At least Chapel's woman wanted to become a vampire.

"For what it's worth," Grey said in that low voice of his, "I'm sorry this happened to Miss Korzha. And to you."

Odd, but the young man's words were touching. "Thank you. I am sorry too."

A few moments of silence passed as they read some more. Grey cleared his throat. "You know, the order duped me as well."

Now there was a bit of new information. "Really?"

The young man looked away. "They used my eagerness to learn about Dreux Breauvrai against me. I should have known they were evil, but I allowed my own interests to blind me. Perhaps Mr. Korzha did the same, and now he is paying for it."

Bishop wasn't quite convinced, nor was he totally unsympathetic. "Perhaps, but that does nothing to help Marika, does it?"

"I suppose not. If I tell you she chose this path for herself, will you threaten me with bodily harm?"

Bishop laughed—a sound caught somewhere between a growl and genuine humor. "She might have chosen to hunt vampires, Mr. Grey, but she never asked to become one."

"You mean she never asked to become Nosferatu."

Bishop shrugged. "Same thing."

"No it's not. Not really."

He was about to argue—perhaps even threaten the man with bodily harm after all—when Molyneux, who was sitting at a table a few feet away, leapt to his feet.

"I have found it!" He gasped, holding up the Latin text he'd been studying. "I have found the cure."

Bishop's own book fell from his numb fingers, spilling to the floor with a muffled thump. His heart was in his throat, too afraid to beat. "What is it?"

The gray-haired man came forward, showing him the pages where Marika's salvation was spelled out in Latin. "It is you, Bishop."

"Me?" But he had no idea how to stop the corruption tearing through Marika's system. He looked up into the priest's face. "How?"

An earnest gaze bored into his. "You must give your blood to Marika. You must make her vampire."

* * *

He was the only one who could cure her.

Bishop ruminated on this as he seated himself beside his bed where he had laid Marika to rest just moments before.

After Molyneux told him the secret to the "cure" he had lifted Marika in his arms and taken her upstairs. Marcus and the priest acted as though the news was good, but Bishop knew better than to agree.

Would Marika take his blood? He had offered it to Elisabetta centuries before and she had rather die than become like him simply because her religion said it was wrong. Marika said she no longer thought of him as a monster, but would that hold true when faced with becoming vampire herself? She would rather die than be a Nosferatu, and Bishop didn't blame her, but Nosferatu was still vampire underneath all the rage and insanity.

Could she become the very thing she had been taught her entire life to hate? Yes, she was learning that not all vampires were evil, but there was a huge difference between knowing that and then becoming one.

She said she loved him, but Elisabetta had said that too. Love meant nothing so far as this decision was concerned. This meant living forever. It meant watching those you love die. It meant being hated by those who could not understand you. He had already brought so much hatred into Marika's life. How could he ask this of her?

Because he had to. It was her decision. Whatever she chose, he would have to accept that, no matter how difficult it might be.

It wasn't merely the blood of a vampire that would cure her. It was only the purest blood that would do it. Only the five of them—that he knew of—who had taken the essence of Lilith into themselves were strong enough to achieve such a cure. The blood grew weaker generation after generation. It was the reason that in most vampire clans—or murders as they were often called—only the purest bloods were allowed to make new acolytes.

It was why, even though she was only a half-blood, Marika could hold her own with a vampire, and why she had managed to resist the Nosferatu poison this long. Saint's blood made her strong, but she would not be able to fight it much longer.

As though she could somehow sense his presence and his thoughts, her eyes opened. They were so big now. Her skin was tight and her lips could hardly contain the fangs within. It broke his heart seeing her pretty face so distorted. He couldn't be repulsed because he loved her. And he wasn't frightened because he would rather die at her hand than any other.

"There's no cure, is there?" she asked weakly. The fangs thickened her speech. The corruption deepened her voice. It was she and it wasn't. It terrified him, watching this poison take her over.

He took her hand—her hot, papery hand—in his. "Yes, there is, sweetheart. Molyneux found it."

Her dark eyes brightened. "What is it?"

He frowned. "You need to drink my blood. You have to become vampire."

She watched him closely, as though searching for some duplicity in him. "Why do you look so sad? I won't let you die to save me, Bishop. Tell me you do not have to give up your life for mine."

A fine pair they were. Both more willing to die for the other rather than live. For years he had thought Elisabetta died because she didn't want to be like him, now he finally realized it was because she had loved him. Loved him enough to die for him.

He wanted someone to live for him. He wanted Marika to live.

"It won't kill me, but Marika, you have to drink my blood. You will become a vampire. Are you prepared to do that?"

She was silent for a moment. "What happens if I don't take your blood."

"You become Nosferatu." *And then I kill you.*

"Then I am prepared to take your blood, Bishop. Yes."

He blinked at her quick response. She hadn't hesitated, not even for a second. "You understand what it means?"

Abnormally strong fingers squeezed his. "I understand that you will not have to kill me and that we can be together. Is there anything else?"

He was confused. "You do not feel that it is cheating one evil for a lesser? You do not believe that you will save your life, yet lose your soul?"

She smiled at him. In fact, she laughed. "No. You are not a monster, Bishop. Your blood will not make me one either. Unless you do not want to change me?"

"Of course I do." He never wanted to hear that plaintive tone of voice again. "I want you with me forever."

"Then hurry up and save me, vampire." Her eyes were damp and bright. "It's what you do best."

He smiled at that. It was going to happen. He was going to cure her and they were going to be together. He would give her his blood tonight to push the poison from her system. Another feeding tomorrow once he had regained his strength would make her a full vampire and bind them forever. It should have scared the hell out of him, but it didn't.

There was a glass on the bedside table. He cupped his hand around it and squeezed hard enough to break off a sliver of crystal. Pulling aside the neck of his shirt, he placed the shard against the base of his throat, near the crook of his shoulder, and cut. A brief sting and then he felt the wetness running down his chest.

Marika's eyes widened, becoming huge black holes in her face. Her lips peeled back, revealing those glistening, murderous fangs.

Bishop frowned, his heart rolling over in his chest. Something was wrong. Was he too late? Had the change already come upon her?

"Marika?"

"Bishop!" That was it—nothing more than a tiny cry of helplessness before she lunged upward on the bed, so fast it was a blur even to him. She grabbed him by the back of the head, bending his neck backward and seized his shoulder with fingers like talons.

His hands came up to stop her, but he was too late. Her teeth tore into him like a wild animal. Pain lashed through him as she knocked him backward onto the bed, fastened on him like a starving wolf.

He pushed, but she would not let go, and pushing too hard might cost him his life if she didn't release him first.

He had never taken anyone like this. Had never experienced anything so painful in his life, but he lay there and let her tear him, let her glut herself on what he freely offered. Her life depended on it.

He closed his arms around her and held her as she fed nosily. "I love you, Marika."

She stiffened at the sound of his voice and lifted her head. Her face was bloody as she stared down at him, horror stiffening her features.

"Bishop? Oh, my God, Bishop, forgive me!" Sobs shook her as she let go of his hair and shoulder. Her fingers fluttered over him like butterflies, wanting to land but unsure if it was safe.

"Someone help!" she screamed. "Please help me!"

Bishop reached for her. "It's all right, Marika." His voice sounded rough and distant in his ears.

Her eyes were so wide as she gazed at his neck. "Oh, Bishop, no it's not."

Before he could say anything else, her eyes rolled back in their sockets and she fell off him onto the bed. He reached for her, but she kicked him, knocking him off the bed to the floor. It wasn't until he tried to get up that he realized she had been right. He wasn't all right, not at all.

From where she had knocked him, he could see a little of her on the bed. She was seizing, her arms and legs flailing as though struggling against some invisible opponent. Perhaps she was. Perhaps his blood was fighting the Nosferatu infection for dominance. Or perhaps he hadn't gotten to her in time and she was becoming a monster even he couldn't stop. She would kill him once the transformation was complete.

He didn't want to die knowing he had failed her.

Bishop watched from the floor as Marika thrashed on the bed. He was too weak to move. She had taken so much. He was bleeding even now, his life leaking onto the carpet. He couldn't help Marika. Couldn't even help himself.

The bedroom door flew open. He turned his head and saw Molyneux and Grey enter the room, followed by Constantin Korzha. Molyneux had sent for him after all. Marika's father went to her. Bishop could hear her heels pummeling the bed, hear the low growls from her throat.

Molyneux and Grey rushed to his side. "*Mon Dieu,*" Molyneux whispered. "Bishop, what did she do?"

She had tried to rip his throat out, that's what. "Wardrobe," he whispered. "Medical kit."

It was Grey who leapt to his bidding and returned with the supplies to treat and cover the wound.

"Any more of that werewolf blood?" he asked. Were it not for the pain talking caused, he wouldn't have recognized that voice as his own.

The priest shook his head. "No more than a few drops perhaps."

"Get it. Mix it with the salve and put it on my neck."

Again Grey rushed to complete the task. Bishop was paralyzed on the carpet as Molyneux pressed a thick square of folded linen to his neck.

"We may be about to find out if vampires can bleed to death," he informed Molyneux.

"Hush. You are not going to die."

Bishop gripped his arm. "If I do, you have to make sure Marika is cured. Take whatever I have left and give it to her. If she cannot be cured, you have to destroy her."

"No!" her father cried.

Bishop swallowed. Goddamn it, it hurt. "It's what she wants, Korzha."

"Bishop, you must be quiet. I insist." The old priest's tone brooked no refusal. "You will survive this and live to see Mam'selle Korzha cured. I promise you."

His vision was beginning to blur, but Bishop fought to stay awake. Grey came back into the room and busied himself with doctoring the torn flesh in Bishop's neck. Bishop lay there, staring at the ceiling.

The thrashing on the bed had ceased.

"Is she . . . ?" His tongue was too dry and too thick to form any more words.

"She is fine!" Korzha's joyful tone would have made Bishop smile if he could. Perhaps the old man wasn't such a bastard after all. "Sleeping, but fine."

Bishop's eyes drifted closed. Marika was sleeping. Alive and resting. *Good*.

"Bishop? Bishop!" Molyneux called to him but Bishop didn't answer. He was drifting. Drifting away. Even the pain at his neck—the stinging of the salve on his torn flesh—couldn't bring him back.

There was darkness all around him, sweet soft darkness, and he was floating in it. Warmth filled him, a sudden sweet sensation that made him want to seize it and follow it wherever it went. He grabbed on to it, let it fill him with peace.

And then there was nothing.

Chapter 18

Marika awoke with a feeling of dread in her stomach and a rifle pointed at her head.

Carefully, she turned her gaze to Marcus Grey, the man sitting in the chair beside her bed holding the rifle. He was his usual youthful-looking self, save for the shadow of stubble along his jaw. He looked like a tired, dirty angel beside her bed.

"Are you planning to shoot me?" she asked, her voice stronger than she expected.

"If necessary I plan to try, yes." He gave her a good looking over. "Judging from your appearance, I do not think it will be necessary after all."

No. Shooting her would not be necessary at the moment. She could feel the differences in herself. She felt more like she used to. Her eyes and skin didn't burn, and her teeth weren't too big for her mouth. But her heart, oh, her heart was too heavy and painful to bear.

She was better, but not totally. She swallowed. Her throat was so dry it hurt. "If Bishop is dead because of me I want you to pull the trigger regardless."

The rifle eased away—but not far. "He's alive." He showed her the bandage on his forearm. "It took blood from Molyneux, your father and myself to achieve it, but he lives."

Relief did not begin to describe how she felt. "Oh, thank God."

Marcus shrugged. "I'm not sure He had much to do with it, but it certainly cannot hurt to be thankful, I suppose."

She watched him watch her for a moment. He acted relaxed, but there was a rigidity to his posture, a certain wariness to every glance and movement. "Are you afraid of me?"

"Not so much now." His honesty was welcome, if not a little disconcerting. "When I saw what you did to Bishop last night I was terrified."

Bishop. When she thought of what she had done to him. All she could remember was the smell of him and then the taste—rich, spicy sweetness filling her. He had told her he loved her and then she saw what she had done. . .

"Does he hate me?" She couldn't blame him if he did, but the idea of it broke her heart.

Marcus scowled at her, as though she were an idiot. "He was prepared to die for you. I think it is safe to assume he likes you well enough."

She almost smiled at that. "You are a very sarcastic man, Mr. Grey."

"My apologies." He didn't sound the least bit sorry. "Usually I'm much more amiable, but for the most part I find vampire courting rituals tedious. Although I must say, you've certainly made it interesting."

She probably should be insulted, but he made it very difficult. Perhaps it was because he was just so lovely to look at, or perhaps because she was just so happy to be alive—and that Bishop was alive—that she didn't care. "Am I cured?"

"Molyneux thinks you will be."

Will be? So not yet. "When?"

"When Bishop is strong enough to give you more blood."

Oh, no. Marika shook her head. "I won't risk hurting him again."

Sighing, Marcus rose to his feet. "Then you will have ripped his throat out for nothing, won't you have? I suppose you'll want him to kill you as well."

Marika blinked at him. Why did he say it as though it was a ridiculous idea? "Of course. I would rather die than harm him again."

"*Vampires.*" He shook his head. "I do not suppose you have given thought to what having to kill the woman he loves will do to him?"

Of course it would pain him, but Bishop would do what must be done. He had promised her. "He wouldn't want me to become a monster." She wouldn't think about the fact that she had become a monster temporarily when she attacked Bishop.

"Exactly!" Marcus thrust his palms outward in

a grand gesture of aggravation. "So why don't you drink his blood, agree to love him forever and then we can get back to the apparently oh-so-insignificant business of saving Temple and stopping the Order of the Silver Palm?"

He was rude, overbearing and, unfortunately, correct. "Do you always speak so frankly?"

"No. But I've seen enough blood to bathe in as of late. I haven't had a decent night's sleep in more than a month, and I've had to accept that there is real evil in the world. It's played havoc with my manners, I'm afraid."

Marika grinned at him despite herself. "I like you."

That seemed to take him back a step. "Perhaps when I no longer have to worry about you killing me, I will like you as well." He gestured to the door with the butt of the rifle. "I will go let the others know that you are awake."

When he left, Marika eased back the blankets and swung her legs over the side of the bed. She was still wobbly, but feeling much stronger than she had after the attack. Unfortunately she was still wearing the same clothes she had changed into that day. Bishop hadn't been able to change her, and neither Marcus nor Father Molyneux was brave enough to make the attempt. She didn't blame them. It was amazing to her that Marcus even dared sit beside her bed, armed or not.

Dried blood made little dark pools of hard crust on her shirt, and she smelled of stale sweat and old fever. Her braid was a mess and her scalp itched. She wanted a bath. Needed a bath.

She hadn't made it halfway across the room before the door opened and Bishop strode into the room.

The sight of him almost took the breath from her. He looked tired, and his hair was disheveled, but he was whole and beautiful.

"What are you doing?" he demanded in that familiar, abrupt tone as he set a brown bottle on the vanity. It was as though nothing had changed between them, as though she hadn't tried to kill him.

Marika burst into tears, surprising even herself. She never used to cry, and now, since meeting Bishop, she seemed to be doing it a lot.

Instantly he had her in his arms and was stroking her back. "Shh. It's all right, Sweetheart."

"I am so happy to see you," she told him, sniffing against his chest. "I'm sorry I hurt you."

His hands, warm and firm, cupped her shoulders and eased her away. She wiped at her eyes and lifted her gaze to his.

"Losing you would have hurt me far more," he told her, his green-gold gaze so full of love, it hurt to look at it. "You will not fight me on this, Marika. You need one more treatment of my blood and you will take it."

She nodded, remembering her conversation with Marcus Grey. "I will not fight you, Bishop. I am terrified of hurting you again, but I will take your blood again if that is what has to be done."

The skin between his dark brows puckered. "You will?"

"I will. I do not want you to have to kill me when I turn Nosferatu. I want to live—with you. I love you."

The strangest expression crossed his face. At that moment Marika would have given anything to know what he was thinking. "Live. For me?"

"For you." Reaching up, she ran the tips of her fingers along his cheek, down the side of his neck, where the evidence of her violence against him was little more than faint pink marks on his flesh. Other than that she would never have known he had almost died at her hand. "With you. Because of you. Will you have me?"

His answer was a kiss—a long, sweet, soul-to-soul kiss that left her tasted, tender and hungry for more.

"I will have you," he murmured against her lips. "In every way imaginable."

As tired and dirty as she was, her body hummed with the possibilities. How could she have come so close to destruction as she had and now be thinking about having him inside her?

"Can I get clean first?" she asked.

Smiling, Bishop backed away from her. "Of course. I need to feed again or Molyneux will have a fit. But first . . ." He handed her the bottle he had brought with him. "Drink this while I run your bath."

"What is it?"

"Blood. I trust you, but before I offer myself to you tonight, I want to make sure you have had an appetizer first."

The bottle of blood bobbed between Marika's knees in the hot bath, waiting patiently for her to open it and drink.

That was all she had to do—open it, raise it to her lips and drink. If she did, then she would be strong enough that when Bishop offered her his blood, she wouldn't have to worry about hurting him again. She would be that much closer to being a vampire—something she never, ever thought she would become.

Bishop said it might be easier for her if she warmed it first. He told her to pretend it was mulled wine.

It didn't bother her that it was blood. She had craved it before, tasted it before. The awful burning of Armitage's essence made drinking anything else easy. And she wasn't hesitant to become a vampire, as strange as that now seemed. It wasn't going to make her different; she knew that now. But she would be stronger and faster and better able to fight alongside Bishop in the future. She would not age, would not die unless she was killed.

It didn't bother her that she would probably never have children—unless vampires could reproduce. That was simply one more thing she didn't know about them. She hadn't thought of motherhood for many years. Back then she hadn't wanted to pass on the foulness of her blood. And now she had other things to worry about, such as Bishop and how they were going to fight the Order of the Silver Palm.

No, it didn't bother her that there was blood in the bottle. What bothered her was the impersonal aspect of it. Blood was life—a gift. When a vampire fed from a person, he was essentially taking part of that person into himself. It was a personal, intimate thing. A moment of delicacy and trust when you held someone's life in your hands. There was none of that when it came from a bottle.

She didn't know whose essence was in that bottle, and having already ingested blood that was slowly destroying her, she was a little hesitant to drink now.

However, if drinking from the bottle meant she wouldn't hurt Bishop again, there was no point in thinking about it any longer. Bishop had brought her the bottle himself, so it had to be from a trusted source—one he had been using himself.

Marika snatched the bottle out of the water, uncorked it and downed the contents in one long, warm gulp.

A lovely glow filled her, blossoming out to her limbs. Her toes and fingers tingled; her mind seemed sharper, clearer.

"That wasn't so bad, was it?"

She turned her head to watch as Bishop entered the door of the bath. His expression was hopeful. How long had he been standing there watching?

"It was easier than I expected," she replied.

He took the empty bottle from her. "I'm glad to hear it. Give me the cloth and I'll wash your back."

She obliged and he lathered it with the sweet, sandalwood soap. It was slippery and warm against her skin, the scent relaxing her almost as much as his touch.

"How do you feel?" he asked as he followed the path of the cloth with slow, kneading strokes of his fingers.

Marika sighed as he rinsed the soap away. "Anxious. Awkward."

He kissed the wet slope of her shoulder. "When you are done with your bath, come join me in the bedroom."

He might not have meant it as a sensual invitation, but Marika's body reacted to it as such. The minute he left the room, she finished washing and wrung the water from her hair. A few minutes later she was towel-dried and walking into the bedroom in a thin dressing gown.

Bishop had obviously meant the invitation as a sexual one. He was waiting for her in the middle of the room, bathed in firelight and gloriously naked. Just the sight of him was enough to make her mouth dry, all the moisture in her body flooding a part much, much lower.

"I thought I might be able to ease your anxiety," he told her.

Smiling appreciatively at his nudity, Marika had to acknowledge he was doing just that. "You are a smart man."

"You are certain this is what you want?" he asked when she came to him, her hands reaching for the smooth perfection of his strong shoulders.

"I want *you*, Bishop. I want us to be together always."

His lips tucked together, then relaxed again. "I'm not sure you answered my question. Was that a yes?"

"It was." Then, hesitantly: "Is this what you want?"

"God, yes."

Marika might have chuckled were she not so aware of the harm she had done to him the last time. "You do not fear me?"

"Fear you?" His hands came up to her face, thumbs stroking her cheeks. "Foolish little halfling. I might fear for you, but I will never be fearful *of* you."

It was that declaration that pushed her to act. No more hesitation or uncertainty. Her fingers untied the sash on her gown, and she let it fall off her shoulders to a soft heap at her feet. They stood before each other, naked and vulnerable.

"This is how it should be with us," he told her, smoothing hair back from her face. "This is how I always want it to be with us."

She knew exactly what he meant. There should always be honesty and trust between them—and nothing else. And when they were to share blood it would be another moment of intimacy they shared—no fear and no unease. When they came together like this again she would know how right it was, and never again have doubts.

She nodded. "I am ready."

"Kiss me," he commanded, then took possession of her mouth before she could reply.

His breath was spicy-sweet, the inside of his mouth wet and hot as his tongue toyed with hers. Her hands slid along the width of his shoulders, up the warm, solid column of his neck to caress the sharpness of his jaw. The skin there was warm and smooth, lightly scented with bay rum. She stroked his cheeks, sliding her fingers back into the silky thickness of his hair. She loved his hair, loved the scent of him, the feel and taste.

Bishop's hands slid down her back with whisper softness, raising gooseflesh with every tender stroke. She tingled from head to toe—the tips of her breasts, even the backs of her knees. Hunger rose from within her, but it was a hunger for him. A hunger that could only be sated by the joining of her body with his.

It was need, pure and simple. She needed to feel him inside her. Needed to know that she possessed him in every way possible and offer herself to be possessed in return. Only when they were finally joined would her heart know peace.

The crisp hair on his chest abraded her nipples, sending little shocks and shivers between her legs. Against her belly, the hard length of him pushed, pulsing when she touched him or moved against him. He was silky and insistent and ready for her.

Knowing that he wanted her brought a flood of moisture from deep within her, dampening her with its shameless heat.

His hands slid down, cupping one quivering cheek of her bottom as the other nudged her thighs apart from behind. One long finger stroked the cleft of her buttocks, teased the sensitive flesh there before easing between the moist lips of her sex. Marika gasped against his mouth as his finger slid deep into her, filling her. Every slow thrust sent a jolt of pleasure shooting through her. She rose up on her toes, widening her legs to allow him even deeper access.

His finger stoked the fire inside her, sending flames of want dancing along her nerves with gentle insistence. The palm of his hand cupped the curve of her buttocks, pressing her tighter against the hard ridge of his sex.

When he removed his hand from between her legs she almost cried out at the loss. Her breath came in sultry pants as his mouth left hers, burning a silky path down her jaw to her throat. She tilted her head, giving him access to bite her, but he didn't. He was going to make her wait for that.

Or was he afraid to take her blood inside him? No, she wasn't going to think such thoughts, not now.

Bishop kept kissing, down her collarbone to her breast. He captured a nipple in his mouth, licking at the crest until it was tight and throbbing from his work. Darts of sharp pleasure shot through her

breast as his mouth pulled, arching her back. The
sensations raced through her, pooling between her
thighs, increasing the throbbing want that flooded
there.

Marika's fingers pulled at his hair, frantically
combing through the dark strands. His teeth nipped
at her aching flesh, drawing a gasp of delight from
her lips. When she thought she couldn't take it anymore, he moved to the other breast, treating it in a
similar fashion until she whimpered in surrender.

She didn't protest when he took them both to the
floor in front of the hearth, drawing her down on
the soft, plush carpet that cushioned her, treated
her skin to a delicious, sensual friction. His golden
flesh glowed, the firelight imbuing him with a
shimmer reserved for gods. Flames caught the gold
in his eyes and the russet in his hair, making him
as bright, beautiful and consuming as fire itself.

He looked at her as though she was his goddess.
In his eyes she was beautiful, perfect and a gift. Her
throat tightened with the revelation. No one had
ever looked at her that way before.

God willing, no one ever would again. She wanted
Bishop and no other for the rest of her days.

For eternity.

Marika shifted under his gaze, the carpet de-
lightfully rough against her back. She was so ready
for him, wanted him so badly. "Bishop, I want—"

He silenced her with a finger against her lips.
"Not yet. I want to taste you first."

He didn't mean her blood. She realized as soon

as she felt his tongue dip into the hollow of her navel exactly where he planned to taste her.

She spread her thighs for him, hips arching as those perfect lips touched the moist curls. His fingers parted her, tongue gliding across her sensitive flesh with excruciating slowness. When he finally reached the tight, aching peak, he licked once and then waited a full heartbeat before licking again. Marika moaned from the torture. She curved her fingers in his hair, urging him closer.

"More," she pleaded. Demanded.

His lips and tongue moved against her, kissing and suckling, nibbling and gently lapping until she was little more than a mindless, writhing coil of pleasure, grinding itself against the hot pressure of his mouth, waiting to explode.

And then he stopped, leaving her panting and quivering. She whimpered a protest as he took her hands and pulled her up onto her knees. Wetness clung to her thighs, sticky and cool. She throbbed for him, ached for him.

Bishop sat on the floor, his back against the small sofa. His sex stood erect in the thatch of hair between his legs, the broad head flushed and damp. Still holding her hands he guided her forward until she straddled him, his flesh pressed against the delicate folds of hers.

She leaned forward to kiss him. The taste of herself was heavy on his lips and she didn't care. He groaned into her mouth as she licked her juices away. Reaching down, she captured the silky length of him in her hand. The thick tip was slick with moisture.

"Do you like the taste of yourself?" he asked, breathless as their mouths broke apart.

"I like the taste of myself mixed with the taste of you," she murmured, stroking him. He pulsed in her hand.

She moved in to kiss him again, but he turned his head, offering her his th█████ rather than his mouth. He held her in his arms, one hand on the back of her skull, pressing her face to the warm hollow between his neck and shoulder where she could feel the heat of his blood beneath the sweetness of his flesh.

Fangs grew and she didn't try to stop them. Opening her mouth, she let them graze his throat, where the heat of him was sweet and beckoning. He stiffened.

He wasn't ready. He didn't trust her not to take too much. Marika lifted her head, tried to pull away, but his hand on the back of her skull stopped her.

His other hand reached down and took the one she had wrapped around his sex. "I want to come inside you, not in your hand."

She shivered, delighting in her own sexual power. "I want that too."

He held her, pressed her face into his neck once more. "I want to feel you inside me," he told her, his voice a seductive rasp. "Take my blood and live for me."

It was an invitation if ever she had been given

one. Sighing, Marika parted her lips, willing her fangs to full length. They sank cleanly into Bishop's flesh. He gasped as she entered him. His fingers fisted in her hair, bit into her back. He held her, stretched his neck so that he was open and vulnerable to her. She could feel him around her, feel herself inside him, and she wanted him to be inside her as well.

His warmth and power filled her, soothed the restlessness in her soul and replaced it with a hunger of another kind. Every nerve seemed to leap to life. Every inch of her wanted to possess him and be possessed by him.

Slowly, she lowered her body onto his, felt the thick length of him fill her, taking both his body and his blood into herself. Her body sang with the perfect completeness of the moment. They were one.

She drank as her hips rose and fell. Bishop's fingers bit into her hips, lifting her up and forcing her down on his slick length. Delicious friction mounted between them, building to a fevered pitch as Marika blindly shoved her body down on his.

His head shifted. She felt the brush of hair against her cheek and then a sting in her shoulder that quickly gave way to a flood of overwhelming heat. He had bitten her. He didn't feed, but the act had the desired effect. It sent her over the edge into the earth-shattering vortex of climax. She cried out against his throat as pleasure assaulted her, felt his arms tighten around her as he stiffened with his own release.

With what strength she had left, Marika lifted her head and lapped at the punctures her teeth had made, closing the small wounds. Bonelessly, she collapsed on top of him and sighed when he stood with her in his arms, and carried her to the bed.

They lay in silence for some time. He stroked her hair while she traced circles on his chest with her fingertip. They were at ease with each other, but Marika anxiously waited for the effect his blood would have on her. Would she go into convulsions as she had the last time?

But instead of feeling as though her body were being burned from the inside out, Marika felt only contentment and the heavy-lidded approach of slumber.

She didn't feel any violence either. No sense of dread. In fact, she felt light and vital. She felt vibrant and alive. She felt. . .

Immortal.

She was cured. She knew in her heart that she was no longer in any danger of becoming Nosferatu. Bishop had healed her.

The soft brush of his lips on her forehead made her raise her gaze to his. Her eyesight had always been keen but now it was so clear she had to blink to make sure it wasn't deceiving her.

"Feel better?" he asked with a smile.

She kissed him, her joy giving her energy she

couldn't have summoned any other way. "Much. Thank you."

"You are welcome, but I did it as much for myself as for you."

She kissed him again. "For us."

His arms tightened around her and she snuggled against his side. "I like the sound of that."

Smiling, Marika closed her eyes as she rested her cheek against his chest. Her earlier feelings of fatigue were slowly creeping back, blanketing her with a comforting warmth. For the first time in several days she was going to fall asleep without worrying about what might happen when she woke up.

"Bishop?" she asked just before letting herself drift off.

"What, my sweet?"

She glanced up at him. "I am glad the order hired me to capture you."

He stared at her a moment before bursting out laughing. "You are the strangest woman I have ever met."

"The strangest *vampire* you have ever met. And proud of it."

"The strangest, boldest, bravest, most incredible woman vampire I have ever met and I love you."

She arched a brow. That was quite the tribute. "Even though I tried to kill you?"

He grinned and leaned in—hopefully for another kiss. "What do you think kept me alive?"

Chapter 19

It was a thankless task, this packing up a house-
hold and moving on with it. That was why
Maxwell had servants to do it for him. All he had
to do was climb into his automobile and have his
driver take him to the station, where his private
car would be attached to the next train bound for
Budapest. From there he would continue on to Italy,
where he would be rewarded for a job well done.

It hadn't been an easy task, he reflected as he set
his hat on his head, but it hadn't been overly ardu-
ous either. Vampires were like sheep. If at first they
did not move in the direction you wished, a little
patience and inventive thinking would soon see
progress, sometimes with surprising results.

Bishop was too concerned about his little dhampyr to come looking for him, and truly, who could
blame him? But Maxwell was a smart man—a man
who knew better than to press his luck. Bishop was

not as smart, but then when you were physically powerful enough to take whatever you wanted, intelligence wasn't a concern.

Even Armitage—who had shown some spark of keenness in the beginning—had turned out to be a disappointment. Thankfully he had managed to make amends for that by becoming the finest Nosferatu Maxwell ever laid eyes on. A shame that Armitage had to be destroyed so soon, but he really would not have been easy to control at all. Bishop had done him a bit of a service with that wicked sword of his. If allowed to live Armitage would have surely returned home to deal with his "creators."

Armitage hadn't even the sense to realize that he had done exactly what Maxwell wanted. Perhaps there was simply something in the demonic strain that made vampires naturally dense.

Or perhaps Maxwell was simply unnaturally brilliant. He smiled into his coffee cup. Yes, he rather fancied that.

"Make certain that crate gets sent ahead," he told the workmen bringing items up from the cellar. Mikael would have need of his equipment in Italy.

Yes, they had made good progress thus far. The English contingent had not only succeeded—with help from the French, nonetheless—in capturing Temple, but in bringing Chapel into the open as well. Their operation yielded a bonus in that Chapel had brought over a human woman. She would be a powerful vampire with his blood in her veins.

All the better for the order.

Armitage was no longer a worry, thanks to Bishop. As for Korzha ... well, perhaps Maxwell should punish his betrayal, but Constantin had proven useful to the cause despite his duplicity, and for that he would be allowed to live. Besides, the order might have use for Korzha's son someday and it would be better if they approached him as friend rather than foe.

And now they had Bishop exactly where they wanted him. It had taken a little maneuvering on his part and they had suffered a few setbacks, but eventually the vampire had merged with the rest of the herd. How lucky for the order that these vampires seemed to fall in love so easily! The woman would soon be a vampire as well. She would obviously accompany her lover in his search for his missing friend—especially since Bishop now knew the order was responsible for other disappearances as well.

They would walk willingly into the order's trap.

Maxwell practically skipped down the steps to the courtyard where his conveyance and driver waited. A footman held the door open for him and he slid inside, covering his expensive suit with a driving robe to protect it from dust and debris.

"Quickly," he told his driver. "I am desirous to leave this place."

"Yes, my lord."

As they sped down the drive, Maxwell watched the rich green countryside pass. It made him think of England, and a wave of homesickness swept over him. *Soon*. Once this was over he could return home and rule from his personal kingdom.

Yes, Chapel and Bishop had fallen into line. Reign and Saint would soon follow. Maxwell congratulated himself on his own success.

Their search would take them both into the order's circle of power, right into the main compound. They would think themselves capable of freeing Temple.

They would be wrong.

It was a mistake that would cost them their lives—and grant the order the power to rule the world. All Maxwell had to do was be patient and wait.

He was a very patient man.

Bishop returned from his quest the next evening empty-handed, but not surprised.

"Maxwell is gone," he informed Marika and her companions as he entered the parlor. "According to the servants, he left at dawn this morning. They wouldn't tell me where he was going."

If Bishop had acted sooner they might have been able to capture the man, but he couldn't bring himself to feel too guilty about it. His attention had been on Marika, where it should have been. And if Korzha was right about the man, Maxwell wouldn't have given them any information anyway—no matter what Bishop did to him.

"They probably did not know," Marika's father told him. "Maxwell is sly. He would tell only those that needed to know and they know the penalty for betraying him."

At that moment Bishop almost felt sorry for Korzha. He knew the order would someday exact payment for his betrayal, either against him or against his family. Marika had already promised to protect Jakob, and since he planned to never let his Huntress out of his sight again, he would offer his own protection to the boy.

Korzha's actions—giving his blood and providing information on the order—had earned him Bishop's respect as well. It didn't make up for all he had put Marika through, but Bishop knew her father honestly regretted hurting her. Marika forgave him, and even if Bishop couldn't, he could appreciate that the man had put his life in danger to help them. To help Marika.

Marika patted Bishop's arm as he seated himself beside her on the sofa. She looked rosy and lovely in her usual trousers and vest. Her dark eyes were bright with the onset of evening and her smile . . . it was only for him. He was dying to kiss her, but not in front of an audience.

Because one kiss was never enough when his lips took hers, and he would not stop at kissing.

"We will find Maxwell, Bishop. And Temple as well." Her voice was determined as she made the vow.

He smiled at her. As soon as she had recovered from her ordeal—which was almost immediately after their joining—she had thrown herself into the challenge of finding Temple. When Bishop said that perhaps he would help Molyneux and Marcus with their investigation, Marika immediately began making plans to leave Romania.

"There is nothing for me here," Marika had told him. "I have too many enemies, and my family will suffer for it. I want to be with you where I belong."

And since he wanted her beside him wherever he was, Bishop didn't argue. He did, however, promise her that he would arrange for her father and grandmother to be protected. It was the least he could do for the people who were now his family as well.

Irina, who had spent her entire life in Fagaras, had agreed to permanently relocate. With Marika gone, the old woman had decided there was nothing left there for her. She would move closer to what family she had remaining.

This chapter of their lives was coming to a quick end.

They weren't married—not in the eyes of the church—but in Bishop's heart they were husband and wife in every way that mattered. He could not—would not—imagine life without her.

"A package arrived for you while you were out," she told him, handing him a box that she scooped up from the floor by her feet. "It was left on the step."

In Bishop's experience that tended to mean one of two things. The box either contained some secret missive or relic—or the head of someone close to him. Regardless, he was leery of opening it.

"I believe I might know what it contains." Molyneux withdrew a folded letter from his pocket.

"I received this from Chapel earlier today." He handed it to Bishop.

Frowning, Bishop scanned the brief note scrawled in Chapel's familiar hand. "An amulet?" He looked up at the priest. "Made from the cup?"

"Perhaps our *bon ami* Temple has sent you one as well."

That would certainly be preferable to a head. "How did Temple know to do this?" he asked Molyneux as he opened the package. "Did he know that someone was after him?"

The priest shrugged in the way only the French can. "I do not know. I had not spoken to him in months. If he did have any suspicions he kept them to himself."

"Is that silver?" Marika asked, peering inside the opened box.

Bishop nodded. Slowly, he reached in and picked up the amulet. Marika gasped and tried to stop him, but he curled his fingers around the cast silver and lifted it to the light to get a better look. It was warm and heavy and sent shivers of power up his arm as he held it.

Marika stared at it in awe. "It doesn't burn."

"No," Bishop replied. "That is because it is made from the cup that turned us. It is the Blood Grail—the only silver I've ever been able to touch without pain."

Her hand hovered over it. "I can feel its pull. It is as though it tugs at me from the inside."

Her father came over and placed his finger on the metal. "I feel nothing."

"I think that is the point," Bishop told him, slipping the amulet around his neck. "Temple didn't want anyone but us to know what it was." The sword, cross and chalice engraved on the front of it was a hint, but probably more to make anyone who saw it think it was merely an old medallion rather than a relic of power.

"Is there a note?" Molyneux asked.

There was. "It's the name of a bank in Rome. And the information for what I think must be a safe box."

"Chapel said he was given a Rome address as well—a house."

Bishop tossed the paper into the fire—after memorizing the information on it. "I wonder if Reign and Saint have gotten similar clues?"

It was Marika who replied—though not in direct answer to his musing. "I think it best if the four of us head for Rome as soon as possible."

Bishop arched a brow. "The four of us?"

She nodded. "You and I, Father Molyneux and Mr. Grey. Father Molyneux has contacts within the church and Mr. Grey knows a great deal about the order. We need them."

Bishop stared at her, smiling. "You amaze me."

She smiled back, obviously pleased by his praise.

"We need to leave this place," Marcus announced, destroying the mood as he burst into the room. His eyes were wide and his cheeks flushed with color. "There's mob brewing a few villages away. They want the Huntress and her demon's head." He shot a pointed look at the two of them. "No offense, but I assumed they meant you."

Bishop rose to his feet. "How long do we have?"

"Until dawn, I think. Thankfully they suffer from the impression that you'll be weak and asleep. If we can get out in the next few hours, we should be gone by then. The only problem will be protecting the two of you from the sun."

It seemed Bishop was the only one who hadn't started thinking of the four of them as a unit.

"We might be able to get a train," Molyneux suggested.

"There is one that leaves at six for Budapest," Marika's father told them.

Marika rose to her feet as well. "Perhaps we could procure a car for ourselves?"

"No need," Bishop told her—told them all. "I have my own car. We only have to ensure there is a train to attach it to."

Marika gaped at him. "You have your own car?"

He nodded. "Of course. How else could I travel without worrying about daylight and being discovered?"

"Excellent!" Marcus enthused. "Now we only have to worry about getting to the station."

"Take my motor car," Constantin offered. "There might not be enough room for the four of you—"

"Marika and I do not need to drive," Bishop reminded him brusquely. Then he smiled. "And thank you for your offer."

Marcus was actually grinning. "This is so much

more adventurous when one doesn't have to worry about transportation."

"Are you rich?" Marika blurted, apparently finding her voice.

Bishop laughed—so did Molyneux and Grey. "That depends on your definition, but yes. I suppose I am."

"So you *can* buy me a new gown after all."

It took him a moment to figure out what she was talking about—the gown Roxana had ruined when she stabbed her. "Many, in fact."

He could tell from the look on her face that she liked that idea. He never should have told her how much he liked her in dresses.

"I will pack my things," she told him. "After taking so much of my life to finally realize what true monsters are, I have no desire to be hunted like one."

"I will take my leave of you then," her father said softly. "Perhaps, Marika, I could have use of your horse to return home?"

"Of course," she replied, going to his embrace. "She is yours to keep. Give her to my brother when he is old enough to ride."

Bishop knew he shouldn't watch—shouldn't listen as father and daughter said their good-byes, but he did anyway. They hadn't had enough time together to miss each other keenly, but someday Marika would want to come back to Romania—or have her father come to them wherever they settled once they found Temple and defeated the order.

And they would find Temple and defeat the order.

When Constantin was gone, the four of them went to quickly gather whatever belongings they had to take. None of them had very much—mostly clothes and weapons in his and Marika's case. Clothes and books for Grey and the priest. Of course Grey carried a battered pistol that Bishop was willing to bet was loaded with silver shot—just in case.

They left within the hour; Marcus and Molyneux in the Daimler with the luggage, and Bishop and Marika in the air. Even though she could now fly on her own, she insisted on his holding her.

"I cannot imagine being in the sky without something to hold on to," she told him and he chuckled, knowing that one day she would have to test her own abilities.

They arrived first at the train yard. Bishop lighted a lantern and hung it outside for Molyneux and Grey to find them, and the two men arrived shortly after—Bishop didn't even have time to kiss Marika properly before they were knocking at the door.

They spent the few hours before dawn in Bishop's train car. Marcus talked to the authorities at the station and made arrangements to have them attached to the next train heading west. The "arrangements" basically meant that he gave the men enough of Bishop's money to ensure their transportation.

Once the train pulled out of the station, Molyneux and Grey left them, claiming that they needed exercise and refreshment.

"And daylight," Marcus remarked dryly. "I'm beginning to feel like a mushroom. You'll excuse us?"

Bishop grinned at the young man, who was beginning to grow on him—but in a nonmushroom way. "Of course."

In the darkened, comfortable confines of the car, Bishop and Marika climbed into the bed at the back and drew the sliding doors around it closed. The bed was designed to be shut up like a little box, ensuring total darkness—and privacy for its occupants.

"Are you afraid?" he asked once she was in his arms.

"No." Her breath was warm on his neck. "Perhaps it is arrogant of me, but I believe together you and I can do anything."

He kissed the top of her head. "And now that I have you alone, there's something I've been wanting to do for hours now . . ."

Soft laughter caressed him as he rolled her onto her back. He kissed her—on the lips and cheeks; on the breasts, teasing her sweet pink nipples into full erection as she whispered encouragement; and lower, removing her clothes as he went until he was between her splayed thighs, lapping at her juices as she shuddered and came in his mouth.

And then he was inside her—where he belonged—thrusting and slowly rocking his body into hers, building the tension kindled between them. Nothing had ever felt so right as being in her arms. Nothing had ever given him the peace, the sense of personal power that Marika did. For centuries he had known he was immortal—but not unkillable. In her arms he knew what it was to be invincible. This brave and bold woman gave herself wholly to him, accepting all that he was and demanding nothing but that he do the same. It was a demand he gladly met.

Her knees gripped his sides. Her hands were in his, pinned above her head, and her neck was open and inviting. He bit her, delirious as she filled his mouth, shuddering as she replied in kind by sinking her fangs into his shoulder. There were no words to describe the ecstasy of biting and being bitten. Feeling her inside him, knowing she was taking him into her with both sex and mouth, feeling the tight, wet heat of her wrapped around his cock as he drew her essence into himself. It was a feeling of completion he had never felt before and never would again.

They came together, clinging to each other like tendrils of ivy as pleasure rocked them both to the very core. For a moment there was nothing but their hearts beating together, and then the world slowly drew them back into her dark embrace.

"I never thought I could love someone as I do you," she murmured a little later, as they lay wrapped together. "I was too busy filling my life with hate before I met you."

He unwound her braid, running his fingers through the soft length of her hair. Even with his eyesight, she was but a shadow in their dark little haven. "You had good reason to feel as you did."

"I thought I had, but you changed all that."

"We've both changed." He laced the fingers of his other hand through hers and laid them both on his chest. "For the better."

"I remember the exact moment it began. It was the day I realized you had tended Elisabetta's grave. I think my heart knew then that it was going to be yours."

That same heart swelled at her admission. "For me it was the day you trusted me with your name."

Her head lifted. He could feel her gaze even though he couldn't see it. Nor could she see him. "I trust you with more than my name."

"I know. It's why I love you as much as I do."

Her lips were close to his—so close he could feel their succulent warmth. "I love you, Bishop. So much it hurts."

"I know a cure for that," he murmured, as he cupped the back of her head with his hand, bringing her down for a kiss.

She climbed on top of him, and as they rolled on toward whatever fate held in store for them, as Marika covered his body with her own, joining them once again, Bishop gave silent thanks.

He was so very glad that he had found his incredible little Huntress—and that she had captured not only his body, but his heart as well.

Avon Romantic Treasures

Unforgettable, enthralling love stories, sparkling with passion and adventure from Romance's bestselling authors